"Shut the fuck up." I'd breath mingled with mine before jabbing a finger into .... I don't even know how you can talk about anyone putting up with me, when I can't even stand to share a room with you." His face was now mere millimeters away from mine.

"Then change rooms. See if I give a shit. Sleep in the corridor for all I care. As long as you save face in front of the coaches, you can do whatever you want, captain." I grit out the final word, but I could feel pins starting to prick the back of my eyes; why did I always have to get teary when I got angry?

"You know if it was fucking possible, I'd have changed rooms by now. Unlike you, though, I care about the public perception of the team and don't want anyone to get wind that we are actually just this malfunctioning unit," he replied through equally gritted teeth, eyes glued to mine.

"Malfunctioning unit." I chuckled in the hopes it would diffuse the tension between us and get him to back off, but it only extracted a deep, raspy noise from the back of his throat. His eyes flitted down to my lips, in a move that if he hadn't been so close I definitely wouldn't have seen. A move I could now never unsee.

Olympic Enemies

by

Rebecca J Caffery

Olympic Enemies

Cover Art by *The Wild Rose Press, Inc.*

The Wild Rose Press, Inc.
PO Box 708
Adams Basin, NY 14410-0708
Visit us at www.thewildrosepress.com

Publishing History
First Edition, 2023
Trade Paperback ISBN 978-1-5092-4756-1
Digital ISBN 978-1-5092-4757-8

Published in the United States of America

Dedication

To all the Queer athletes paving the way.

Chapter One

Lucas

What they say about the Olympic Village is true, well about the condoms at least. They are truly at your disposal and to get more all you have to do is ask.

As we arrived at the Village we were handed a swag bag and the first thing I pulled out was a strip of ribbed ones. Not that I imagined I'd be using them; I didn't get through a strip a year at home.

This information would probably shock most people. I'm not a stereo-typical twenty-something who gets wasted every weekend, bringing home a new guy every other night. The rigorous focus and training I apply to being an athlete doesn't just stay on the mat. It's how I've managed to finish almost two degrees and help my family stay afloat financially. Being an Olympian won't last forever and I'm not idiotic enough to think I don't need a back-up plan for the future, unlike our Team Captain Oliver Ramsey.

Since I am the only openly gay member of Team Great Britain this year, the press has been desperate to pap me with a bloke. They'd take anything from me at this point: pictures of us stumbling out of a club or us holding hands at lunch—literally anything—but, so far, they've had no such luck.

Tom Daley's all settled down with his husband and

child and they'd like me to be the next gay athlete to set that kind of example, but I was having none of it. My focus hadn't wavered from the goal of gold for the last seven years and I didn't plan to let it any time soon. It was safe to say I was a constant disappointment for the press.

They'd have a field day if they knew I was just going to toss these condoms in my bedside drawer and leave them for the cleaners to get rid of once the games were over.

For a final second, I let the condoms distract me from the beauty of the Olympic Village and the fact I was there. I'd made it. Even if that did mean having to be in close proximity to the guy who went out of his way to make my life hell.

Even surrounded by hundreds and hundreds of British athletes, I could still pick Oliver Ramsey out of a crowd. Not because he was the tallest or the loudest, but because whenever I searched for him he was always there looking right back at me, eyes mocking me as I stood on my own with my duffel bag waiting for our next instructions.

I tore my eyes away from where they'd become locked on him to marvel at the Olympic Village. France had done a beautiful job, the buildings alone were stunning. I looked up to see eight full floors of British flags hung over the balconies and pride flared in my chest.

The men's gymnastics team was shuffled to the side by one of our coaches, Carson, so he could hand out our room passes. That's when the dread kicked in. I'd heard the stories, I'd read the articles, I knew how this worked. I was about to be given a roommate. This was going to be absolutely nothing like sharing a room with my twin.

"Okay," Coach Jacub started once we were in a quieter space. "Thirteen days till the opening ceremony. In your bags you'll find the training schedule for the next two weeks, plus time off for you guys to relax and also for family day." Time to relax, meant time to study. At least I had something to work with in terms of fitting in a couple of hours here and there to work on my master's dissertation. I still couldn't believe that the Opening Ceremony was just thirteen days away though. The thought of walking out into that true Olympic atmosphere was enough to make me lightheaded, but the fuzziness only furthered the buzz of adrenaline and excitement inside me.

That high was quickly dulled. "Julius and Tom, you're in room four hundred and nine," Coach Carson said as he handed them two hotel-style key cards. They trudged off to their room, only turning back once to shoot a glare to their best friend that said, 'unlucky man'. Carson had really fucked me and Oliver over if he was about to shove the pair of us in a room together for almost three weeks. Brayden, the alternate on the team, wasn't arriving until next week so the likelihood of us being put together was zero. I turned to look at Oliver as he turned to look at me, the air between us palpable with five years of treacherous history.

Just last year we were snapped arguing at a party and the year before that the press had leaked private texts of Oliver's about how much he disliked me and my attitude towards being a part of a team.

"Lucas and Oliver." Carson gritted his teeth as he handed over our key cards, before slapping a heavy hand on Oliver's shoulder. "I assume, as team captain, I don't have to ask you to behave, right?"

Oliver, with a forced looking grin I knew only too well, nodded at him, and mocked a salute earning him a fond shove. Oliver the golden boy. "You got it, coach. We'll be fine. Won't we, Lucas?"

I nodded, hard, but, in my mind, I couldn't stop any of the thoughts about putting up a screen in the middle of our room to keep him on the other side. I'd like to say a big fat no thank you to having to wake up to the sight of him every morning.

The rooms were incredibly simple: two beds, wardrobes, dressers, and an en-suite bathroom. Each side of the room was identical and backdropped by plain white, cinder block walls I couldn't wait to cover with a huge British flag and the posters and pictures I'd bought from home. The only pop of color in the room were the bedsheets; they were navy and pink and covered with the Olympic logo and cartoons of all the different sports. It was exactly like I'd seen from every other athlete on Instagram as they'd arrived for the 2020 games, where I'd longed to be three years ago with no luck. It was probably the only sentiment my new roommate and I shared.

"Look," Oliver started, disturbing me from my internal thoughts about making it to the Olympics. "Can't we just put all this shit behind us? We're at the Olympics now, we need to focus on training if we're going to win. Neither of us wants a repeat of 2020."

We'd both been in the running back then. I was just eighteen during the first round of trials for what should have been the 2020 Olympics. I was too young and, even after six years of solid training, the nerves had gotten the better of me. My floor routine had been flawless, but despite that I'd flunked the two other apparatus they'd asked me to perform on. Oliver had been there, watching me fail and then progressing to the next round while I cried in the changing rooms.

He didn't make it much further though. He picked up an injury during the final selection process and was ruled out completely. The 2024 Olympics were set to be a redemption year for the both of us. Not even the distraction of having to share a room with Oliver would ruin that, I'm sure even our captain would agree. Although he'd probably let himself be distracted by his friends anyway. Friends was not a sentiment we shared. Well, except for Alicia.

"I have no problem doing that," I replied, and I didn't. There was never a second I wasn't focused on the games. They'd been all I'd desired since before I could even remember, from when I'd begged my single mum working three jobs to pay for me to go to a gymnastics club. At nine years old I had no idea how much clubs cost and was an overly disappointed child when she'd said no. "Can *you* do it? That's the question. It's not me that keeps getting caught partying in the press."

He whirled around to face me, alarmingly blue eyes narrowed in my direction, shock evident at my words. "Fucking hell, I'm not going to apologize for having fun. It is allowed, you know? Maybe if you gave it a shot your parallel bars wouldn't look so uptight."

"Says the guy who struggles with a simple airflare on floor. Pretty sure all that alcohol has fucked up your coordination."

Oliver drunk was somewhat worse than Oliver sober. Sober he knew when to stop being a dick, drunk all restraint went out the window. I'd stupidly allowed myself to get drunk with him and the other guys once at an event last year. Oliver and I, well, we'd ended up almost coming to blows after I'd stepped outside for some air. I thought he was going to hit me, he'd had his fingers clutched in the collar of my shirt, his other fist balled at his side. Then he'd pulled away. Shame the people outside the bar had already caught the action on Snapchat. It was too late to stop all the news sites reporting we'd been in a scuffle. I hadn't touched a drop since. Coach screaming down the phone to me the next day was enough to put me off for life.

"Obviously not too shabby considering I was chosen as team captain. Didn't see your one-trick pony routine earning you that title." Oh, Oliver was good, he knew exactly where to aim his malicious words.

This floor routine had gotten me through the devastation of not being chosen for the last Olympics. My trainer had posted a video of it to Instagram and it'd gone viral. Ever since it had only been getting better. This year I was tipped to do incredibly well on floor, which terrified me, but I had my idol's footsteps to follow in.

Oliver observed that his words had had the desired effect and slipped into the bathroom. So I took my chance to decorate my side of the room. I started with a small British flag which I hung over my bed with blue tack and then quickly, whilst I could still hear the water running, I blue tacked my most treasured poster underneath it. Max Whitlock lived on my wall at home and he'd live on my wall here too. He kept me motivated and driven, something that wouldn't be taken away from me. Not even if Oliver was going to be sleeping mere meters from me.

He was the most incredible gymnast and the fact the bookies were betting I'd follow in his footsteps and win gold on floor was completely overwhelming. I heard the lock slide open and quickly repositioned the flag, covering up any evidence of the poster's existence before crossing my legs on top of the duvet to make myself look less shifty.

"Making yourself at home?" he asked in a snarky tone I swear he only saved for me.

I rolled my eyes and reminded myself I needed to focus and that started with ignoring the smarmy faced git. Instead I distracted myself with unpacking the stupid amount of tracksuit sets I'd brought with me to be able to stay comfortable. I'd hardly packed anything else, except the mandated suit for any press events I would be summoned to do. I'd brought no clothes for the wild parties which were thrown here, the ones I'm sure Oliver and his pals would be attending.

"I should get used to this silence, shouldn't I?" he asked, only for there to be a loud knock at the door saving me from having to answer him. Voices that were unmistakably the two other members of our team yelled Oliver's name from outside. I had this awful feeling living next door to them and constantly being in the training room with them meant I was never going to escape this trio. It filled the lone wolf in me with dread.

Chapter Two

Oliver

The hammering at the door continued, but I couldn't tear my eyes away from Lucas and his smug, holier-than-thou face as he ignored me to get on with his unpacking. I tried to forget about his existence as I headed for the door to the two guys who completed me as my best friends. "Can't I have a minute's peace before I have to deal with you two idiots?" I shouted through the door as they continued to pound on it like wild animals.

"Open up," Julius hollered, banging once more before he threw the door open himself, revealing the stupid grin I always expected from him. His blonde hair looked completely wild, which suggested he and Tom had napped instead of unpacking. Typical. "Well, at least neither of you were naked." He smirked teasingly, though the likelihood of us being naked at the same time or in the same room was zero. Lucas was beyond prudish and I was almost ninety-nine percent sure he was a virgin.

I remembered watching his coming out interview and everything in that moment had suddenly made sense. My first thought was now I understood why he hadn't been papped with a girlfriend before, my second was he was pretty damn brave considering there still weren't many out athletes, and the third was if he'd ever had sex.

What was he like in the sack? That thought was something I'd never shared with anyone.

"We've actually started unpacking our suitcases, unlike you," Julius said, gesturing to my untouched cases abandoned on the floor.

"Just having so much fun rooming with my best pal, you know?" I said in the most sarcastic drawl I could muster, only for it to elicit no response from Lucas the bore. It ground on me more than words could explain. If he only bit back more than once in a while he may do okay on this team. He really was no fun at all. He always had this focused look on his face, like the world was so serious twenty-four hours a day, three hundred and sixty-five days a year.

He was nothing but cold to me, to the team, and sometimes even to the coaches. I knew why he hated me, though, I'd beaten him to what should have been his first Olympic qualifiers. He was butt-hurt because, when it came down to it, I was better than him. Not that it had gotten me anywhere. I'd bombed my vault and sustained an injury which almost ruined my career, so who really lost out?

I started to unpack my bags as the guys made themselves comfy on my way too small bed. The top layer of my bag was packed with framed photos of my grandparents and me, my friends and me, and then one which immediately caught Tom's attention.

"Awww, you brought this one with you? You're such a big softy, cap'n," he remarked as he prized the framed picture of Tom, Julius, and me from my hands. It was my favorite picture of us; we all looked so happy with gold medals strewn around our necks at Worlds last year. The win pretty much guaranteed our spots on the

Olympic team.

I snatched it back off of him and stood it up on the side table next to my bed. "Suck ass," I shot back at him which caused both boys to snicker.

"Only if it's yours," Julius winked. If only he knew, if only anyone knew. Even I was still unsure how to explain it. I was pretty sure my grandparents knew, but I'd never gone out of my way to ask.

"Make yourselves useful and put these pictures up on my dresser, please." I dropped the frames into their laps only to be met with the most unpleasant groans of disapproval at my actions.

With both of them distracted, I pulled out the final picture, the one wrapped in my grandma's silk pillowcase, to be protected at all costs. Carefully, but quickly, I shoved it under my pillow where it had lived every night since the accident and where it would stay the whole time I was here.

The photo of Amber and me at our sixth form prom was too hard to look at now, but I couldn't be without it. The girl I'd fallen in love with at sixteen. The girl I'd kept out of the limelight when my athletic career took off, only to lose her four years later. She had been my escape from the world when the cameras never stopped flashing, but with her now gone I wish I could have shared every bit of her just so I could have been allowed to grieve for her publicly. Julius and Tom were my saviors; they'd pulled me from the brink of depression when she died, pushed me back into the gym, and gave me a reason to live. I could never thank them enough.

As a couple, we'd shared so many secrets and now she was gone they weighed me down. The only time the weight disappeared was when I was flipping on the bars or holding a position on the rings. It was complete freedom, but there was one secret I shared with her I'd never be free of.

"You good down there?" Tom asked from where he stood over me, all the frames now neatly lined up across my dresser. At least the pair were useful for something and they'd actually done a good job.

"All good. Why are you guys here again?" I asked, shutting off my thoughts completely. More than anything right now, I wanted to be out of my own head, not thinking about Amber, concentrating on being here with the guys and winning.

"We were thinking about getting dinner and then maybe some weight training so coach doesn't kill us for jetting off to Prague for the weekend." Admittedly, we maybe shouldn't have gone on a booze filled holiday the weekend before we flew to Paris for the Olympics, but we did make a pact afterwards not to drink at all for the month so we could focus on winning gold. Coach should really start trying to see things from our swings and roundabouts approach to life.

"Hey, before you leave, do you mind if I plug my streaming stick into the TV? You're welcome to use it whenever you want, I just need to be able to watch *Brooklyn Nine-Nine* whilst writing my thesis," Is of course what Lucas said to remind me he was still in the room. So he still had his addiction? Good to know. I remember hearing him talk about it like crazy during his interview for the cover of *Vogue* a couple of years ago. It was the only thing the reporter could get him to talk about outside of gymnastics and making it to the Olympics. The humor kept him calm during rough deadlines, that's what he'd told the journalist.

I looked up at Julius and Tom in time to see Julius roll his eyes at Lucas. Julius was a lot more impatient than I was, probably best we got out of here as quick as possible. "Sure, hook it up," I replied, only for Lucas to turn his back on me again and return to his side of the room. I wished I could figure out how to break him out of this bubble, his bubble. It made me so angry I couldn't find a way to get him out.

"So, dinner?" Julius pushed, his feet shuffling impatiently on the spot.

"Sure, sure, I'm coming. Let me just grab my jacket and water bottle and we can go." I herded them towards the door and opened it, clearly signaling for them to wait outside. I shut the door behind them and walked over to my bed so I could grab my abandoned jacket and bottle from the flight. "Do you want to join us?" I asked, only almost out of courtesy. It wouldn't be any fun if he did join us, but I had to ask, I had to keep trying to convince him to be part of this team. It was my job as captain, after all.

"Still full from the sandwich I ate at the airport, probably gonna get an early night as well so I can get up and fit in a run before breakfast." He held up the pair of pajama pants that he was clearly about to get changed into so he could spend the evening, alone, in bed.

I shook my head and didn't wait around to gauge his full reaction to me inviting him. He never had any time for the team. It sucked, for both him and us.

"Evan's not coming?" Tom asked as I stepped outside and pulled the door behind me with a slam, Tom didn't sound surprised though. None of us were anymore. Lucas actually made more time for Brayden, the alternate on our team, than he did for any of us.

"Nah, getting an early night, so you're stuck with only me boys," I said, only for Julius to let out an unsurprised laugh, so I smacked him on the back of his head. The three of us had come to share a mutual understanding that Lucas was only out for himself, but I think if Julius could make a point about this whenever he opened his mouth, he would. Coming from a family with six brothers, he had the strongest belief in brotherhood, but no amount of wittering on at Lucas would convince him to leave his bubble.

If the sport had taught me anything in the many years I'd been involved, it was that you needed to be friendly with your teammates to survive. Most people had to force it but not us three. For Julius, Tom, and I it had all come naturally. Being part of the 2024 team was a bonus. Lucas was overly dedicated to his training and his degree and nothing else. He had no place for friends. Even when he won gold last year at Worlds, he'd still abandoned us to go home.

I pitied him; it must have been lonely at the top with no-one to share it with.

Julius pulled out his vlogging camera and hit record as we walked down the corridor of the village dorms. His YouTube voice bounced off every door and perked something up inside me; it made me feel lucky to have friends I got to compete with. Even if they did feel the need to capture every moment and make them as dramatic as possible.

"What's up guys?" he yelled into the microphone with the ridiculous wave he did at the start of every video. "We are all moved into the Olympic Village and me and this pair"—he tilted the camera at me and Tom and we both waved, completely used to this happening now—"are heading down for our first dinner. No training today after all the traveling, but you can guarantee we'll be back to crushing it in the gym tomorrow. I'll try and get some footage of the wonderful food they probably serve here and rope these idiots into a Q&A session over dinner. Over and out for now. Oh and definitely tune in tomorrow for a challenge video I have ready for the boys." He flicked off the record button and shoved the camera back into his pocket.

Both Tom and I stared at him, wordlessly, as he stalked down the corridor without us.

"Did he just say challenge?" I asked.

"I think he did," Tom replied. "Care to let us in on what you're going to force us to do on camera?" Tom shouted after him, Julius completely unaware that we'd stopped.

"What are you talking about?" he asked as he halted about ten meters down the corridor in front of us, finally noticing we weren't following him.

"You, forcing us to do some weird challenge thing," I said, this time louder so he could actually hear us complaining.

"What can I say? The fans love you guys and when Tom did all those backflips on the trampoline and then fell off I got like ten thousand new followers." Julius shrugged mischievously and waited for us to catch up with him.

"And I got a chipped bone in my elbow. Please don't break any of my bones just two weeks before the games, I beg you," Tom pleaded over dramatically. I'm sure Julius was gutted he'd put his camera away, he always missed the best bits.

"Both of you won't be doing anything too crazy,

coach would beat my ass if I let his all-rounders crash out of the competition." They both snickered as I used what Julius had coined my captain's voice, in the hopes it would tone down their crazy side at least a little.

"How much do you think I would have to pay your boy Lucas to get in on something?" He never stopped pushing. "One of my subscribers had this amazing idea for a stunt, but I'd need all four of us to execute."

"I think you'd have to rig the competition so he wins every medal possible for him to even consider a starring role in your little home movies. And he's not my boy." In my head I knew it would probably take more than that. Much, much more. Like maybe a brain or personality transplant.

"Hey, you make them sound like pornos. They are entertainment for all the people who love to watch this hot bod work out and whom appreciate my constant sense of humor." He gestured to himself like he was some model on the runway.

"Damn, did the boy just say whom? When did he go to university?" Tom smirked, before Julius punched his arm and then jogged down the stairs at a rapid pace to avoid any retaliation.

"He did, incorrectly, but at least he tried," I replied as I hurtled down the stairs after him. "Also, please can we not talk about university again? Not only am I going to have to deal with Lucas stressed about the games, but also his damn master's thesis," I groaned over the banister loud enough for the pair to hear as they chased each other like children.

"Well, if it gets too tough, we'll drag your mattress into our room and you can sleep on the floor. You never know though, there are still two weeks to go before our qualifiers. Lucas may have a change of heart," Tom's positivity was so unrealistic I snorted as I laughed. That was never going to happen.

Chapter Three

Lucas

My hands and feet had pummeled across the floor a thousand times before Oliver, Tom and Julius decided to join us in the training room. They caught my eye as Coach Carson pulled me to the side to discuss whether we should switch up the final move of my floor routine. It had already gone from being a double layout in the video which went viral, to a twisting double layout at Worlds which I had then perfected for the Olympics. Yet, coach still wanted it to be more, he was adamant I was capable of more.

"This routine scored 15.655 at Worlds and that was after a .1-point deduction when I took a step after landing the triple twist." The words went in one ear and straight back out as he searched for a video of the Arabian he wanted to add to my double layout. Carson was relentless and whilst I normally appreciated him constantly pushing me to do more, the Arabian felt out of my reach.

"Your difficulty rating right now is what, a 6.8 and you're executing it perfectly, scoring between 8.8 and 9 every single time for execution. Adding the Arabian into your double layout would take the difficulty up to a 7, maybe even a 7.1, if you made it a triple layout." Carson showed me the move he was talking about and it was perfect, not a single bent arm or step on landing in sight.

It had probably taken months to perfect and he wanted me to add it to my already set-in-stone routine with just twelve days until the qualifiers.

"If I tank the landing my execution score will plummet. Is it really worth the extra 0.2 in difficulty?"

Carson looked bemused at my tone, eyebrow raised as for the first time, probably ever, I was objecting to a harder move being added to my routine.

"You'll be asking me to try and do a quadruple twist next."

"Well, your three and a half punch front is superb, there's probably room for an extra half a twist in there."

I tipped my head back as laughter bubbled out of me, catching the attention of Oliver, who looked over at the pair of us in shock before he shook his head and chalked up in preparation for being hoisted onto the rings.

Oliver was the worst, but it never stopped me admiring him physically from afar. Last year he made it onto some world's hottest twenty-somethings list, ranking like tenth or so out of fifty. Not that I bought the magazine. Still, even I could admit he was gorgeous, like jaws dropped when he stepped into the room kind of gorgeous. With his bottomless sea blue eyes, swished back brown hair, and a chiseled to perfection jaw, he had that typical hot guy look. Then you looked closer and there was an auburn smattering of freckles across his nose and cheekbones and a fan of dark brown eyelashes which would put any girl's falsies to shame. Okay, so maybe I studied the picture, but could anyone blame me? If he wasn't such a jerk, his confidence and his leadership skills would make him beyond attractive, but alas, he was.

His rings looked amazing though. I watched as he

held a flawless iron cross, impeccable concentration on his face before he pulled himself up into a swallow hold.

"So?" Carson said, his voice clipped, telling me he'd probably been speaking to me the whole time I'd been hopelessly distracted by tensing muscles and clear blue eyes.

"I'll try it, okay?" I gave in, at least it would get him off my back for an hour or two. Who knows, maybe I did have the move in me?

"Good, because we are going to need this score to be high to have a chance of medaling in the all-around team final. Plus I'm going to need you to have this done so you can help Brayden with his floor when he gets here." Brayden wanted nothing more than to be good on floor, but even at nineteen he was built to be more of a rings guy or like Julius, amazing on pommel.

When my back slammed on to the padded mat for what felt like the hundredth time I wanted to be done, but the Arabian was getting there and the one time I sort of landed it had fired something up inside of me. I'd chugged down a protein shake for lunch and returned to the corner of the mat. Looking across the floor before I launched into the layout never got old, even when every muscle in my body throbbed.

A couple more on the mat before dinner and I'd probably have been able to get it down a little more. Then I could begin figuring out how difficult it would be to add in after my wide arm handstand, or if I needed to fit in another set of tumbles before this closing move. My head was swimming with ideas, drowning out my brain as I stared at the opposite corner. I needed to chat with Carson before I changed anything, but I'd rather have an idea before I discussed it with them. Maybe if I moved my handstand and air flares to the middle of the routine, before the triple front punch, it would make more sense.

"Don't you think it's time to move off of the mat for today?" I heard him say behind me; of course he'd chosen this moment to interrupt. "I could do with getting some practice in and I'm sure your other routines could use some work," Oliver said as he sidled up and stood behind me as I went to take my millionth run up of the day. I tried not to let his words ruin my focus, but now I knew he was there, I was distracted.

"Excuse me?" My eyes were still glued to the mat like if I zoned in on it enough Oliver would disappear and I'd smash the Arabian double layout.

"I need to use the mat," Oliver reiterated like I hadn't heard him the first time. "Your high bar needs some work before the competition, doesn't it?"

He knew exactly where to hit me. For a pair who weren't friends, we knew each other inside and out on the mat, all of each other's strengths and weaknesses, and he knew I'd been struggling on the bar. I finally diverted my eyes to meet his, a sheen of sweat dripping down his brow, his blue eyes a shade of denim that had been washed too many times. "Coach okayed me to work on the mat all day, he's added a new move to my routine and I need to master it before I can move on. Plus, if I master it now, I'll have more time to help Brayden with his when gets here. That good with you, *captain*?"

"I'm just saying, it might be nice for you to share the floor with us. Just because it's your specialty doesn't mean you get to hog it and only share it with your shadow whenever he decides to rock up. He does realize this is the big time right, why isn't he here yet?" He shared a knowing look with Julius and Tom who had joined us on the side of the mat, a bemused smile on Julius's face as Oliver rolled his eyes.

I let out a noisy breath, almost at the point of giving in when Oliver started to push again. "Your teammates are asking you to share. Any chance of that happening sometime before they lock up the training room tonight?"

"I guess you'll have to wait till tomorrow then." I quickly looked away from him so I didn't have to see how annoyed they looked before I took off across the mat. My mind screamed at me: half twist, double flip, keep your body straight, and then land. I flew through the air and when my feet hit the ground, apart from the tiniest wobble, I opened my eyes to see all three men stood opposite me, gobsmacked, confirming I'd smashed it.

"I mean, I can kind of see why Carson's let him have the floor today. He owned it," Tom commented, earning him a swift elbow to the ribs from Oliver.

"Whatever, I'm going to work out," Oliver grumbled before he disappeared into the gym off the side of our training room, the other two boys splitting off as well, with Julius to the vault and Tom to the pommel horse.

At least it got them off my back till tomorrow. Or at least that's what I'd thought, until I remembered there was no escape from Oliver now that we shared a room.

"Hey, I get as team captain you think you have a say in my training, but you don't, and I'd appreciate it if you didn't try to interfere," I said as we sat down on our respective beds for the evening, breaking the awkward silence which had settled around us.

"If that's what you thought I was doing, then you

21

really have no idea. Maybe if you stopped focusing on yourself for a second you'd realize how strong our team is. We have a real chance of qualifying for the all-around team finals, but we can't do it if you carry on this solo mission. Both Julius and Tom are the best all-rounders Team GB has seen in decades, why can't you just get on board?"

Just get on board. Like it was so easy. Like I hadn't banked on myself for literally everything since I was old enough to remember. Did he have any idea what it was like to be a fourteen-year-old being told by their mum that she couldn't afford to send him to gymnastics club for the year. Then having to get not one, but two jobs to try and help out? Mum thought it was so I could go back to gymnastics, but really it was so I could keep food on the table and make sure my baby sister never caught on to how poor we were. Lucy was still naïve to it, even at fourteen, but it was my three-year-old sister, Lauren, I wanted to shield the most. I resented having to work so much as a child, but it built me to always go at it alone in order to support those around me. The Olympics were no different.

"Are you even listening?"

I hadn't been. I'd tuned out, my eyes focused on the picture of me, mom, Lucy, and Lauren at Disneyland. I'd paid for it with my first set of endorsement money so I could give my baby sister, at eight-years-old, her first family holiday.

"You're so selfish. We're supposed to be a team. I don't mean to be cliché, but there's no I in team and we aren't going to win if your only focus is individual gold."

"Sorry, did you just say selfish? Are you fucking kidding me? You know absolutely nothing about me—"

"And whose fault is that?" Oliver interrupted, thrusting himself to his feet. "You've made it impossible for any of us to befriend you. It's like there's this wall around you which blocks out the rest of the team."

"I don't want to be friends. It wasn't a requirement for me to be on the team the last time I checked."

He stormed across the room to me to stand in front of my bed and whilst my blood boiled, I wasn't about to engage in a fight which would probably get me kicked off the team. That was exactly what Oliver wanted. So instead I took a deep breath, relaxing my shoulders and he seemed to get the message; I didn't want to fight about this anymore.

"Look, I'm not asking for a lot, just for you to maybe make a little more effort with the guys. Did you see the team which went to the Rio Olympics? Nile, Louis -"

I snickered a little and some of the redness eased from his face, the anger draining from his cheeks as he caught on to why I was laughing. "Didn't realize we were discussing One Direction, would that be pre- or post-Zayn leaving the band?"

He laughed, only the tiniest bit but I was counting it, before he attempted to straighten out his face enough to say, "I just don't think it would do you any harm to try a little bit harder to be part of the team." For a second I was distracted by his beautiful smile, which for once was aimed at me, until his phone bleeped and he shrugged on his Team GB jacket and took off like there was a rocket up his ass.

I blinked and he was gone, taking probably the one moment of niceness we were ever going to share with him. A tiny pang of sadness struck my heart, but then I realized I was being left in peace and could get at least an hour's worth of research done. Balance was restored.

Chapter Four

Oliver

"Incredible, the twisted handstand into a dismount never fails to astound me," I said, congratulating Julius as he performed yet another flawless pommel horse routine.

"Well, you know, I'm not named the best all-rounder on this team for nothing." He took a dramatic bow, before clapping chalk in both mine and Tom's faces. Some gratitude.

"I'm like one hundred percent sure that's my title," Tom replied, as he dusted the chalk which coated his nose and cheeks off, leaving him with just a white cast across a thick layer of sweat. "Well at least I won't need the make-up artist to powder my face before we go on camera," he chuckled.

"Who is this with again?" Julius asked. "I read the press calendar at like half-five this morning. Not sure Estelle quite understands the time difference. For some reason she thought Paris was like five hours ahead rather than just an hour when she called me this morning." Estelle may have been a bit of a common sense ditz, but she had an English degree from Durham and she wrote like Jane Austen. Plus, she wasn't afraid to stand her ground with Julius. He needed that in a girlfriend.

"Some French sports mag. Every day they're

publishing a piece about sports in the Olympics and we're the lucky four to be chosen to talk about Gymnastics." I'd glanced over the questions they were going to ask us this morning, the usual things—what got us into gymnastics, what we are looking forwards to at the Olympics. All the stuff we'd spieled out many, many times before.

"Talking of the four of us, where's Lucas? I'm shocked he wasn't in here before us again," Julius added like I hadn't already noticed he was missing. My muscles had tensed with every step I'd taken on the mat, like Lucas's phantom was following me around. It was, after all, his apparatus apparently.

"I have no clue. He'd already left this morning when I woke up. I saw him at breakfast with Alicia, but not since then." I glanced up at the clock. We should have left to walk to the briefing room at least ten minutes ago, but I knew, as captain, if we showed up without Lucas, that people would talk and none of us needed any bad press just eleven days before the qualifiers.

"How is sharing a room with him?" Julius asked as he mounted the pommel horse once more, incapable of standing still for a single moment. He'd been like this the whole time I'd known him; the teachers at school hated him for it as he was constantly tapping or rocking on his chair.

"Quiet, he doesn't say much. Just sleeps and studies to be honest. Most of the time I don't even realize he's there." I shrugged as Julius made neat work of the pommel, his hands never slipping off the grips once, concrete concentration as he swiveled up and down the horse.

"Why do you sound so surprised?" Tom sighed as

he reached for his bag from the floor. "Maybe I should talk to him?"

I tried to interject and say nothing would help, but Tom just waved his hand at me to stop me in my tracks.

"I'm just saying, I don't think he's going to listen to you with your history and the fact you can't keep your temper around him for more than two minutes." Tom, the most level-headed of the three of us, would never let me live down the big argument of 2022. At least that fight had been kept out of the press. Tom had jumped in the middle of the verbal abuse Lucas and I had been hurling at each other before I did anything I'd regret.

We were at the Nike launch party, where Lucas had pretty much been the guest of honor as one of the new faces of the brand. Turned out I couldn't take seeing him on billboards around the country and national TV adverts as I tried to watch my favorite show. Something about seeing those big green eyes and auburn locks every single day had caused me to lose it, especially as I'd downed several glasses of champagne.

"Sorry, sorry, I know I'm late," Lucas panted and the image in my head of him in tight Nike shorts vanished. "Let's get this over with."

Julius cleared his throat as he dismounted the pommel horse, clearly waiting for some kind of explanation as to why Lucas was late, but I knew one wasn't coming. "Come on, let's just go please. We're already fifteen minutes late," I said firmly before anything kicked off between the pair.

Four stools were already set up when we arrived and Janice, the journalist, had a crease in her forehead which told me she wasn't happy we were late. "Whenever you boys are ready, we'll get started." She clicked record on the taping device and the ping echoed through the room as we all perched on the tiny stools.

She plowed through the questions as we gave the most stereotypical answers. All the gymnasts who'd inspired us over the years, Lucas discussing his gymnastics group in South Essex as per usual. Like we hadn't heard about it enough from when Max Whitlock was on the scene. Then the tone shifted, Tom talking about how his dad had always been his inspiration. I'd heard the story a thousand times, but he hardly ever brought it up to the press.

"Dad was a gymnast when he was younger. He had incredible potential, but he broke his back early on as a teen and although surgery fixed it, the doctors told him he'd never be able to compete. So he became a coach, much to my mom's despair as he had me tumbling across the playroom as a toddler. If Team GB had hired him as a coach he'd probably be here right now with us." Tom laughed, a glossy sheen spread across his hazelnut eyes as he talked about his hero.

"What about you guys? Are any of your family involved? They must all be so proud of how far you guys have come," Janice asked as she finished making notes on what Tom had said. "Oliver, what about your folks?"

"Well, as I'm sure you're aware, my mother passed away during childbirth and my father isn't around. My grandparents supported me through my teens and early twenties and are incredibly proud. They'll be flying out next week. They love the Olympics, and are big fans of all the water sports." I pushed down the lump that had formed in my throat, it already felt scratchy, like shards of glass had cut into it from her words. Janice just smiled appreciatively, her cheeks rosy after her slip up about my mum. It was common knowledge in the press that she wasn't with us.

"My parents and girlfriend, Estelle, will be flying out for the games. Estelle has been my biggest supporter since we first got together over nine years ago. She came to the Tokyo games and you can bet she'll be in the crowds again this year. She's incredible." Julius shot Janice the proudest smile, he truly adored that girl.

I loved Estelle, Amber's big sister, but since Amber's death I'd struggled to spend time with her. Until the funeral we'd been each other's biggest comforts, then the funeral passed and I couldn't bear to be around her or the rest of the family. Even hearing her name hurt; it was like something clenched around my heart when someone bought her up. It was a constant reminder of what I'd lost.

The clench around my heart moved up to my throat and my eyes swam with tears at her memory. She would have loved being here today, as Paris was her favorite city after all. I'd loved to have seen her in the crowds and, well, if she was here today it wouldn't have just been her coming to support me.

"Anyone special in your life?" Janice asked, and I followed her line of sight through my bleary eyes to where she was looking at Lucas. Normally the press skirted around this topic with him. He came out as gay years ago and even though we had progressed with LGBTQ+ athletes, it wasn't enough. In the joint interviews I'd done with him, I'd either seen the reporter being really lewd about his sexuality or completely avoiding the subject. How hard was it to just ask if he had a partner or boyfriend? I felt for him; it was part of the reason I never discussed my bisexuality. I guess I had it easier.

"I uh, well, I…" he fumbled over his words, tongue-tied as he struggled to give his answer.

I was fairly sure there wasn't anybody in his life, not that I'd been keeping tabs on him. I'd just never seen him with anyone or read about him being with anyone in the papers. Just before our argument at the Nike party, I'd watched this guy hit on him at the bar. He'd offered to buy Lucas a drink, even stroked his hand up Lucas's thigh seductively. I'd never seen anyone flinch back so quickly. He had dashed to the bathroom, not even offering the poor guy an apology.

That's when I'd cornered Lucas in the bathroom to tell him exactly what I thought of his stupid Nike advert. Okay, maybe not exactly what I thought—some of those thoughts belonged to my bed late at night—but I'd given him a piece of my mind about it. I'd had my fists clutched at the collars of his crisp white shirt as I bared my soul, no idea what my next move was going to be. Thank heavens Tom had been in the stall opposite us and had quickly jumped in and pulled us apart.

"No handsome fella?" Janice pushed, leaning forwards into the one-sided conversation. Lucas shifted on his stool, arms folded across his chest defensively. She'd clearly hit a nerve and whilst I wanted her to push, because I too wanted to hear his answer, I did feel bad for him. If she'd pressured me to talk about a girlfriend, I'd have reacted exactly the same. This question also wasn't on our approved list, which was frustrating.

He shook his head and I watched as his Adam's apple bobbed repeatedly. The topic clearly made him uncomfortable. How had I never noticed this before? "No," he added to the shake of his head. "My main focus right now is the Olympics." Well, we all knew that.

"So we can put out an alert after the games that you'll be on the lookout for a man?" She grinned, shooting him a cheeky wink which I couldn't help but think was a little unprofessional. "What's your type?" she asked. "Just so the male population are aware?"

Lucas glanced at the door. I recognized the look— he was contemplating bolting—and the team captain in me kicked in. I may not have liked the bloke much, but no journalist had the right to make anyone uneasy, especially a member of *my* team.

"I'm sorry, but can we wrap this up?" I signaled with my hands for her to cut the tape recorder and thankfully she complied without me having to call the team's agent over. "Thank you so much for having us, but we do have to get back to training as our qualifiers are less than two weeks away."

"Thank you, Team GB. I'll have a copy sent out to you before it goes to print tomorrow. Are you guys okay for us to get a couple of snaps for the double page spread before you head back to training?"

The color which had drained from his face at her questions had now returned to a soft, embarrassed glow radiating from his cheeks. He gave me the tiniest of nods, so I agreed to the pictures.

We lined up next to each other, me and Lucas on opposing sides of Julius and Tom. It was always best for us to keep our distance even when I was practically saving his ass from a journalist. Then she made us wrap our arms around each other against the stupid green screen, which she'd probably turn into some cheesy Parisian background. Across the back of Julius and Tom, Lucas and my arms met and at first I wanted to push his arm away to mess up whatever face he had pulled for the camera. But then the struggle on his face from the interview flashed up in my mind: the way he'd tugged at his lower lip with his teeth, the fear in his eyes. So, instead, I squeezed his forearm, which I'm sure was super weird, but felt like the reassuring thing to do in my head.

It wasn't until we were back in our shared room in the evening, both of us tucked up in bed, the night sky consuming the room, that I realized how much he'd needed it, because into the darkness he whispered, "Hey, thanks for earlier. You didn't need to save me like that, but you did and I'm really grateful."

He couldn't see it, but a soft smile spread across my face and rather than a snarky remark, I whispered back that he was welcome and no matter what, I'd never let anyone feel uncomfortable like that. Then, for the first time, I felt like a worthy captain.

Chapter Five

Lucas

I woke up exhausted, the back of my eyes stinging from the lack of sleep and restless tossing and turning all night. I'd laid awake for hours in the darkness, Oliver's words still lingering in the air between us, clouding my thoughts and preventing me from getting any sleep.

I knew he'd sensed it from the start. I'd caught his eye as he looked down the line at me fumbling over my words, trying to dodge any kind of questioning about my love life. I always contemplate lying, saying there was somebody but it was private, but why should I have to? Why did there have to be somebody in my life? I had all I needed between gymnastics and my family.

My twin would always tell me about her boyfriends, serious or not. She'd always wait for me to tell my own stories, but they never came. I had two or three peer pressured one-night stands at Uni, but that was it. One night, when Lucy had come up to my university in Colchester, she'd asked the dreaded question as we tried to sleep.

"When are you going to get a boyfriend?" the then eighteen-year-old Lucy had asked. She'd been in a relationship for about five months at this point with someone from her university in Chelmsford. She was desperate for us to share yet another experience together.

I'd pondered my answer. She'd told me a few years later she thought I was aromantic or asexual because I just never seemed interested, but that wasn't the case at all. It wasn't that I didn't desire sex or a relationship, I just didn't see the point. I took care of myself and my family and I didn't need anyone else in the mix who could disrupt my life. I especially didn't need anyone diverting my attention and focus away from getting to the Olympics and providing the life my family deserved.

So I had told her I wasn't sure. "I don't know, Luce. I haven't met anyone here who's caught my eye. I've been busy with classes and training and driving home every weekend to help at the pub."

"You don't have to, you know? mum would hire some local students to work weekends, she can cope." I knew Lucy meant well, but I didn't want mum to have to just cope. I didn't want her to be back in the position of being exhausted from working three jobs and having no time to spend with her kids. Especially as Lauren was still only twelve. I had wanted to help out in any way I could so she could run the pub from home with enough employees and with the money to do the extensions and upgrades she wanted. I was so close to making that happen.

Lucy hadn't asked since, so I think the question from the journalist had startled me. Although, it was Oliver's act of kindness which kept me awake all night. I couldn't for the life of me understand why him saving me had made me feel so warm and safe; it was his job as captain after all. He'd just never really extended that out to me. So the question of why now had played on my mind all night.

However, as Oliver emerged from the bathroom the

following morning, the kindness was gone. Instead it was replaced with a bemused grin I knew all too well. "We have an interview with Sky Sports News today, please do try not to be late."

Before I could stop myself I shot back, "Are you kidding me? I was fifteen minutes late and I apologized."

"What was so important you made the whole team late for an important interview? One which was an honor to be chosen for," he asked, like it was any of his business, when it really wasn't.

I didn't want to tell him, and quite frankly I didn't feel like I had to, but I knew it was going to be the only way to get him off my back. "My twin sister is a nurse and she works ridiculous shifts. She called me on her break to let me know she couldn't get the time off work to be here for the opening ceremony, so now she and my family aren't flying out till the day before our first competition. I was a little bit upset, so I needed a moment to collect myself. Is that okay with you? I said I was sorry yesterday, it won't happen again." He was lucky I was apologizing again after he'd already had too many.

"You see, this is my problem with you—" Oliver started.

"Do we have time right now to hear all the reasons you dislike me? Didn't *The Sun* already leak that list?" I stood up from my bed so I could grab a pair of sweatpants and a hoodie and get the hell out of this room. I was not in the mood to hear his team spiel again.

"Look, I'm sorry they can't make it to the opening ceremony, it sucks. But, we have commitments and you being late made us all late and it's just beyond unprofessional. All I'm asking is for you to think about us, for once. The Olympics isn't just about you."

A wave of rage washed over me and I couldn't control myself as I stalked into Oliver's space to really make my point clear to him. "Why don't you just go fuck yourself. I've had enough of you talking down to me, calling me selfish and inconsiderate just because I won't dance to the beat of your drum. I've worked my whole life for my family, to keep food on our table, to get to the point where we can afford to actually live in our own house so my mum never has to worry again about us being evicted like she did our whole childhood. I do everything for them, everything, so don't you dare make it out like I only do this for myself. I'm sorry you can't understand that or the fact I don't want friends, but I'm here to win and I can't afford to get distracted. I'm so glad you're capable of juggling a social life and training, but I don't have time for it." I all but screamed at him as my words forced him to walk backwards to the point his back hit the wall.

"I'm not asking you to be our friend," he screamed back. "I actually couldn't think of anything worse. What I am asking is for you to have just a little bit of respect for us as your teammates." He took the deepest of breaths and then exhaled into the small amount of space we were sharing, before he straightened his shoulders to make his next point. "Have you ever noticed we've always shown up for everything you do? When you became one of the faces of Nike, we were there at the celebration party. We showed up for your Fitbit commercial shoot when you had the range with them. I even came by myself to your fucking *Vogue* shoot a few months ago, because that's what we do as a team, we support each other. We are the only people who understand how grueling and exhausting it is to be an athlete, yet we still find time in the day for one another. You don't even stick around for the after parties when we've won medals."

"I still work, you know? Outside of being a gymnast, I'm a barman at my mom's pub and you know I'm still a student. I have papers to write, exams to sit, and lectures to attend."

"You choose to do that shit. You could have just stopped at your undergraduate degree. I mean what the fuck even is a Master's in Political Administration?"

I'd never told him anything about my master's, so I had no idea exactly how he knew what course I was doing, but in the moment it was beyond the point.

"Being an athlete doesn't last forever, you know? Is it so awful to want to have a couple of degrees under my belt so when I'm too old to compete anymore I can find a new career to support my family in the future?" I couldn't understand how people didn't think about these kind of things, like a back-up plan in case I get injured.

"What future family? Your freak out yesterday tells me you can't even talk about a partner without choking. What happened? Someone break your heart beyond repair? Get over it, we've all had bad break-ups, doesn't mean you get to fuck up all the time."

"I doubt anybody could ever put up with *you*; you're a constant pain in my ass. Can you not get off my back for one bloody moment and just let me get on with my training? I've been doing this on my own for the last eleven years, I don't need your captain complex interfering now."

My back collided with the wall before I could even recognize that I'd practically been flung across the room. All of a sudden I was being pinned to said wall by the straps of my work out vest. Oliver's fists curled around the straps causing them to dig into my armpits whilst he made no attempt to move. His skin was mottled and his nostrils flared as he stared down at me, rage flickering across the whites of his eyes.

"Shut the fuck up." I'd clearly hit a nerve. His hot breath mingled with mine as he panted against me, before jabbing a finger into my shoulder. "I don't even know how you can talk about anyone putting up with me, when I can't even stand to share a room with you." His face was now mere millimeters away from mine.

"Then change rooms. See if I give a shit. Sleep in the corridor for all I care. As long as you save face in front of the coaches, you can do whatever you want, captain." I grit out the final word, but I could feel pins starting to prick the back of my eyes; why did I always have to get teary when I got angry?

"You know if it was fucking possible, I'd have changed rooms by now. Unlike you, though, I care about the public perception of the team and don't want anyone to get wind that we are actually just this malfunctioning unit," he replied through equally gritted teeth, eyes glued to mine.

"Malfunctioning unit." I chuckled in the hopes it would diffuse the tension between us and get him to back off, but it only extracted a deep, raspy noise from the back of his throat. His eyes flitted down to my lips, in a move that if he hadn't been so close I definitely wouldn't have seen. A move I could now never unsee. We'd been in this position before—me convinced he was going to punch me—but this time, as I watched every inch of his face move, it didn't seem to be the case at all.

Whatever he was feeling as he licked across his bottom lip, it startled me. If I was an outsider looking in on this moment like it was a TV show, this would be the bit where they'd kiss. This was the end of season two of *Brooklyn Nine-Nine* for Amy and Jake where there was so much lust in the air they couldn't help but give in.

That wasn't us though. He wasn't Jake and I had no desire to lose myself in him, in the moment, like Amy does. I definitely didn't. No matter how much there was something tugging in my gut saying, 'what's the harm?', I knew what the harm could be—complete distraction and me walking away from the Olympics a complete failure. Losing everything I'd ever worked for.

His blue eyes sparkled in the fluorescent lighting of our room and I knew if I didn't move soon, we'd both become wrapped up in this moment and then each other and nope, I couldn't do that. So, with my hands flat on his chest, I pushed him away. He stumbled slightly, but when he looked up at me again the haze had worn off and the spell was completely broken.

"Oh fuck," he groaned, his eyes hooded as he frantically tried to avert his gaze to anything other than me. Finally his gaze found the door.

I steadied myself against the wall behind me as he turned on his heels and hot footed it out of our room, leaving me behind, panting and frustrated. The only sound I could hear over my heart thumping in my chest was his heavy footsteps as he sprinted down the corridor away from me.

Chapter Six

Oliver

What the heck had I been thinking?

Why the hell did I think sticking my tongue down his throat would help our already rocky relationship? If I was honest with myself, which I really didn't want to be, I'd been thinking about doing this for ages, maybe even years; but I'd resisted thus far, so why was now any different? How had I let myself get so close to kissing him again? I fucking hated it. I hated him.

At first I'd just wanted to shut him up, to stop him mocking me. There had been this glint in his pretty eyes which had almost dared me to kiss him. I'd almost taken that dare. I'd been seconds from leaning in and claiming his mouth. It would have been the stupidest thing I could ever have done.

It was the heat of the moment. That's what I had to keep telling myself. It was always the heat of the moment with Lucas Evans. He'd never let anyone get close enough under any other circumstance, the only time we ever really properly spoke was in the midst of an argument, or if he really had to in the training center.

Something about this time had felt different though. Maybe it's because it'd come off of the back of the weird little conversation we'd had in the dark last night or because right now there was no escaping him, but it felt different. Like maybe I should have kissed him just to see what happened next. I could almost guarantee he'd still have pushed me away, but it still intrigued me. Maybe it was because this time around it looked like he actually wanted to kiss me too.

Kissing another guy had never played on my mind like this before. I'd been with my fair share in the last few years, but they'd been anonymous one-time things in the bathrooms of seedy clubs. Most of them I hardly remembered in the morning, just a dull throb of pleasure under a humongous hangover.

This kiss, well this kiss would probably have lived with me forever. Lucas and his stupid grass-green eyes weren't going to be something I could just forget. Even more so with him sleeping just a couple of meters away from me every night.

As I escaped out of our room, I felt like I'd been reduced to a teenage boy running away from a crush. Lucas wasn't a crush, not at all.

I fished my phone from my pocket and realized it was literally only six-thirty a.m., and the run I'd woken up early to go on had been forgotten about in a blur of horny angst.

As I sprinted down the corridor with only my sliders on my feet, I realized a run was now out of the question. Instead, I decided on the next best option: waking up the guys and forcing them to have an early breakfast with me.

Hovering outside their room, I shot them a text, hearing both of their phones ping on the other side of the door. Rather than patiently waiting for either of them to reply, I started hammering against the wood instead. Underneath my horny filled rage, I hoped the pair didn't actually resent me for waking them up at this ridiculous hour. A shuffle of feet towards the door confirmed I'd been successful and seconds later I was met with a groggy looking Julius and an equally tired looking Tom.

"Dude, come on. Are you kidding me? It's not even seven yet, where's the fire?" Julius mumbled out whilst trying to stifle back a yawn.

Tom rubbed sleep from his eyes before squinting at me. "What's wrong?" he asked as I fiddled with the hem of my shirt, my thoughts swamped with the feeling of Lucas's lips on mine. Damn Tom for always knowing when something was going on in my head.

"Nothing, just didn't sleep well," I lied. I'd actually slept incredibly well, which was why I'd woken up at the crack of dawn refreshed and ready to go.

"Tell me about it." Julius slipped a dirty shirt he'd just picked up off the floor over his head before he jutted his thumbs out at Tom. "This one arrived back at one this morning after a couple rounds with a certain Australian high jumper."

I rolled my eyes. She was one of the many female athletes I'd seen Tom try to hit on since we'd got here. He hadn't shut up about her for the whole of dinner last night.

"You can talk. I came back and he was video calling Estelle and let me tell you, Ollie, I saw things I can never unsee." Tom shivered and I didn't even want to begin to imagine what he'd seen.

"I put a sock on the door," Julius argued in protest.

"I thought you were joking. It was one am," Tom shot back. Thank God for these two idiots. Often they argued like toddlers, but right now I needed all the playful arguments between the pair to keep my mind off of Lucas.

"Okay, calm down," I interjected before they woke up the whole floor. "It's still not even seven yet, let's not wake everyone else up with your childish behavior. Shall we head to the canteen and get breakfast instead?"

We trudged down to the canteen, only to have to wait another twenty minutes for it to open for service. Unfortunately, in that time I'd already been given a blow by blow, quite literally, of Tom's engagement with Kacey, and just before I could be any more shocked by my friends, Julius revealed something huge.

"After I hung up from Estelle last night, I bought an engagement ring online."

Tom's jaw dropped and his fork fell into his plate of scrambled eggs, the clattering attracting the curious eyes of all the other early risers. "I'm sorry, why the fuck did you not tell me this last night?"

"Before or after you caught me tugging at my own dick?" Julius smirked. "I wanted to tell both of you together, okay? Me and Estelle are planning to stay on in Paris for a long weekend after the games finish and I'm going to be a sappy asshole who asks her in front of the Eiffel Tower." His smirk turned to this soft, whimsical smile he always wore when he spoke about Estelle and a tiny pang of jealousy tugged at my heartstrings.

"Oh man, I can't wait to be in this wedding party," Tom joked. No doubt it was going to end up being a huge affair. He clapped his hands on Julius's shoulders. "Seriously though man, congratulations. It's about bloody time, to be honest."

"Yeah man, so happy for you. Even if part of me can't believe that out of the three of us, it's you who's going to be engaged first, asshole." I was happy for him,

I really was, but fuck this wasn't fair.

"Well, maybe if Tom stopped sleeping around for a minute and you actually looked for a girl, we wouldn't have that problem, would we?" Julius replied jokingly, but even amongst his humor he shot me a knowing look, like he understood why I hadn't yet, even after four years.

I smiled, sadly, back at him, only for both boys to be quickly distracted by a mop of chocolate brown curls and the screechy voice of the one and only Alicia Jones. And, of course, not far behind her was Lucas. Julius followed my line of sight as the pair breezed past our table without a single word. Lucas looked away quickly as he caught sight of me and then he blushed, like to the point his cheeks looked like they were on fire.

"And what does he have to be looking so flushed over?" Julius asked. He just couldn't help himself. "Did you catch him up to no good too? Is that why you're so grouchy this morning?" he followed up, before stuffing a spoonful of porridge into his gob, flakes of oat spilling out the corners of his amused grin.

"How the fuck would I know?" I grumbled back, averting my eyes to the half-eaten banana I'd discarded on the table, my appetite gone. "If he hooked up with someone, he definitely wouldn't have done it in our room." I shrugged; I couldn't allow myself to seem too fazed. There was no way in hell the guys could find out about what had almost happened. They'd never let me live it down.

Tom eyed me suspiciously, but Julius just took my answer for fact and continued to munch his bowl of slop loudly, before he swiveled his seat around to get a better look at Lucas where he was now seated.

"Who do you think the lucky guy was?" he speculated absentmindedly.

Normally, I'd engage in these kind of conversations, we do it at events all the time. We'd sit and watch athletes and B grade celebrities sneaking in and out of charity galas to fuck. It became a game of predicting who'd be getting off with who during the night, it was the highlight of most of our work events. Now that it concerned me, well, I had no desire to get involved, especially when it came to thinking about Lucas kissing someone else right now.

I kind of had to get involved though, because if I didn't join in they would get suspicious and with us sharing a room it would be really easy to make the connection between the two of us. Well, if they both didn't already know we couldn't stand each other.

"I literally have no clue. Who does he spend his time with apart from Alicia? I haven't seen him with anybody else, never mind another guy," Tom added to the discussion. I wished it was over already.

Without even thinking I said, "Who gives a fuck? Let him suck whichever dick he wants." I chomped down on the final bit of my banana, a pit of regret settling in my stomach about waking them up.

It worked though, shutting them up about Lucas. I quickly turned their attention to the Sky Sports News interview later that afternoon and then to how much work Julius's floor still needed. However, naturally, talking about floor routines circled us straight back to Lucas and before I knew it, his name was being thrown around the table again and I could feel his ghost against me. Was I going to have to experience this every time I heard his name or saw his face? If so, I should just fly home now before my focus went completely to shit.

"Hopefully, he won't be hogging the floor again today," Julius commented. "You spoke to him right?" he asked, his spoon scraping the edge of his bowl, the noise grating against my ears.

I was so desperate for this conversation or any conversation concerning the strawberry blonde boy to be over.

"Yeah, I spoke to him. Look, I need to shower and get ready for the day. I'll see you guys in the training room in like an hour, okay?" I didn't wait to hear their replies as I grabbed the banana skin and lobbed it in the bin while exiting the dining hall at full speed. On the way out I scanned the hall, noticing both Lucas and Alicia had already left. They'd been in their gym gear, so I guessed they were on the way to work out together before practice.

I was wrong. As I trudged through the door, he emerged from the bathroom, dripping wet and in just a towel. The sight woke something up inside of me.

I still remembered the first time I saw Amber; she was sitting across from me in our year eleven Biology class. I'd stared at her for the whole class, missing whatever the teacher was saying. She was a true wonder of this world.

I'd just rocked up to this new school, where there were over four-hundred kids per year group and I stuck out like a sore thumb. I was already toned and muscular, like a guy who'd gone through puberty super early thanks to a combination of being strict with my diet and training to become a gymnast since I was just eight years old.

However, she hardly noticed me, not like I noticed

her. I really had to work hard to get her attention. But, the first time I saw her, well it was like a black hole had opened up above my lungs and sucked all the air out of them.

This felt something like that, but it was more of a stab of anxiety to my lungs rather than a black hole. He wasn't a girl I desperately wanted to notice me or a guy who intrigued me beyond belief. He was a thorn in my side, a constant annoyance, and someone whom I had stupidly almost kissed. Yet the air still continued to drain out of my lungs as water trickled down his pecs and his curls matted to his forehead. With the lack of air to my lungs came this crazy thought about kissing him again. A desire I quickly suppressed as I mentally shook myself.

"Hey," I said, because it was literally the only word I could form on my tongue right then in the awkward atmosphere between the pair of us.

"Sorry, I thought you were still at breakfast. I'll be out of here in literally two minutes." He went straight to his drawers and started to rapidly search through them for something to wear, his towel hanging loose around his hips, giving me the perfect view of the dip in his back and the top of his ass.

"It's still your room. You don't have to rush out." Even though I wanted nothing more than for him to leave so I could step into the shower and relieve myself from all the thoughts I'd been having while his naked chest continued to gleam in the fluorescent light. "Look, we don't have to talk about what happened, okay? But we do still have to share this room and it can't be awkward, otherwise our focus is just going to be fucked up." That morning, in a matter of minutes, mine had gone from ready for a run and pumped for a day in the training room, to feeling like a hormonal teenager with a ton of angst coiled inside of me.

It was even worse as I practically drank him in while he tried to get dressed without looking at me or like he was performing some kind of strip show in the small space. He didn't reply, just wordlessly nodded at me as he pulled on his trainers and grabbed his key card before he slipped past me to exit the room.

"Just don't try and kiss me again," he whispered as his whole body brushed against mine to get out of the room. The door slammed behind him. He'd noticed, of course he'd noticed. I'd been about as subtle as a bee trapped in an enclosed space.

I'd thought about Lucas in an 'he's attractive' kind of way before, but the way he'd whispered those words was the single sexiest thing I'd ever heard. Goosebumps littered my arms and my dick strained against the constraints of my sweatpants. I wanted more of Lucas, there was no doubt about it.

It wasn't going to happen though. He'd made that clear and I had to respect that. So, instead, I settled for my hand in the shower, but the vision getting me off was Lucas all over every inch of me, his lips, his tongue, his hands, his dick, all on me. When I shut off the water, I locked the vision away, tossed the key into the Pacific, and swore to myself I'd never think about him like that again. Lucas Evans was off limits.

Chapter Seven

Lucas

We avoided each other like the plague throughout training; it wasn't possible for us to be further apart. When he was on the high bar, I was on the parallel bars in the opposite corner and when we both headed to the chalk pit at the same time, I turned quickly on my heel like if I got any closer I'd get scorched. The callouses which coated the palms of my hands were the price I had to pay to keep my distance from him. They were worth it.

I'd avert my eyes every time he looked my way and I made small talk with the coaches to prevent him coming anywhere near me. He'd never cause a scene in front of them; he'd lose his captaincy. If I could do this for just over a fortnight, we could go back to the UK, back to our own lives and spaces, and pretend the stupid near kiss never happened.

I left the training room after the six-hour practice without speaking a single word to any of my teammates and decided to skip out on eating dinner in the dining hall that evening.

I grabbed a salmon salad from the canteen in a to-go container and left before I had to entertain a run in with the three of them. Apparently I couldn't even look at Oliver anymore without blushing like a love drunk idiot.

Julius had clearly caught on to something and there was no way I'd let either of them play on my mind like this.

I needed a distraction, something which would help me switch my brain off from Oliver and his stupid lips and his stupid friends just so I could focus on this damned paper for five minutes. I really should have postponed my master's for a year when I found out I'd made the Olympic team. It would have saved a whole heap of stress right now.

I picked up my notebook and remote from the dresser and dropped them onto my bed beside my salad. *Brooklyn Nine-Nine* would fix all of this. I had a good few episodes of season ten to catch up on and when they were over, I would just go straight back to the beginning for the thousandth time.

The thick mattress beneath me offered a ton of comfort as I slipped under my duvet. At home I would never work like this, but without a chair to sit at the dresser here, this was my only option to get any work done.

My Roku stick, however, had other plans for me. As I loaded up the device it returned to a paused video. One of Julius's YouTube videos. He always had his camera out, even during training, but this video looked like it had been recorded in the corridor of our dormitory. I recognized the patches of Olympic logos on the walls behind them.

Curiously, I resumed the video and almost immediately regretted it. They were venturing down the corridors and into the dining hall before Julius set up the camera at the end of their table, so all three of them were in the shot.

"So, I've managed to gather both Tom and Ollie

here to answer some of your burning questions." Julius looked directly into the camera as a couple of passers-by in the background tried to get a look in on what they were doing.

"Bribed, more like." Oliver coughed before spooning a heap of brown rice into his mouth.

"So, Lottie8762 would like to know firstly if Ollie has a girlfriend and secondly what we are most excited for at the Olympics?"

I watched for Oliver's reaction. How he pursed his lips to think about his reply and then smiled. It almost looked forced. Almost. "No girlfriend over here, Lottie, and I'm mostly just happy to be here with these guys. A lot of people think gymnastics isn't a team sport, but without Jules and Tom, I don't think I'd be here."

Tom then added, "Personally, I can't wait for us to win gold. Our team is incredibly strong this year and I have no doubt we're going to win a good few, with some individually and hopefully a team medal."

"Next question comes from WeHeartLucas!!" I heard my name and my heart lurched into my mouth. I'd never really been in Julius's videos before so this had to be from someone who followed the sport. "They want to know when we are gonna get Lucas in the vlogs and is he just as gorgeous in real life as he is on TV?"

I couldn't help but think Julius had picked this question on purpose. Especially with how much Oliver had been bugging me to hang out with them and all the off-hand comments I always heard Julius chucking around.

"What do you think, boys? Shall we try and get the one and only Lucas Evans in on the vlogs?" Julius asked, in what I now recognized to be his on-camera voice. It sounded higher pitched and cheerier than he did in real life. "We haven't managed it yet. I'm not sure why." Sarcasm ran through his every word, but it was masked with this flashy smile so viewers who didn't know him wouldn't pick up on it.

"I think he's just a bit camera shy," Oliver said quickly, and my heart lurched again, this time not so anxiously. Was this going to be a thing now? Him having my back and it making me feel this weird safe warmth. "And, to answer your second question, I'd say how you see him on your screens is pretty accurate." He then smiled his widest smile at the camera, pearly white teeth on full display for the whole world to see.

As the camera zoomed in on his face ridiculously, he appeared in front of me in real life. "Seeing double?" he asked, with a smile similar to the one on the screen. I rapidly pressed home on the remote as I wished it was that easy to get rid of him in real life. "Sorry, I forgot to close down the app earlier."

"Don't worry about it. I said you could use it whenever, so." I shrugged and opened my notebook, ready to work before hitting the Netflix app.

"Hey, can we talk please? Me and the guys tried to find you in the dining hall, but, well, you weren't there." His eyes found the plastic container full of salad and gestured to it. "Well, at least you aren't skipping meals to avoid us."

"If you wanna fight again, can you at least let me finish a couple of paragraphs of my thesis first?"

He perched opposite me on the edge of his bed, far enough for me to be comfortable, but as he leant towards me, I knew he wasn't planning on leaving this alone. "Okay, look, I don't want to fight again," he started. "I'm sorry I called you selfish yesterday. As team captain I should be building you up, not tearing you down. All I want is for you to hang out with us a little, maybe engage in conversation with us in the training room every now and then."

My resistance to his request was beginning to wear thin and with his calm tone of voice, for once, I was struggling to say no. I had started to see his point and being reminded of these videos only hammered it home. Had I missed out all these years by keeping myself separated from every team I'd been a part of? Not just this one, but the guys I'd been to five different Worlds competitions with. Even club meets. I bailed on everything except the actual competitions. I always went straight home or to the library to study or to the pub to work. I never made the effort. I actually had no understanding of what it was like to be part of a team. What if it wasn't that bad?

"I don't want to fight either." I slowly closed the notebook laid out in front of me. "I hear what you're saying, okay? I know you're trying, I just don't know how to do this. I'm sorry." If I took my eye off the ball for friends, especially teammates who I had to spend every second with in the gym, would it all just crumble around me?

"All I want is for you to try, that's it." He punctuated his words by switching to the end of my bed, his hands resting on my unused notebook. "So, what exactly does someone who wants a Master's in Public Administration write about?" he asked with a grin. It was mischievous, but not malicious, like he actually cared about my answer.

"When my gymnastics career comes to an end, I'd

like to have some kind of idea about what I'll be doing with my life." He tilted his head at me, his grin slipping as he took his hands off of my notebook. I quickly realized how defensive I sounded. "I love politics." I restarted my answer in the hope he'd let the first one slide. "I've always loved politics: British, American, Canadian, you name a country and I'll tell you about their political system. More than anything, though, I love policy and this master's degree would be another step into that world. In the next five years I'd like to be some kind of policy analyst."

"What does that even mean? Do you wanna be Prime Minister or something? Has an athlete ever done that before?"

I rolled my eyes at him, but I couldn't stop the smile which graced my lips.

"No, I definitely don't want to be Prime Minister. I'd like to be an adviser or analyst to a politician, someone who combs through all the policy before it goes through the Commons and the Lords."

"Sounds like you've got it all mapped out." He quickly reached across me and grabbed the remote, turning off *Brooklyn Nine-Nine.*

"Hey! I was gonna watch that," I replied, but he just threw the remote further away on to his own bed.

"Me and the guys are going to go for a jog. Julius is talking about McDonald's too. Clearly he didn't have enough dinner and seeing as you haven't actually eaten yet, would you like to come with us?"

Like was a strong word in this context, but I had a feeling Oliver wasn't planning to give up on this issue. So I abandoned my laptop and notebook in exchange for my trainers and shrugged my team jacket back on. "Lead the way," I replied before I could give myself the chance to change my mind. The thought had already crossed my mind several times between my bed and the door.

Julius and Tom were already outside waiting for Oliver. Before I could even close the door, Julius was giving me the once over with his Cheshire cat grin.

"You joining us today, Evans?" Julius commented the second I stepped out into the hallway.

I was so close to just retreating back into our bedroom and locking the door behind myself.

Luckily, Oliver stepped in to save me. Again. "Oh yeah, he hadn't eaten yet and he has nothing better to do, unless you count studying to become the Prime Minister." He winked at me and I giggled, like teenage-girl-giggled, which caused both of the other guys to look at us like we'd lost the plot.

"Well, you're always welcome to join us," Tom said, out of the three of them he always wanted to keep the peace the most.

The other two, well; it was Oliver's job as captain to have me be a bigger part of the team and if it was up to Julius, well, he'd probably put me on a plane right back to the UK.

"Let's get going then." Oliver ushered us down the corridor and into the lift. "Julius has this route which apparently takes us to the Eiffel Tower and back if that's cool?"

I nodded, unable to form words right now. *They're just your teammates,* I reminded myself, but funnily enough it didn't make me feel any better. In reality they were the people I'd tried to avoid hanging out with for the last half a decade.

For the first ten minutes we jogged in pretty much

silence. Tom set the pace from the front and I lagged a little behind just in case they did decide to chat. Quietly jogging through the Parisian streets made it easy to forget the three of them were there. At least until we got in front of the Tower and the guys found space on the grass in front of it for us to take a water break.

"So, are you enjoying being at the Olympic Village?" Julius asked, a wide smirk spread across his face.

"Jules," Oliver warned. There was no way he'd have told them about what almost happened yesterday, no way at all.

"What, I'm just asking? I noticed he was looking a little hot and bothered this morning, that's all. We're all adults here, Ollie." Julius took a long sip of his water, but kept his eyes trained on me expectantly waiting for an answer.

This was bullshit. I didn't owe this guy an answer for anything and what did he expect me to actually say? 'Sorry, I looked so flushed, your best friend had just had me pinned to the wall and I'm pretty sure we both got a boner from it?' Yeah, that would go down so well with the whole group.

"It's pretty good. I haven't seen a ton of it between training and studying, but I'm hoping to go see a couple of the other events in our down time." It was probably the most neutral response I could have offered Julius, but it didn't stop him from probing further.

"Anybody caught your eye since being here? Tom's currently chasing after this Australian high jumper. I heard through the grapevine the blonde Canadian cyclist is gay, Brett I think his name is. Is he your type?"

I knew who he was talking about, but whether Jesse

was gay or not was none of any of our businesses. To my knowledge he wasn't publicly out, so it wasn't for me to speculate about.

He wasn't my type anyway. I wasn't sure what was, but it wasn't him. "Nah, not a fan of blonds."

Julius's face completely dropped.

"Burn," Tom quickly added before Julius squirted water at him. I hadn't meant for it to be, but when I came to think about it Julius one hundred percent wasn't my type.

"It doesn't really surprise me to be honest. Blonds have more fun and fun isn't really your kind of thing is it, Lucas?" Julius was really going for it today.

Half an hour into this hang out session and I already resented Oliver for forcing me to come. Luckily, I'd come prepared. In the lift I'd typed out an SOS message in my group chat with Lucy and Alicia. SOS always meant call straight away. All I had to do was click send and one of them would get me the hell out of here.

"You just can't help yourself, can you?"

Julius just rolled his eyes at Oliver in response. "I'm just trying to get to know our teammate, that's all. I've never seen him with a boyfriend before so I'm just curious as to what his type is. Isn't that what we do here? I wingman Tom all the time, maybe Lucas just needs a little help." He spoke almost as if I wasn't there and as my finger hovered over the send button on my phone I wished I wasn't. "So?" he pushed.

My finger hit send and I contemplated what I would say in reply if either of the girls weren't by their phone. Just as I went to open my mouth to reply my phone started to ring out. I pulled it quickly from my jacket pocket to find Alicia's name flashing away on the screen.

I showed them all the screen and quickly pushed myself up from the grass. "Sorry guys, I'm gonna have to take this. She only ever calls without texting first if something's wrong." My legs moved quicker than I knew they possibly could and when I was a safe distance away I answered the call.

"What's wrong?" Alicia asked, she sounded out of breath and I hoped I hadn't disturbed a late-night training session or work out.

"Stupidly agreed to go on a jog with the team. Julius tried to dig into my love life and I needed to get out of there. Thanks for calling me. Also, you okay?"

"What's there to dig into, it's still non-existent right?" I could always count on my best friend to make me feel better. "Unless I missed something?"

"Nope, nothing, still non-existent. Don't worry."

"Good to know. We still on for dinner after my evening practice tomorrow?" she asked. I'd almost forgotten we'd planned that.

"Yep, sounds good. See you tomorrow, love you."

"Love you too." I quickly hung up before jogging my way back to the Olympic Village. I scurried back to the sanctuary of my room and my master's notebook, throwing in headphones to do as much work as I could manage before I pretended to be asleep when Oliver got back.

Chapter Eight

Oliver

So last night hadn't been a success and whilst I wanted to be angry at Lucas for storming off, Julius hadn't really helped in easing him into our friendship group. What Lucas would have to learn himself is that Julius was always like that. He was nosy and had no boundaries when it came to literally anything with his friends. He thought with his dick instead of his head, but his heart was in the right place. I didn't think he'd purposefully tried to embarrass Lucas. I actually thought it was his owned fucked up way of letting Lucas know he was happy talking about guys and him being gay.

I just had to convince him that if he was to try again, things would be easier now he'd caught a glimpse of Julius. The thing was, I kind of felt like Lucas had that kind of side to him too. He'd always been quick witted enough to snap back at me during our arguments. He just had to bring some of that to the table with Julius.

"Hey, so me and the guys are going bowling after training. Do you wanna join us?" I asked him as we got dressed for the afternoon's training session. I'd left him alone all morning as he studied in bed with headphones in, but if I didn't ask now, it would be one more day lost.

Everything in how he glared back at me as he slipped on sweatpants over his gym shorts told me he couldn't think of doing anything worse. "What? So Julius can take the piss out of me again? No thanks."

"He wasn't taking the piss, I promise. He genuinely takes too much interest in both mine and Tom's sex lives too."

"I just can't do it," he said as he pulled out the backs of his trainers so he could slip his feet into them. "I can't sit and make small talk, I don't have it in me. I've tried and it's clear I'm just too awkward and sexually inexperienced to be friends with you guys. What does Julius want me to say? I haven't had sex in two years, I've never had a boyfriend, and I don't think I'd know what my type would look like even if he was standing in front of me."

"Maybe if you put yourself out there a little." Lucas groaned, loudly and I held up my hands. "Okay, okay, so you aren't interested in a boyfriend. I get it, you're only here to train and study. You've made that loud and clear. But even if you aren't looking for a man, would being friends with your teammates hurt?" His shoulders slacked and maybe I'd started to break through his resolve.

"If I come out on your little bowling adventure, will you stop harping on about guys and being part of the team? My ears are starting to bleed."

I'd take it at this point and instead of replying, I nodded, dropping the subject in favor of the pair of us walking quietly down to training.

I'd held my breath throughout the whole of practice just in case he decided to bail, but as I dismounted from the rings for a final time, landing perfectly, he was there waiting on the side, ready to go.

"He's coming?" Julius asked as I peeled off my

gloves and chucked them into the gym bag I'd brought with me.

"Yeah, he is. Can we like try and just tone it down a little tonight? You've moaned for so long he hasn't made any effort to be our friend or part of the team, but when you're full-on Julius it can be a little intimidating for people who don't know you."

"I'll be on my best behavior." His words didn't sound the least bit reassuring and the smirk that pulled at his lips filled me with regret about even inviting Lucas.

"Lucas, my man." Julius wrapped his arm around his shoulders. "You ready to get your ass whooped on the lanes?"

"Who said you're going to win?" Lucas replied as he shrugged off Julius's arm. "For the last two years bowling has been my little sister's favorite thing to do on the weekends I'm home from university."

"I'm thinking we need some stakes here, like if I get more points than you I win something and same if you do." This could go two ways, either Lucas would win and finally put Julius in his place a little, or Julius would win and Lucas would end up doing something ridiculous as Julius's prize. Like having to spill all of his sexual secrets.

"Sure, what are you thinking?" I was completely surprised. I didn't have Lucas down as a betting man at all.

"If I win, I want you to film this YouTube floor challenge with me which my viewers have been asking to see." That was pretty tame, I'd take it.

"Sure and if I win, I want food brought to me every time I need to study." That made much more sense. I'd found his salmon salad from the night before untouched when I'd returned from our jog. He needed a bit more encouragement.

"Fine by me. Tom and I need to go sort out a problem with our opening ceremony tracksuit. Somehow we both have size small, and they aren't working out for some reason."

I laughed, because I couldn't imagine six foot one Julius with his wide shoulders trying to fit into a size small jacket.

"We'll go on ahead and claim a lane and order some food. Meet you there?" Julius had already taken off across the hall, but Tom nodded at me and I took that as an okay for me and Lucas to leave.

"I knew you had a twin sister, Lucy right? But I didn't realize you had a little sister till I saw the picture on your dresser. What's her name?" I asked as we set off on our walk to the bowling alley.

"Yeah, she's eleven years younger than me. Her names Lauren, she's going through her tween faze where she knows best about absolutely everything, but at the same time she's very different to a lot of girls in her class. It's a tough balance." He adored her, I could tell by the softness in his voice as he spoke about her.

"Sounds a lot like her big brother."

"In some ways. In others not at all. She's outgoing almost to a fault. She's not afraid to say what she thinks, even if it's to the wrong person. She's in year seven and I think it's making her a little unpopular. She doesn't care though, I don't think…"

"Definitely sounds like her big brother to me. I think you've got a ton of fighting talk in you. You might wanna bring it tonight. The thing with Julius is, he only bites because he wants you to bite back, and once you do he won't bare his teeth as much. Or he will, but you'll always have a comeback."

He nodded along like he understood what I was trying to say. I hoped he did.

We secured the lane for the guys, ordered a big sharing platter of food, and by the time they'd arrived we'd already drunk a slush puppy each and were fired up, ready to bowl.

Julius beat him by one point, but all-night Lucas had kept up with his banter. He'd listened when I'd told him to bite back against Julius and I'd been right. Julius had lapped it up and they'd ended up laughing and joking as we bowled.

"I'm looking forward to claiming my prize," Julius said like he meant it and I knew he did. He'd been wanting to get Lucas on the vlogs for ages and now he'd trapped him into doing it.

"Good night, Julius." Both boys threw waves over their shoulders towards us as they entered their rooms, leaving me and Lucas in the corridor alone.

The door clicked behind the other two and it was like a live wire switched on between Lucas and me. All night I'd been watching him as he bantered with my friends, giving Julius as good as he got and just generally relaxing into the group. It was all I'd wanted from Lucas. A week ago I'd have said it was because I wanted him to be a good team player, but now, well now I wasn't quite sure. All the arguments between us had given us a reason to talk and without them, well I needed to find another reason.

If I tried to put my finger on why, I'd probably put myself in the position of thinking about how I wanted to keep him around because he was gorgeous, and I liked how hot he was when I got him all riled up, and maybe I wanted to make something more of that. It was a stupid idea, but sometimes all of the best ideas were a little bit stupid.

"Good night?" I asked as he searched for the key card in his pocket to let us into our room.

As he slid it in and the light lit up green, he opened the door and stepped in. "It was pretty okay. I guess, well, I dunno, I just guess…" He trailed off, eyes scanning me as if he thought I held all the answers to what was playing on his mind.

"You guess what?" I asked as I pushed the door closed behind us. "You guess you actually enjoyed spending time with us? That Julius isn't actually that bad? Or you guess you've realized you're lucky to have such a great roommate?"

"If you thought any of those answers were about to come out of my mouth, you're delusional." Maybe I was, but the way he hovered in front of me made me question his thoughts on the last one. We'd hardly taken two steps into the room and if he came any closer he'd have me pinned up against the door. I wasn't sure at this point if I'd object.

"You sure about that? Who wouldn't want to room with a guy with a six pack you get to ogle every time I step out of the bathroom?"

"Who said I was even looking?" He took a step towards me and almost closed the gap between us. "All I see when you step out of the bathroom is that you have a habit of leaving your boxers all over the floor."

"You know you are."

He rolled his eyes at me, but the way his cheeks-tinged rouge told me he'd definitely been catching a glimpse every now and then.

"Are you going to stop being a dick and hang out with us more now then?"

"Just when I was starting to even consider liking you, you have to start this again. I'm trying aren't I? Why can't that just be enough?" We'd been seconds away from being flush up against each other, but I'd pushed too far, to the point he'd started to walk away from me, throwing his team jacket down on the bed.

"Consider liking me? Are there stages to your process of becoming friends with people, is this why your only pal is Alicia?" The words flew out of my mouth as he pulled down his sweatpants, taking his gym shorts with them, leaving him in just his boxers. His eyes lit up with rage as he looked back up at me and I'd definitely pushed too far.

"Fuck off, Oliver. I've literally gone out of my way tonight to do what you asked. I should have been working on the dissertation I have to hand in in less than two months' time, not messing around at a bowling alley."

I should have been absorbing the rage, firing back angry comments about how he'd made an effort for one night, whoopie doo, but I could not stop staring at his muscular thighs and the way his boxers clung to every curve.

"Oliver?"

"I'm sorry what?" Having him stripping in the middle of this argument had done me absolutely no favors, because I couldn't even remember what he'd been saying.

"You're such a dick, like what is the actual problem here? I've promised I'll try more, how much more can you ask from me?"

I wondered if anybody else had ever asked for something like this before. It didn't seem like it. He seemed completely determined for us not to be proper friends.

"You aren't even listening are you?"

"No, I got completely distracted by your thighs, I'm not going to lie. You're so fucking hot."

"Shut up." His tongue dipped out to wet his lips. He didn't want me to shut up at all. I just had to tease all of those wants and desires out of him.

"Make me," I replied.

And he did. He full force hauled himself at me, his lips clashing against mine as we walked backwards till my back hit the wall. The clank pulled him out of the kiss and he looked at me with the most bewildered eyes, almost as if he couldn't believe he was doing it, kissing me.

"It's okay." I wasn't quite sure what I was reassuring him about, whether it was okay for him to kiss me again or to pull away, but either way something burned inside of me to make sure he knew.

Testing the waters, he leaned back into the kiss and in a completely unlike me move, I let him take the lead. As his lips brushed against mine his hands found the hem of my shirt to hold onto. I wound my hands around his neck to keep me from pushing him further, but he took it as a cue to deepen the kiss.

His fists greedily pulled at my shirt and a whimper escaped his lips as I pulled back a second to tug the t-shirt over my head. "I don't know what the fuck I'm doing," he mumbled into my naked collarbone. Words like that would normally ruin the mood for me, but as I tipped up his chin to figure out if this meant he wanted to stop, I realized I had to make this good for him.

I leaned into him again, captured his lips softly before licking over his bottom lip so I could gain access. His legs tangled around mine to the point our bodies were perfectly entwined with each other. Every party of my body was on fire at this point, tingling at every point of contact between us as a thick air of lust clouded around the both of us, leaving me a little lightheaded.

"Fuck," I groaned as I detached my lips from his and christened his jawline with rough kisses, then a soft place behind his ear, and a sensitive spot on his neck, to the point I had him whimpering. If I wasn't hard before, I definitely was now. He quickly followed suit by removing his shirt, leaving him in just his boxers.

"I don't know why, but I was expecting you to be the kind of guy who wore like tighty-whities or a thong. Not that I'm saying you're uptight or anything," I muttered into the side of his neck as I kissed my way across his chest, nipping and licking as I walked him back towards the bed, his body hitting it with a cushioned thunk. I practically had him writhing beneath me.

"Fuck you," he grunted as I grabbed at his clearly defined erection beneath his briefs. He was a whole lot bigger than I thought he was going to be. Thinking of him being a bit of a short arse had me under the impression he was going to be short all over. Not that I'd given it too much thought.

"Actually, I think that's what I'm about to do to you, mister." I grinned as I peeled off his briefs and slipped out of my sweats, leaving us both incredibly naked.

I watched something which looked like worry flicker across his face as he tugged at his bottom lip with his teeth as he laid beneath me. His brow wrinkled and his eyes searched mine for the answer to whatever I was about to do next. Or maybe if I was going to do anything at all. Everything had moved so quickly from us screaming at each other to me not being able to keep my hands and lips off of him. Now we were completely butt naked, practically rutting against each other. It was easy to see how it could be overwhelming for him.

I reached out and took his hand, pulling him back into the moment, silently I hoped he wasn't about to shut me out completely. "Are you okay?" I asked carefully, prepared to climb off of him if this wasn't what he wanted. There was no way I was going to do anything he didn't want. That would be fucked up and it'd only make things so much worse between the pair of us.

He ran a jerky, unsure hand through his curls and pulled at them almost exasperatedly as he contemplated his decision. But, as his eyes brightened and he looked up at me, thrusting forward so our dicks bobbed against each other, I knew this was a go. "Just literally do anything, I swear just having your hands on me feels good right now."

"You have the condoms they gave us right?" He nodded and pointed to his bedside drawer. "Sorry, I gave mine to Tom, his need seemed greater than mine at the time. He pulls way more than I do and I'm just going to shut up now." I retrieved the condom, tore it open, and rolled it on.

"How can I make this good for you?" I asked as I retrieved some lotion from my drawer and lubed up my fingers.

"You're asking the wrong person, I don't know. Literally anything. What do you like?"

I wasn't sure myself, but something inside of me longed to make this good, for both of us. So I did exactly what I'd seen them do in porn.

I coated my fingers until they were slick and he was squirming underneath me. Then I flipped him on to his stomach and told him to get on all fours so I had a better vantage point to his ass. This was probably going to be the only time I was going to get to do this, like a once in a lifetime opportunity. So, whatever I did next, it needed to be memorable.

"Is this okay?" I asked, looking down at him in probably one of the most vulnerable sex positions. Internally I cringed, because I couldn't believe we were about to try and do this on a tiny single bed, but there was no way I'd let that deter me. His beautiful, muscular body was breathing shallowly below me, it was enough to have me coming all over him before I'd even got a single digit inside of him.

He moaned deep and throaty as I dragged a cold, wet finger down the crack of his ass. "Sure, fucking sure, just hurry up and get inside of me." I didn't need to be told twice.

Chapter Nine

Lucas

I collapsed face first into the pillow beneath me, his hands still braced at my hips as I breathed in his stupid bergamot cologne. It hit me, all at once, this was not the kind of mistake we could come back from. This wasn't a kiss or me stupidly getting on my knees to blow him, this was full blown sex.

"Fuck," I swore as I started to feel him softening inside of me, his heavy breathing the only noise in our room. "What the fuck, Oliver? What the fuck did we just do?"

I instantly peeled off of him and jumped straight out of his bed. Every muscle in my body ached in the most incredible way as a sense of euphoria I'd never felt before shot through me. Neither of the feelings were enough to override the pit of dread which had started to churn in my stomach. It twisted and turned, to the point I was sure I was going to be sick.

The whole world stilled around us as he flopped onto the bed and instead of waiting for his reply, I fled to the bathroom in the desperate hope that when I returned he'd either be gone or this whole debacle wouldn't have happened. Of course, I knew that wasn't how this worked so, instead, I settled for resting my forehead against the coolness of the mirror, balling my fists at my side as I tried to resist the urge to smash it.

With the door locked behind me I ran the tap until the water was as cold as ice and splashed it over my face. Unfortunately, no amount of water could cleanse the visions of Oliver naked and balls deep inside of me from my mind. Even over the sound of the running water I could still hear every primal grunt. My hips ached with how hard he'd gripped me.

It was just sex. That's what I had to remind myself as my hands grazed over the bruises. It happened all the time; I'd literally heard it coming from the room on the other side of us last night. All I had to do was go back out there and act casual, pretend this happened all the time, and that a one-night stand meant nothing to me. Especially not with Oliver Ramsey.

I had to admit though, it did feel good to loosen up a little. Especially after how hard coach had been on me when he saw the shambles I'd made of my rings this morning.

Training. That's what would distract me from thoughts of Oliver. But even as my mind looked into the gym, he was still there. I thought about being back in the UK instead and he was still there, this time in my bed at home. I blinked rapidly to get rid of the image. Then I thought about my family, my twin, and the pit of dread turned to longing. I missed her a lot, I just wanted to call her and tell her everything right now, but I knew she'd be way too excited about me shagging one of the hottest Olympians in the village.

I was sure, as I leant against the sink still naked, this was why they told us not to sleep with fellow Olympians, especially teammates. It was so easy to become distracted by them and tomorrow we couldn't just forget about this when we still had to share the same training center. Why had I thought this was a good idea?

"Hey, Lucas?" Oliver called through the door as he rapped his fist against the wood. "I need to piss. Can you hurry up?"

It was enough to draw me from the mini pity party I had been throwing for myself, but as I pushed open the door, I could hardly look at him. I trained my eyes to the ground as I searched for my clothes which were sprawled all over the floor, before grabbing my trainers so I could get the fuck out of there.

As I hauled my ass into my sweatpants and struggled to get my head through the right hole of my shirt, Oliver popped up again. I realized he hadn't even bothered to shut the door behind him as he pissed. I guess us sleeping together had pushed every boundary out of the window.

"You going somewhere?" he asked.

"To meet Alicia," I was so glad we'd planned this late dinner for tonight; it was the perfect excuse to get the heck out of here. "Don't wait up," I called over my shoulder as I slipped on my jacket and bolted out the door.

I found her tucked up in an empty corner of the canteen. It was quiet. Normally I'd love this, but right now I craved the buzz of other people to take my mind off of what had just happened.

"Who's rattled your cage?" she asked as I plonked myself across from her. She had a tray of my favorite pasta in front of her, but right now it looked completely unappealing. My appetite gone, just like my dignity.

I imagined saying something along the lines of: 'Well, funny story, but I just had Oliver's dick inside of me. You remember Oliver right? My teammate, roommate, nemesis, yeah him.' Instead, I just shook all the visuals of him out of my head and tried to push past how I could still feel the ghost of his lips on my neck.

"Nothing, it's all just coming around so quickly now right? Coach Jacub yelled at us way more than usual today. I sucked on rings, and Tom isn't nailing his vault still. Plus, Julius ripped yet another leotard getting cocky with his floor routine." At some points it had been brutal and my whole body was in desperate need of a sports massage. I just wanted to win though; gold this summer had me pushing through all the aches and pains.

"God, tell me about it. Jackie has been kicking our ass. I slipped on the beam today and when I looked up she was at my side. For a second I thought she was checking I was okay, but instead she just screamed at me to get my ass back up on the beam. Although, FYI, I'd love to see Julius rip a leotard. I'm surprised you aren't more over the moon about seeing his ass. After Ollie he's the hottest man on your team."

I cleared my throat.

She just rolled her eyes at me playfully. "I'm talking about available men, unless you're telling me you're gonna turn for me?"

Not likely when my brain was still full of images of stupid, gorgeous Oliver. Who did he think he actually was kissing me like it was absolutely nothing? Like I'm not the kind of guy who just wanted to train hard and win. I didn't do this pining for hot guys thing.

"You sure you're okay?" she asked. "I lost you for a minute then." Alicia could read me like a book. Not surprising when we've shared everything for the last eleven years with each other. From the day I pushed my way into the girls' gymnastics club in Essex—because there wasn't a local boys club—she convinced her parents to start a fundraiser for them to install some rings and parallel bars. Alicia, being the sassy tween she was back then, got all the other kids' parents to support the idea. We did everything together, and when we moved house just a couple years after we met, I ended up at her school for year nine; from there we were completely inseparable.

"I had sex," I blurted out in the quietest possible voice, scanning the room quickly to make sure nobody around us heard.

"About time," she replied, shoveling a chunk of pasta into her mouth. "You know I slept with that Canadian cyclist dude the first night here? Well, he came a knocking again last night and to be honest I'm thinking about emigrating." She gushed like it was nothing, and maybe for other mid-twenty somethings it was. I wished it could be that easy for me. Maybe not even just for me, but for gay hookups in general. They were pretty hidden across the Olympic Village.

"No, shit, it wasn't just sex. I slept with Oliver."

She scanned me up and down, left to right, like she was checking if it was actually me she was talking to, before her jaw dropped, dramatically, just like in all the movies. "I'm sorry." She paused for a second to take all of my words in. "Did you just say Oliver? Like Ollie, hot gym stud, Ollie? Ollie the most gorgeous Olympian to walk this village, nay this earth, that Ollie?" She spiraled, hands flailing around in front of her, her voice getting louder every time she said his name.

"Yes, that Oliver," I said through gritted teeth. Even though he'd been inside me I still refused to call him by his dumb nickname. We weren't friends. "Can you keep it down? You must know this isn't something I want broadcasted to the world." Not just because I didn't want people to know the ins and outs of my sex life, but because Oliver wasn't out. In my eyes and pretty much the whole world's he's straight, only ever pictured in the papers with girls. I wasn't quite sure how he defined or if he was out to anybody else. I still wasn't sure how I'd missed it. Oh yeah, because he always seemed to be out to ruin my life.

"Holy shit, what was it like? God I've dreamed about seeing him naked, he must have the body of dreams. How big was his—"

"Stop, literally stop. It was a dumb mistake. I only told you because it was eating me up. It won't be happening again. I don't even know how we are going to go back to sharing a room."

"He's welcome to sleep on my floor or you know, in my bed," she suggested with that mischievous glint in her eye, which once scored us a thousand-pound donation to our gym from our local MP. "Should we start sharing men?"

At that I swiped the final piece of garlic bread from her plate and stood up. "I'm going to head back to the room in the hopes he's now asleep, shower, and pass out. See you tomorrow." She blew me a kiss, and with the promise of training together I headed back to my room.

Disappointingly, he wasn't asleep. He was curled up in his bed with training footage of his vault on our shared TV. He was shirtless as usual, but for the first time I noticed all the freckles across his broad chest and how hairless his pecs actually were. He definitely manscaped. I tried not to drink him up, but I couldn't help it. It wasn't that I'd never noticed how stunning he was, but I used to think he was flawless. Now that I'd seen him up close and personal, I knew he wasn't. I'd felt a scar across his shoulder and he had a huge mole on the side of his neck which I definitely hadn't kissed multiple times.

"Round two?" he mocked in an attempt to break the icier than usual air around us.

I almost laughed. Almost. Instead, I grabbed the towel from the back of my bed and attempted to hide in the bathroom from him once more.

"Hey." The unusually soft tone to his voice caught me off guard, almost making me jump a little. "Are you freaking out? You wanted it right? It was just sex. Happens all the time."

"Yep, just sex," I repeated back to him. The thing I'd only done a handful of times before. Nothing special or sacred, just sex. "It's fine, Oliver," I confirmed and his stupid smile reappeared as he took the footage off pause. His eyes, however, lingered on mine and he traced them up my body, the movement sending a shiver down my spine. Was this how it was going to be from now on? Long looks and goose prickled skin?

He used to just get on my nerves, but now he set every single one of those nerve endings on fire. As he looked over me once more I couldn't help but think about how good his hands had felt as they roamed up and down my body.

"Good." He nodded and trained his eyes back to the screen before he added, "You need someone to scrub your back?"

And with that I slammed the door behind myself and prayed I drowned in the shower.

Chapter Ten

Oliver

"Just you and me this morning, old chap." The ice was in desperate need of breaking, but with Lucas keeping his distance from me as we walked to training and the glare he shot me at the remark, I was not going about it the right way.

"Oh the joys." The sarcasm in his voice should have put me off, but it only motivated me to close the distance between us and keep at him so things didn't get crazy awkward just because we'd slept together.

So I went for the one topic I knew he'd converse with me on. "You working on your floor today?" I asked.

"Nope, not till tomorrow as Alicia has some free time and she said she'll go over it with me to see if there is anything more I can do to make it better. Plus I think my back needs a break from it. It's still aching from trying to figure out how to land the Arabian double layout." I'd seen him land it several times since he first started working on it, it was gorgeous. "What about you? What's feeling strong right now?"

"My rings are feeling particularly strong this year, but my pommel horse is shaky. I always feel good on the horizontal bar. But my parallel bars suck right now. And, of course, I don't have a floor routine to rival yours." I laughed and he actually smiled back at me. "You know if your back's giving you trouble, I'll happily give you a massage."

"You never stop do you?" He groaned. "I bet you don't offer Tom and Julius massages."

"Trust me, nobody wants to massage anything of Julius's and if I offered it would only inflate his ego." It was already the size of a house. "Is there anything you're struggling with right now?"

"Rings and high bar are definitely my least favorite apparatus right now, but I think I have a good enough routine for us to still qualify all round."

"I don't think we have to worry about that at all. The best eight teams qualify for the finals and we will easily be amongst them." The bookies had us positioned as the fourth best gymnastics team here.

"It would be so incredible right? It's my dream to qualify for the individual event on floor, but if we could make the event happen too, god my mum and sisters would be so proud. All the struggles would be worth it."

His words just before our first fight here rang out in my head. How he'd talked about their financial problems when he was little and how he'd gone out of his way to support his family to make sure his little sister never had to face hard times. That was some superhero shit. He deserved this win. It was easy to see why he worked so damn hard right now; he didn't know any other way.

"Are they flying out?" I asked as we walked across the gravel towards the training center.

"Not until after the opening ceremony, which sucks, but Lucy could only get so long off of work as she's a nurse, and mum has the pub to look after," he replied as he opened the double doors for the both of us.

"You know, I can't believe I've never met Lucy

before, never mind the rest of your family. I've met all of Tom and Julius's family." I was hoping, with some prompting, he'd start to share more and open up.

"I never had a big interest in bringing her or any of my family into the limelight. I struggle with it enough. You remember the *Vogue* shoot you came to? I've never felt more exhausted than after the final photo of that interview. I'd rather do a twelve-hour practice than go through one again."

"Why though?" I asked. I'd never thought of the press in that way. The shoots, the interviews, and the brand deals were always so much fun for me. I loved the social side of things—it kept me level-headed when training was hectic and there was so much pressure in the run up to big events like The Olympics.

"Well, in case you didn't notice, I'm kind of a private person."

I almost snickered at his words, but it ended up coming out as more of a repressed snort as I tried to contain it.

"It's not even just that. I'm good on my own, I like my own company. I'm not sure there is anything interesting to share." He shrugged his final comment off and I knew best to leave it for now. He'd given me something and that was enough.

We walked into our training room and it was clear the women's team hadn't cleared up after they'd used our space last night. Their beam still lurked amongst our apparatus.

"Been a while since I've been up on one of them," he commented and his words triggered the Julius in me.

"I dare you to get up there and give us a little performance." My words sounded way flirtier than I'd intended them to be, which led to him shooting me a glare straight back. "I'll give you a hundred quid." He still looked at me like I was messing with him. "All I'm saying is I'd like to see you do a couple flips or like one of those aerial things."

The James Bond theme tune rang out across the hall, pulling us from our conversation, but as I watched Coach Jacub disappear into his office, I couldn't help but push. "Now you can prove it,"

"One hundred pounds for a few tricks on the beam…Is it even worth it?" He peeled off the gloves he'd put on to be ready for the rings, dropping them into his shorts pockets. I was worried that was it, that our morning was over and maybe he was retreating away from me again.

Then he turned around and I was hit with the confident grin he saved for the corner of the floor. I knew it wasn't just about his skills on the beam, but the fact he was about to prove me wrong and take my money in the meanwhile. I drank in the grin and just couldn't find the energy to care about losing the money. It would be worth it.

"Two hundred pounds and I'll give you the massage I promised earlier," I challenged him.

"If I fall off this thing and break something, I'm gonna sue. Just so you know." Yet he still placed the palms of his hands on the beam as he prepared to push up on it. "You know I trained at a girls' gym till I was like fifteen, right? I mastered the beam before I'd even been up on the pommel horse."

Of course he had, it was probably why he was so bloody good on floor. The women's routines had a beautiful, artistic side compared to our power routines.

Especially someone like Alicia, it was like watching a paintbrush on a canvas when she performed.

"If you fall, you don't get the two hundred quid," I replied, but he said nothing, just pushed himself up on to the beam. His legs spread perfectly into the splits and all the blood in my body rushed to my groin. His eyes were still trained on me as he swung his legs round, almost seductively, and went into standing.

He performed a full spin like it was nothing, like his feet were glued to the six inches of wood below him. "Was this worth losing two hundred pounds over?" he asked, arms fully extended in the air as he steadied himself for what I was sure was going to be a flawless flip sequence.

"Every penny," I commented as I leant back against the chalk pit and followed the curve of every muscle as he flipped once, twice, and a third time to the other side of the beam without a single wobble. I'd always admired him on the floor, to the point I don't think I appreciated he could be just as good on any other apparatus. He'd truly proven me wrong; His balance was impeccable.

"So, I used to be able to do an aerial walkover when I was like fifteen, but I'm sure I still have the trick in my inventory." He closed his eyes to concentrate, the tip of his tongue poking out the corner of his mouth. Then he just went for it. The aerial itself was perfect, but as he landed his foot missed the beam and he toppled straight off the beam. But, like the knight in shining armor I so clearly was, I dashed across the mat to make sure he didn't completely crash.

I completely overestimated my own strength though and as I steadied his fall, I couldn't prevent my own and we both landed in a heap on the ground, a heap that couldn't stop laughing. My shoulder twinged, but even that wasn't enough to stop me chuckling at the position we found ourselves in.

We both sounded exactly like teenagers and as I slyly stroked up his thigh I felt like one too. With no-one around to catch us it couldn't possibly hurt to have a little fun by messing with him a bit.

"Oliver," he warned as I reached around to cup his ass. "What are you doing?" he asked, almost accusingly, but he made no effort to move from underneath me. Slowly, I felt his fingers creep under the back of my shirt, his callouses rough against my skin.

"I'm catching your ass, duh, just like I said I was going to." I smirked hard into his shoulder, I could feel his heart racing against my chest and damn there was something so erotic about how it thumped at a ridiculous rate when my hands grazed over him.

"You're such a dick." But, still, he made zero attempt to pull away from me. Instead, he surprised me as he slotted his leg more comfortably in between mine so our thighs were flush up against each other.

"How inappropriate would it be if I kissed you right now?" I was curious to see how far he'd let me go in an area which was basically our workplace.

"Very, I think there are cameras in here and the position we are in right now is compromising enough." His fingers trailing over my abs right now said otherwise. At least he hadn't just straight up said he didn't want to kiss me. It was a win.

"Ollie, Lucas?" Jacub bellowed from across the room. We'd fallen behind the beam so he probably wasn't able to see us as we laid on the floor. But, as I looked up from under the beam, I could see him crouched down on the floor with an eye full of my hands on Lucas's ass. Fucking fantastic.

Lucas groaned into my neck, the vibrations only worsening the raging erection in my gym shorts. As Jacub made his way over to us there was no way I could rearrange myself without being seen so I'd have to just face coach with a really obvious boner.

"What's going on here?" Jacub asked as we both emerged from behind the beam. "I feel like I've just walked into some alternative reality and caught you two messing around in the gym. Something we need to know?"

"Absolutely not," Lucas replied before I could even compose a reply.

"Not what it looked like to me. From where I was standing, I'm pretty sure Oliver had his hands all over your ass." There was no kidding Coach Jacub here, but I could sense Lucas did not want this to get out so I'd push for whatever he wanted if it kept us on good terms.

"Just being an idiot, sorry, coach. I dared Lucas to get up on the beam and he fell, so rather than let him crash I tried to catch him but we ended up in a heap on the floor. Nothing else going on."

"If you boys say so." Jacub wasn't convinced. He was still eying us wearily, as if he'd actually caught us naked and going at it on the mat. In my eyes there was nothing we could say to convince him.

"Can we go?" Lucas asked through gritted teeth, the embarrassed blush which had tinged his cheeks had turned to a full, red-faced frustrated glow. Jacub nodded and gestured towards the exit and Lucas took off at the rate of knots.

"Hey, wait up a second," I called after him as he

tried to stride away from me. Lucas being the shortest on the team made it easy for me to catch up with him. "Wait!" I reached out, clutching at his wrist so he couldn't get away from me. "What's wrong?"

"Are you kidding me? That was humiliating, that's what's wrong. Now coach thinks there's something going on between us. What part of a private person did you not get, Oliver? I feel mortified right now." His cheeks were stained with anger and embarrassment.

"Would it be so bad if there was something going on between us?" I asked. "You were there the other night, the sex was pretty hot, you can't deny it."

He looked like he was about to though, but then I licked my lips impatiently and he flushed further. "What are you saying, you want to sleep together again? Why?"

"Again and again and again," I added because why the fuck not. I could see, from the sparkle in his eyes and how the tip of his ears burnt red beneath his auburn curls, he was considering it. "It would be such a good arrangement considering our current sleeping situation. Easy access and all that."

He gagged. "That makes it sound so gross." Then he scrunched his nose up in complete disgust. Maybe this was the wrong approach towards Lucas.

"Okay, but come on, would a friend with benefits situation really be so bad? We fuck well together." My choice of words definitely didn't help, his face only looked more disgusted with me. "Did you really not enjoy it?" I asked, because the vibes he was giving me right now was screaming I'd been an awful lay.

"It's not that at all. It was good, fun, but like, I don't know. It's not really me. I can't afford to be distracted now."

"So you don't even want to give it a try?" I asked.

"You wanna take a walk?" he came back with, like it was the answer to my question.

I got the feeling this was all that was on offer right now and if that was the case I would take it. "Sure."

For a while we walked in silence, every now and then exchanging glances with each other like school kids afraid to talk about what was going on in their relationship. I'd realized the friends with benefits suggestion may have been too much for Lucas, but I thought I'd be able to convince him. Maybe I was wrong.

"I don't want the coaches to know we hooked up," he made clear. "Like, that can't happen. I'm here to work with them as an Olympian, not for them to know the ins and outs of my personal life." It made sense, just an hour ago he'd clearly laid out he was a private person.

"Next time."

"Oliver, I'm serious."

"Okay, we'll be more careful and make sure nobody finds out. At the end of the day, us sleeping together is nobody else's business anyway and I wouldn't want it to be either. I'm just a little less tetchy about it."

"I just…I don't know. What's the point? Like what do we gain by doing this?" Of course, Lucas needed a reason to do this, something that would be good for his future. It was how his mind worked, he was forward thinking almost to a fault.

"Can't it just be for fun? Like to unwind after a long day of training or because you have some extra energy to burn. Think of it as another form of exercise. You'll burn a ton of calories and all that dopamine running through your body will keep you in a good mood."

He shook his head, but a smile tugged at his lips

which he wasn't able to control. I loved that I amused him, even if I did have to wind him up to do so. He said nothing in reply though, so rather than push I changed the topic to something he was more comfortable talking about.

"Why did you go to university?" I asked as we took a left towards the Velodrome. This place was huge, how far did he actually want to walk before he considered my proposal? "Like obvs you want the qualification, but you have good A-Levels, why wasn't that enough?"

He looked at me like I was about to shit on his degree again. "Didn't we already have this conversation? I told you I want to be a policy analyst."

"No, no, but like before when you were like seventeen and looking at your future. What made you want to go to university?" I didn't want to push, but I'd been thinking about it a lot recently, especially because I'd seen him studying and we'd talked about his life after gymnastics. Those kind of thoughts hadn't even crossed my mind.

"I think, having grown up seeing my mum as a single parent struggling through three jobs to give her kids a good life, it made me want to be better. She taught me I could do anything I wanted if I put my mind to it, just like she did by hustling and giving her kids a good life." He paused for a second as we walked through a busy area of the main section of the village. Once the crowds passed, he continued. "I want to be able to give my kids the best shot at life like my mum did. I've always loved politics and I did it at A-Levels, so university seemed like the right path. Has it been a lot trying to do it alongside training? Yeah of course it has, but it's been worth it. If I fall tomorrow and obtain an injury which ends my career, I'll have almost two degrees to help me get back on my feet."

"Oh, so you have secret children now?"

"Shut up, you know what I mean. I want them, you know, though. Like not soon, but after I retire from gymnastics and I'm in a steady job and relationship or whatever. Or maybe I'll do it on my own. Who knows, but I want kids."

It shouldn't have surprised me, considering Lucas was so family orientated, but picturing Lucas with kids was a crazy thought. He'd be a good dad though. After everything he'd told me about working his ass off at Uni and in the pub, his kids would love him. They'd want for nothing; Lucas would be thriving.

"I respect that. I know I've been a dick about it, but I do. You're going to do great things. I've never met anyone like you. So driven and motivated, I just wanna help you have some fun. You deserve to be happy too, you know?" Burn out was one of the things we were always warned about as athletes, taking breaks and getting proper rest was encouraged and between training and studying he wasn't relaxing. There were of course other selfish reasons I wanted him to chill out a little, but I'd spin it whatever way he needed to hear.

He heaved out a sigh. "I'm trying, okay? I really am. You sound like my sister."

"I'm sure her kind of chill out activities are a little different to mine," I replied with a chuckle.

"You'd be wrong there. All throughout Uni she was like 'when are you going to get a boyfriend', 'I hope you're enjoying yourself on nights out', 'have you bought anyone home recently?' It was annoying." He didn't sound annoyed though. I wasn't sure he could be at his sisters, as he seemed to adore them.

"So, what do you say?" This was going to be the final time I asked. I wasn't going to push him into something he didn't want to do, but I had a feeling he did want this, he just didn't know how to say yes.

We started to approach the dorms, as he contemplated the answer. I held out the door for him and he pushed the button for the lift to take us to floor four. There was pure silence as we journeyed upwards and then walked into our dorm room.

Maybe it would be easier if he didn't have to answer with words. "If I kiss you again, are you going to run out on me to a fake dinner with Alicia?"

He snorted and rolled his eyes, but he didn't pull away as I threaded my fingers through his curls and brought his forehead to rest against mine.

"Oliver, what are we doing?" he mumbled, his eyes a glossy green as he searched mine for answers. This close up I could see the circle of yellow which encased his irises and how fair his eyelashes truly were.

"Well, I'm hoping we're about to kiss." I chuckled as he started to cave, winding his arms around my waist until his hands found themselves in my back pocket.

"Seems like a really stupid idea to me." Before I could even say anything, he was leaning in and I was doing the same.

This kiss was different to the first one. Last time it had been rough and eager, but this time it was soft, sweet even and felt like it could go on for a lifetime. We didn't have a lifetime though, and if we were going to do this it had to be strictly sex and nothing else.

"Come to bed with me," I whispered against his lips. He shuddered. I waited for a beat for him to say no, but when he slipped his hand into mine I knew it wasn't coming.

Chapter Eleven

Lucas

"Okay, so go easy on me. Remember I don't have the skills you have on floor, but I'm thinking I could maybe up my double twist into a triple twist," Julius said from the opposite corner of the mat. His floor routine was currently his lowest ranking apparatus and for some crazy reason I'd agreed to help him instead of working on my own routines.

"Just get on with it. I've seen you perform before, it's not awful." He shot me the middle finger, but before I could say anything he took off across the mat leaping into a series of flips, landing his first power move, a double back. His routine was packed with them, but when I watched it was choppy as there was nothing breaking up all the power moves. He was losing points for not doing any other elements. There was no groundwork, no handstands, no held positions. A look of utter determination crossed his face as he lurched into attempting to land the triple twist as his final move, but it only ended in him landing smack bang on his ass.

He dusted himself off quickly and walked back to the top corner to attempt the move again. Each time he tried he didn't land it. The final time he smacked the ground frustratedly with his hand as he stood up. "I don't understand why I can't get it."

"Am I good to touch your chest?" I asked as I walked to the corner he stood in.

"Are you this polite with all the boys?" If this had been a week ago I'd have quickly pulled away and told him to get fucked, but I'd come to realize Julius was like this with everyone. Just like Oliver had said, he was annoyingly right about this.

"Do you want my help or not?"

He bit his bottom lip and held his hands up to let me proceed.

"I don't mean just touch your chest randomly, I mean whilst you're doing the routine. You need to be getting more height as you go into your triple twist, otherwise you're going to keep falling out of it early."

"Hang on, so you want to get in my way as I flip across the mat?"

I nodded. "You need to feel what it's like to land it and to see exactly how much height you need to get to make it through all three twists. Once you've done it the first time, it'll feel easier."

"Well, you are king of the floor." He caved and stretched up on to his tip toes, ready to go.

I positioned myself about two thirds of the way across the floor, estimating where he'd come out of his cartwheel series into the triple twist.

"Ready?"

I nodded and in a blink of an eye he was thundering across the floor. I timed it just right; as he got to me, his triple twist began and I got my hands just under his chest to push him up further so he could get all three twists in.

I counted them and the moment he hit the third he landed, perfectly. "Oh damn, that felt good. Was that three?"

"Yep, you killed it." He really had, if he could get the move competition ready then our team score on floor would be amazing.

"Well, whilst we're here and my camera and tripod are in my bag, what do you say to me cashing in on my bowling prize?"

Like I had a choice, a bet was a bet and I owed Julius one weird floor challenge.

"What actually is it you want me to do?" I asked because I still had no clue. Oliver had explained it to be some kind of mirror challenge which sounded like it could be an absolute mess.

He began to set up two tripods with cameras stacked on top of them on two different sides of the mat as he explained to me the challenge. "Basically we have to do an exact mirror image of a floor routine. So we plan what we are going to do and then we do a couple practice runs to see if we can keep them in time with each other. I'll film the practices and then the full run and hopefully it'll make for a good video."

We planned out a simple, but powerful looking routine with a tiny bit of my flare in the middle to really challenge Julius. In the practice he smashed through the layout into a double pike and then a roll over; He even quickly mastered a lay out of back flips. But, when it came to the air flare, his ass hit the floor more than I'd ever seen it. We both just laughed it off as Julius told me it would make for great viewing.

Our full run through ended up going really well and, after just two takes of it, Julius was beaming about the footage and opening his laptop so he could upload it and view it better.

With the filming done and Julius and Tom both

reviewing the footage, I slipped away to take a moment in the bathroom. Well, it was more like a wet room with its shower. It wasn't that being friends with them was exhausting, but I was just so used to being able to knuckle down in training and lose myself on the apparatus for several hours.

I was just about to lock the door behind me when it opened a crack and Oliver slid inside with me, the most mischievous grin spread across his face.

"What are you doing?" I squeaked. I was just about to push down the toilet seat and sit for a couple seconds in peace.

"What, can't I just want to come hang out with you in the bathroom?"

I shook my head at him and narrowed my eyes. He was such a rascal.

"Okay fine, I snuck in here because apparently watching you on the floor is a bit of a turn on for me and now I want to blow you."

"This is the worst idea you've ever had." I watched as he locked the door behind himself. There was absolutely no way someone wasn't going to catch on to the fact we were both in here together. I hadn't exactly announced I was going for a piss, but this was a small training hall and there weren't many other places for us both to be.

"Probably, but I'm here now. Are you really going to turn down a blow job?"

This fucking guy. The cheek of him. I was completely prepared to say no, but then he brushed a hand across my cheek and traced my abs with the other one under my shirt. "I can't believe we wasted so long fighting at parties and events when we could have been doing this."

"You blow many guys in the bathroom?" His eyes danced as I leaned into his touch and they told me this wasn't his first run in a bathroom at all.

"I'm taking this off now." He slipped my shirt up over my head. I did nothing to protest because, even though this was an awful idea, my dick was already hard and my skin craved the touch of his hands and lips all over it.

His lips lingered on my own for a second before he started to trace a familiar path down my neck, across my collarbone, around my nipples and then down my chest. "Oh fuck, Oliver," I moaned before I remembered we were in a public bathroom with our teammates and coaches, so I quickly slapped a hand over my mouth.

His thumbs snuck under the waistband of my gym shorts and boxers and in one fell swoop, they were around my ankles. "Is this okay?" He pulled me back into a fierce kiss whilst his hand teased the inside of my thigh.

It was more than okay. It was incredible, no one had ever made me feel this level of want before and I couldn't imagine anyone other than Oliver setting every nerve ending of my body on fire like this again. I nodded against his forehead as he pulled away from the kiss.

The pulse in my neck thrummed so hard I could feel every beat as he dropped down to his knees in front of me. He took the full length of me to the back of his throat and I got completely lost in the way he hollowed his cheeks and then peeked up at me, blue eyes shining through a fan of dark lashes.

My hand searched for something to grip onto whilst the other bit into the flesh of my palm to keep anything audible from slipping out. I quickly found the rim of the sink to hold onto, as I allowed the wall to support the rest of my body. Oliver slowly pulled off of my dick, before teasingly licking over the slit, then dragging his tongue up my shaft. He was such a dickhead. His eyes glistened with delight as he watched me try not to draw any attention to what was going on in here. It was all fun and games as he took me to the back of his throat once more, until someone outside started to pound on the door.

"Hey, anyone in there?" Julius called out as he wrapped his knuckles against the door once more and *fuck* I wanted to die. What the heck were we supposed to do when Oliver was on his knees, mouth around my dick, and we were both half naked?

Oliver looked up at me with wide eyes, like he wanted me to make the decision on what we were going to do, but quite frankly I'd never found myself in this predicament before and had no idea what the plan was going to be. I gently nudged him off my quickly softening dick and wordlessly communicated he should go to the door. Neither of us could guarantee who Julius had seen come in here so it was just easier if Oliver spoke to him.

"Hellooooo? Come on man, I need to piss." As Oliver stood I pushed his shoulder. Literally a second ago I'd been close to coming down the back of his throat so I was in no fit state to handle Julius.

Oliver's eyes darted frantically to the door as Julius tugged the handle up and down again. "Julius?" Oliver called out from the other side of the door.

"What the fuck are you doing in there man? I'm about to piss myself."

Oliver looked back at me but I just looked away.

This was moments away from being an absolute disaster. It had the potential to ruin everything.

"I, erm, sorry man. I think the egg salad at lunch has fucked with my stomach. I might be a while."

I wanted to laugh so much I had to clasp a hand over my mouth to prevent it from spilling out and alerting Julius to my presence.

"Gross as fuck, but do you need anything? I could go see if there's anything to settle your stomach in the first aid kit or like an electrolyte drink or something?" It hadn't been the reaction I'd been expecting from Julius, I thought he'd take the piss, but maybe this caring side was something only his best friends got to see.

"Nah, I'm good. I'd go find another bathroom if I was you. I need a minute and it fucking stinks in here." I was a second away from losing it. Oliver could have given a whole book ton of excuses and he'd gone with 'I have diarrhea'.

"Okay man, give us a shout if you need anything. I'm going to run across to the canteen to use the toilets there." I listened as Julius walked away. I counted several beats before I started to laugh. I finally pulled my boxers up and retrieved my shirt from where it was resting in the sink.

"I told you this was a bad idea," I said in between chuckles. Imagine if we hadn't fucking locked the door, Julius would have walked straight into a disaster of a scene. If he found out, Tom would have too and his reaction probably would have alerted the coaches which were currently in the gym as well.

"I can't believe you didn't even get to come. I'm guessing me talking about shitting myself was a complete and utter buzz kill?" As if he even had to ask,

I was already dressed again and what had once been a raging erection was soft and tucked back into my gym shorts.

Something weird vibrated through me though. It was a mix between excitement and adrenaline, the kind I was used to experiencing when I stretched on to my tiptoes in the corner of the mat as I prepared to dive into a series of power moves. It wasn't something I'd ever joined together with sex, and then, like in this situation, the thrill of getting caught. It felt dangerous, but not the kind I wanted to run from. It's probably what scared me the most—I wasn't yearning to run from Oliver and this mess.

"Just a little," I replied as I splashed water across my face to cool off. "How the fuck do we get out of here though?"

"I'll go first, then you count to thirty and leave. I'll make sure Tom and the coaches are distracted."

"Sounds like you've done this before." It slipped out before I could even stop myself. I wasn't sure I needed to know about Oliver's previous sexual encounters. I'd already kind of figured out for myself this wasn't his first time with a man, but that didn't mean I needed to hear all about them either, though.

"Messy blow jobs on a bathroom floor are a key part to someone's clubbing experience." He winked at me as he unlocked the door and left before I could say anything else.

Oliver continued to surprise me and I hated it. This hadn't been what I'd agreed to with myself at all. When we'd discussed the friends with benefits thing I thought 'you know what, even though I'm not truly desperate to get laid—especially with Oliver Ramsey—why not?' As long as I could do that and focus on writing my dissertation and training, it couldn't hurt. So far, so good, but every time Oliver revealed this side to him which I kind of liked, one where he wasn't constantly having a go at me or being a dick, something like 'What if?' popped into my head. There could be no what ifs, none at all.

I'd completely forgotten I was supposed to be counting to thirty, but I assumed it had been long enough. When I cracked open the door I realized I had nothing to worry about at all. Tom, Oliver, and the coaches were all crowded around the entry way to our training center and as I got closer to them I could see why. Brayden had arrived.

Oliver scowled at him, as if the first thing Brayden had done upon his arrival was kick his dog. I wasn't sure what that was about at all. None of us had really known Brayden long. He'd come out of nowhere and before we knew it, he'd flipped his way into the alternate spot on the team. For someone who was only nineteen it was a crazy achievement.

"Hey, Lucas." He flashed me the brightest of smiles, interrupting whatever conversation the four of them had been having. "How's it going?"

"Not bad. You happy to finally be here?"

He nodded and grinned harder at me. It wasn't a cocky grin, more of a look of admiration. It was probably how I looked at Max Whitlock the first time I'd met him. At least Brayden didn't stumble over his words when he was around me.

In the few training sessions the five of us had shared together, the guys had ribbed him for trying to copy me on floor. Back then I'd said nothing because none of them were my friends, but now here we were, somewhat friendly, and I wasn't sure I how fitted into the line of banter.

"Ready to go. I know I'm only an alternate, but I want to be as prepared as I can be. You never know what might happen."

Oliver grunted and rolled his eyes, which earned him a shove from Tom, but Oliver was having none of it.

"We should get back to practice." He hadn't been saying that ten minutes ago.

"Hey, you okay?" I asked as I followed him to the chalk pit. His brow furrowed so hard and when he met my eye his blue eyes were dark and stormy. "Is there beef between you and Brayden?"

"I hardly know the kid, it's all good." His tone was gruff, like he wanted me to drop it. "You good?" he asked in return. His eyes flickered to the bathroom door and I knew what he meant.

"Yeah, all good, don't worry about it." The way he hovered told me he knew I was already worrying about it.

"Talk to me," he said as he scooped up another load of chalk to make us lurking around look less suspicious.

"If—and I mean if—we continue to do this, Oliver, we've gotta be more careful. That's twice now we've almost been caught in compromising positions."

He started to grin and part of me wanted to back out of this deal before it was even made, but the rest of me, well, reluctantly, it was having fun.

"I can do careful," he replied before he sauntered back to the parallel bars, stripping out of his sweatpants leaving him in the smallest gym shorts I'd ever seen him in. Fucking dick, he was doing this on purpose. I'd just signed a deal with the devil, hadn't I?

Chapter Twelve

Oliver

Just like everything else in his life, Lucas did nothing by halves in our new arrangement. Yeah, he'd been hesitant at first, but the night after the toilet incident, I'd let him take the lead again. Which had led to us exchanging blow jobs in the shower. He was really beginning to make the most of our arrangement.

It was just all completely behind closed doors, locked in our bedroom with no chance of anyone catching us. I understood his reasoning, but it was hard not to reach out and touch him whenever I felt like it.

We'd fallen into a bit of a routine though. We did what we'd started doing every night, chose an episode of *Brooklyn Nine-Nine,* turned the volume up as loud as we could get it without it being obnoxious, and got down to business without the worry of Jules and Tom next door being able to hear us.

"I swear to god I'm not going to be able to practice tomorrow," Lucas panted from on top of me.

"I don't think you can use that excuse when Carson or Jacub asks why you're sitting out. Jacub pretty much already knows there's something going on between us and I'm almost certain he's told Carson about what he saw us doing the other day," I replied as he rolled off of me to lie beside me.

"Well, that's not humiliating at all," he groaned. "Like they've always been completely fine about me being gay and on the team, but you know some people can be different when you're flaunting it in their faces."

I didn't think we had to worry about homophobia with them, but I could feel his anxiety.

"I don't think you need to worry about it. If anything they were pleased. They pretty much said they were glad I was sticking my dick in you because it was bringing you out of your shell."

"They did not?" He flushed the deepest shade of rouge, and it was almost adorable that he thought they'd actually say something like that to me.

"You're right, they didn't, but it was worth it to see your tomato face again." I leaned in and pecked him on the lips, before I licked the strip of sweat which had dripped down his nose.

"You're so fucking gross, get off of me. I need to piss." He pushed off the arm I'd draped over him and rolled out of bed.

As I peeled off the condom, knotting it at the end before lobbing it in the bin, I realized we'd reached the end of the strip. "You know when you don't go to practice tomorrow could you go down to reception and ask for some more condoms? We're completely out now."

He chuckled to himself as he entered the bathroom and I decided it was best just not to ask why. As I tugged on my boxers there was now a huge wet patch on my sheets again, which was just great. How did we always end up having sex on my bed and not his?

I stripped off the sheet, but it had soaked straight through to the mattress and flipping it would have been an effort I couldn't be bothered with. So I stuck a towel, one from Lucas's wardrobe to be more specific, over the wet patch and covered it with a fresh sheet. It was then that I had a genius idea.

It seemed like the perfect idea in the heat of the moment as my eyes had followed his ass into the bathroom. I'd pulled the wooden bedside table out from in between our beds and then in one swift movement I collided his bed into mine with a loud crash.

However, as he returned from taking a piss, I realized I may have made a mistake. His eyes landed straight on the bed where I'd tried to join both our duvets together to make it at least look somewhat appealing to sleep in. Then they darted straight to the big empty space where his used to be, as he bit his lip in what looked like panic.

"I just thought it would be easier. Like if we're going to do this I need a bit more space to not feel like I'm shagging you in my childhood bed," I said in the hopes it justified my actions.

"When you put it like that I'm not going to protest. Although, now I'm thinking about it, what was your childhood bedroom like? Were you like a sports fan, did you have like big buff footballers on your wall or were you like a nerd?" he asked as we climbed back into bed. I wrapped my arms around him as he got himself comfy on my chest.

"I lived in my grandparents' spare room for the first ten years of my life, thinking I was just having a sleepover. They'd try to get me to unpack, but I was always insistent I was going home soon. Then when I started secondary school in London I think I finally accepted it. I mainly had band posters to be honest."

"I know your mum passed away, but what happened to your dad?" The hand I had rubbing his back stilled. "You don't have to tell me, sorry."

"No, no, it's okay. I just guess I haven't really spoke about it before. Julius's parents are friends of my grandparents so they've always known and I'm fairly sure Julius explained the situation to Tom so I didn't have to." I shuffled the pillow behind me so I could lie down properly. "After my mum died I think he did try to be a good father, but they were both so young at twenty-one and twenty-two and I just don't think he could hack it without my mom. So when I was like three or four months old he dropped me off at his parents place so they could have me for a weekend and then just never came back for me."

"Oliver." His hand slid over mine and laced our fingers together, squeezing hard. "I'm sorry."

"I'm not, my grandparents gave me the best possible life they could. They made sure I was fed and clothed and when I wasn't happy at school they paid for me to go to a private school when I was fifteen. Then I met Julius. He was a couple years ahead of me, but he'd just signed with an agent for gymnastics and I basically just followed him around and signed with the same agent."

"It's pretty cute, how inseparable you two are." He smiled up at me, resting his chin on my chest. His eyes were half closed though and as I peered at the digital clock on his bedside table I could see it was after three in the morning. The opening ceremony was later this evening, he needed some sleep.

"We are, I can't imagine us not being friends now. And Tom, well we met him not long after and it was just like a perfect fit ennit."

He nodded against my chest and let his eyes fall closed.

"You should sleep, it's ridiculously late."

He leaned up and pressed a soft kiss to my lips and I sighed into it. I wasn't even tired, but I didn't mind being his pillow if it meant he slept happily. He resettled himself on to my chest and I watched as he slipped into the most blissful looking sleep.

I'd never pictured being in a friends with benefits situation with Lucas and as I looked down at him snoring softly on my chest it hit me just sex probably didn't look anything like this. I ran my fingers softly through his curls and in his sleep he shuffled closer to me until he had a leg thrown over my thigh.

Lucas Evans was killing me and it was fucking ridiculous. He'd always been gorgeous, but it was so much easier to despise him when he was moody and set on going at this alone. Now, not so much. Learning about him and his family and everything he wanted from his future, it made it hard to push him away and hate him again. This wasn't just sex.

He'd started to open himself up to me, he felt comfortable talking about his fears and hopes with me, and everything good or bad about his past. Yet I still sat on all my secrets, not only just to him, but also to my best friends. I wasn't even out. The two most important people in my life didn't know this whole other side of me, and if I thought about it too hard it would probably eat me up.

My phone vibrated under my pillow and with my free arm I pulled it out to see what was going on. It was almost four in the morning so I couldn't even think of anybody who'd be texting me. It wasn't a text, though; it was a Sky Sports News notification.

—*Abbie Heston, Canadian cyclist, comes out as a lesbian the night before Olympic opening ceremony.*—

Well fuck. Had she been reading my mind? Not that I'd been thinking about coming out to the whole world, but maybe to my best friends would be a start. She was so brave, to just put out a Twitter statement and let it go to the world. The world didn't seem to be falling apart either. I clicked the link to the actual tweet and all her replies were filled with love and support. I wasn't surprised, this was her third Olympic circuit and she was a legend.

What would they write if this was me? I wasn't Abbie, with five gold medals to my name, or Lucas with his world-renowned floor routine. I couldn't help but think me being bisexual would become the only thing I'd be known for, and I'd have nothing else to fall back on. I didn't spend two thirds of my life training to be known only as 'the bisexual gymnast'. I just wasn't sure what else I had to offer.

I was the captain who was overlooked by the incredible floor guy and the two all-rounders, I just about had an A-Level or two to rub together. Who was I? Maybe I should have considered going to university. *Fuck.* I was being ridiculous. After this I'd have a gold medal and it wouldn't matter what they printed about my bisexuality.

Chapter Thirteen

Lucas

Waking up in Oliver's arms on the morning of the opening ceremony for the Olympics was something I'd never pictured happening to me, not even in my wildest dreams. Yet here I was, playing the little spoon, tucked up under his chin in our crappy, makeshift double bed. When had this become my life? Or maybe the real question was, how? I couldn't say I minded though, not when everything inside of me felt completely relaxed, even on what should be one of the most nerve-wracking days of my life.

"How you feeling?" Oliver asked as he rolled me over by the waist to face him before he yawned his disgusting morning breath into my face like he did every morning. Waking up like this had been a thing for the last almost week or so and I was already attached to it. This was what worried me about relationships. Not being able to let go of things, like when we had to go home and this, whatever this was between us, would be over.

"Ready. There is a crap ton of adrenaline rushing round my body right now, but it's more excitement than nerves. Does that make any sense?" He pulled his arm from under my waist to allow me to snuggle properly into the nook of his shoulder.

"I don't think you ever make any sense, but sure

thing." He chuckled and I slapped his bare stomach, which only caused him to laugh more. "Nah, I get you, it's a big day. I think everybody is going to be feeling a mixture of nerves and excitement." He dropped a soft kiss into my curls and I almost combusted. How did people do this daily? Wake up with their partners like it was normal, feeling so ridiculously happy. I had no clue what all of this meant, but I was happy to continue doing it if it made me feel like this.

"I'm just gutted my mum and sisters aren't here. Like I know they'll be watching at home, but like I dunno, it feels weird to know they won't be in the crowd. I bet you're excited to see your grandparents though?" I knew he was trying not to show how excited he was, but I could feel it all night with how restlessly he'd slept. He was like a kid waiting for Christmas, waking up every hour to check the time. "You're allowed to be excited Oliver. This is a big fucking deal."

A grin spread across his face and it only made me smile too. I was a little jealous, but so happy he had support here. Especially after what he'd told me last night about his dad leaving him with them. "I really am excited and I'm excited for family day tomorrow."

The day which I'd have no part in. It was going to be a shit one, but I was going to see Alicia's mum in the morning and then go on a nice run around Paris after. I'd found a beautiful route on Google. Then I'd spend the rest of the afternoon working on my seriously neglected Master's dissertation.

His smile turned to a frown and I hated that he'd caught on to my vibe.

"Stop looking at me like that, I'll video chat with my sisters in the evening, it's fine. They'll both be watching at home and mum's already said she'll have the opening ceremony on every screen in the pub." It wasn't completely fine, but there was nothing I could change about this situation, so I just had to roll with it.

"I'll be right next to you tonight, anyway, you can just look at this gorgeous face. Why would you even need to look into the crowd?"

Had he always been this funny? It wasn't just his humor though, it was the fact he was using it to take my mind off of the situation.

"If you say so." He quickly pulled me into a kiss and before I knew it we'd lost most of the day to our bed and it was time to start getting ready for the evening ahead.

I put a 'get pumped' playlist on loud from the TV as we stripped and got into the shower; Luckily, we were both so wrung out it was strictly just a quick body and hair wash. He shaved in the mirror as I dried my unruly curls with the hairdryer, both of our bodies crammed into the tiny bathroom. The thing was, I no longer minded sharing the space with him. I actually loved it, and the thought alone was incredibly perturbing. He watched how my face changed in the mirror and mouthed a quick 'you okay?' before he ran beard oil through his neatly trimmed stubble. I nodded quickly, smiling at him as he blew me a kiss in the mirror, and I finished drying my hair.

"You putting any product in them or leaving them all loose?" he asked, gesturing to my curls as I put the dryer back in the cupboard under the sink. I'd come to learn he preferred when I left them unstyled as it made it easier for him to run his fingers through them, but there would be constant photos tonight so I probably needed to refine them a little bit.

"Just some mousse to keep them from being in my face." He handed me the product a little reluctantly, before smothering moisturizer around his face and down his neck.

After taming my curls, we both grabbed out team uniforms for tonight. They were a little different to our training uniforms and the uniforms we'd actually wear when we were waiting to perform. These were a royal blue pair of joggers and matching zip up jacket and white vest top. Of course they were all covered in British flags.

My hands shook as I did up the team jacket, to the point Oliver had to take them between his own to steady them. He pulled the zip up himself and pressed a kiss to my lips. It was soft, as though he wasn't expecting anything more than just a kiss. Like he'd done it just to say everything was going to be okay, that we were going to be okay, today and every other day whilst we were here. It was a promise of some sorts. One that, as we were about to venture towards one of the biggest nights of our lives, I didn't have enough time to read into. It was probably for the best.

"We ready?" I asked, tucking my phone into the pocket of my jacket.

"Ready. We'll knock on for the guys and then meet up with the women's teams. How's Alicia feeling?" he asked as he grabbed the key card to our room so I didn't have to. Such a gem.

She'd been blowing up my phone for the last couple of hours as she and her teammates got ready for the night. They put a lot more effort into their appearances for this event. "She just sent me this." I pulled out my phone and showed him the picture of her and the three other girls on her team. All of their hair pulled back into these gorgeous fishtail plaits, with red, white and blue-ribbon weaving in and out of each side. They all had blue glitter eyeshadow on and a letter box red lipstick. They were stunning.

"I should probably have at least powdered my face huh?" Oliver commented, and we both burst out laughing just as we got to where Julius and Tom were emerging from their rooms. They shared a questioning look between them, but Tom quickly shook his head.

"Ready to go?" Julius asked, and the excitement really began to buzz as we cheered going down the corridor. This was it, our moment.

They say there are moments in time you'll remember forever. Normally they're like your wedding day or the day your children are born, not a sporting event. But, walking into the Olympic arena as they called for the British teams, all of us in our colors, this was one of those moments for me, regardless of what came next. Win or lose, I'd made it. We'd made it. We were here and the next week was going to be amazing.

The atmosphere was electric, everything I'd ever dreamed of, and when I looked beside me to Oliver and then to Tom and Julius, everything felt right. It felt good to be next to them, all four of us sharing in this crazy wonderful experience, together. The three of them were staring into the crowds of British flags as if they were trying to spot their family. It was impossible to see faces, but it must have felt good for the guys to know their families were there with them.

There were tens of thousands of people in the stadium and millions watching at home, yet all I could see was Oliver walking beside me, my whole body itching to take his hand in mine. There was no way in the world I would do it, but as he side eyed me and flashed me a soft smile, I knew it was what he wanted too.

Our fingers brushed together, his pinkie linking with mine and we were lucky, lucky to be lost amongst hundreds of our teammates so no one could see. I wasn't sure Oliver was ready to be out; it wasn't something we'd talked about. But it felt like something was blossoming between us. It was more than sex. It was us sharing a bed every night, talking more and more about our lives. It was us finding any way to be close when all we were supposed to be right now was Oliver and Lucas, gymnasts, teammates.

I turned to look at him in the same second he turned to look at me and his eyes glistened. He looked as overcome as I felt as we continued to wave at the crowds with our none linked hands. I could feel wetness leaking from the corner of my eyes and I tried to blink the tears away, but they'd started to stream down my face. I couldn't even find the will to care that I was crying in front of him right now. I was so happy, happier than I'd ever been in my whole life. The years of hard work felt worth it as the arena continued to erupt into applause as a new country stepped inside. If this was how I felt now, I couldn't even begin to imagine how I'd feel when I stepped out to perform my floor routine for the first time at the Olympics.

We were close to the end of our circuit of the arena when Oliver let go of my finger, but he quickly slipped his hand into my pocket and stole my phone to take pictures and videos of everything around us. I watched as he caught a stunning one of the GB flag being flown up in front of us, I looked at him curiously and he just mouthed the word 'memories' at me. Who was I to argue with that? I never wanted to forget this feeling.

As we exited out of the tunnel and found coaches Carson and Jacub huddled waiting for us, the excitement dam between the four of us broke down. I don't know who pulled who in first or how it happened at all, but in the next second, we were all hugging. All four of us in this tight circle clutching at each other like our lives depended on it. And maybe they did right now. Maybe Oliver had been right all along and we couldn't do this without each other. Maybe I was only just seeing it for real now.

Tom's face was wet across from mine and Oliver was screaming into the circle about how excited he was. Julius squeezed my arm and I looked up at him and he grinned, blindingly. It was the first time I felt like he was welcoming me into the team. I'd take it, better now than never after I'd been a martyr for so long.

Eventually the coaches had to pull us apart as we were blocking the way for the other teams. "How we feeling?" Coach Carson asked as he led us out the exit of the arena to a private minibus to take us back to the dorms.

Everybody was a little bit speechless so I gulped out, "Overwhelmed, but so fucking excited." The coach gasped and I chuckled. "Sorry, I just don't even know what else to say. Best moment of my life hands down."

Everyone murmured in agreement and for the short ride back to the dorms we all sat in pretty much silence reflecting on the most amazing evening. By the time we left Julius and Tom at their room, I was exhausted. So exhausted the second I stepped into the room I started to step out of my clothes. I pulled on a fresh pair of boxers and climbed straight into bed.

"Not even going to brush your teeth?" he asked. Eventually I'd need to piss before I slept, so I'd brush my teeth then.

"I'm so exhausted right now, but my mind feels so alive at the same time. I think it's going to take me several days to comprehend what happened tonight." It was complete magic, walking around the arena tonight felt like heaven on earth.

He disappeared into the bathroom himself and I pulled out my phone, replied quickly to some messages in the family group chat about how excited they'd been to see me on the TV before I switched into my camera roll.

I swiped through the videos we'd taken of everybody walking and the crowds and all the British flags we spotted. Most of them were for the social media we had to put up tonight, but I was going to treasure these videos forever. I only stopped swiping when I got to some selfies Oliver had taken during the ceremony on my phone. The first one was of him and the other guys, but the second was the four of us all pulling ridiculous faces. It was the perfect representation of our team, maybe I'd even post it to my own personal Instagram over giving it to Team GB. The final one was of just me and him, not a single silly face in sight. Just bright smiles and me looking at Oliver like he was the best thing in my life. In the next one he was looking at me like I could give him the world. Given the chance, I probably would.

I quickly locked the phone before Oliver got back from the bathroom, but the softness in my eyes at the way I leant into his every touch in the photo had unnerved me. There was no way I could fall for Oliver, like none at all. We weren't a good fit, we couldn't be; we were teammates and most of the time we hated each other.

Yet when I looked around our room, all I could see were bits of us and how we worked so well. I'd started to put all his dirty socks and underwear in his laundry bag, he'd scrawled dicks and stupid little comments all over my master's notebook, and on the TV was our now joint favorite episode of *Brooklyn Nine-Nine,* the Halloween Heist episode from season five. I quickly turned off the TV and shoved my phone back under my pillow before he emerged from the bathroom.

"We not watching *The Proposal?*" he asked as he climbed into bed, his breath now minty fresh. I forgot I'd said we'd watch his favorite damn film tonight.

"I'm ready to sleep." He took my word for it and slipped easily into the big spoon position behind me.

Except I didn't sleep, even as he snored softly behind me, his whole body coated to mine like a second layer of skin. I just laid there for hours telling myself all these feelings were just from the euphoria of the night, not because I felt anything towards Oliver Ramsey.

Chapter Fourteen

Oliver

"Yep, I'll text you the address. The table's booked for two, yep, all good. I'll see you then," I said as I hung up the phone and stepped out of the bathroom to find my two best friends making themselves right at home on the bed I'd torn apart from Lucas's when they'd come a knocking.

"Your grandparents?" Tom asked from where he sat opening a couple bottles of beer for us. "I thought Jules's folks had already spoken to them about the booking? They've spoken to mine."

It would be so easy to lie and say yep, my grandparents, but today had already thrown me a curve ball or two so it would be so much easier if I got the guys in on the game to help today flow much easier.

"No, it was Debbie, Lucas's mom."

"You have her number?" Julius asked.

It had been pretty tricky to get if I was honest. I'd gone down what I thought would have been the easiest route and messaged his twin sister on Facebook. Turned out she wasn't my biggest fan and had almost blocked me after the first message. But, when she'd given me a chance to explain my motives, she eased up a little.

"Yes, because I've been arranging for them to come out here early and surprise Lucas, but then he fucked off

116

out to run at ridiculous o'clock this morning and hasn't come back yet so it might all have been for nothing." I'd paid for his sister to take some unpaid leave from work, and found a temp barman to help out at the pub, before splashing the cash so the three could fly first class to Paris and land this morning.

Debbie had cried a lot when we'd spoken on the phone and whilst she couldn't understand why I was doing this, she was beyond grateful. I just couldn't wait to see Lucas's face when they were all re-united. I knew how gutted he was that they couldn't make it.

"Why?" Julius asked, taking a sip of his beer before offering me the third open one.

I'd have killed for a beer, but my nerves were so on edge I'd probably have been sick. I should have just convinced Lucas to hang out with us this morning instead of him going to see Alicia and then this stupid run which seemed to be taking forever. I glared at Julius because I hoped this wasn't about to be him being shitty about Lucas again, especially after the moment we'd shared yesterday as a team.

"I'm not asking to be a dick, I'm just curious as you hadn't mentioned it to any of us."

"I wanted it to be a surprise and neither of you know how to keep a secret."

Julius went to protest, but he didn't have a chance to as Lucas burst through the door, panting and sweaty.

"I'm sorry, I thought you'd be gone by now." His eyes went straight to our bed, frantically checking they weren't still together. It had somewhat pained me splitting them up, but there was no way I could have excused them being pushed together to these two idiots. "Don't mind me, I'm drenched in sweat from the run and the midday sun. I'm going to hop in the shower. Have a great lunch."

"Come with us," I said a little panicked, grabbing his arm as he went to step into the bathroom. If I didn't ask then it would be too late.

"What?" he asked hovering in the door. "Are you serious?"

"Yeah, you're coming to lunch with us. I've booked your spot, I just didn't have a chance to ask you this morning because you ran out of here. Right guys?" Lucas's brows cinched in confusion as he looked behind me, but I checked quickly and both of them were nodding. "Shower and wash your hair quickly, I'll dig out some clothes for you."

He looked completely unsure, but the creases in his forehead started to ease and eventually he nodded. "Okay, uhm, sure. I'll shower, give me five minutes." He closed the door behind him and I went straight to his closet, picking out his black slacks and a teal blue shirt from my side of the closet as well as some underwear and socks.

I knocked lightly at the bathroom door and he slipped the lock back so I could slide in with his outfit. I hung them on the back of the door and took the shortest of seconds to admire his ass as he scrubbed shampoo through his curls. It was probably a really inappropriate time for me to be wondering what my grandparents were going to think of him, but it was the thought on my mind as I watched him shower.

My mind wandered to introducing them to Lucas; would they sense something between us? They knew me inside and out. I wouldn't be surprised if they did.

"Did you piss whilst he was in the shower?" Julius

asked as I left the bathroom. Had I really been gone that long? Clearly Lucas's ass was pretty distracting.

I nodded. "Yeah, to be honest, neither of us really care anymore. I often take a leak with the door open. I think he's just used to it now." I shrugged, before slipping my key card to the room into my wallet so we could leave as soon as Lucas was ready.

"Living with you would be an absolute nightmare, I definitely feel sorry for Lucas having to do it for three weeks. Like there are so many crumbs in your bed right now and it kind of smells, I don't know what like but it's sort of sweaty. What have you been doing in here?" Whilst I'd had time to separate our beds, I hadn't had time to change the sheets on them and I felt kind of bad that he was laying on the ones we'd fucked on this morning.

Lucas returned from the bathroom not long after I'd left, now dressed in his formal clothes. He'd towel dried his hair to the point his strawberry blonde curls looked tight. He was so fucking cute. I still wasn't sure when that had happened, like when did I start thinking everything Lucas Evans did was cute? It was an automatic response now, and every time I realized I was doing it I could probably have vomited.

Everything was changing and I had no clue what I was going to do when I had to start acknowledging these feelings properly.

"Okay, taxis here. Lucas, you need shoes and then we can get out of here," Tom said, and he shrugged on his dinner jacket as Lucas slipped on his fancy shoes which he wore to interviews.

Lucas didn't say anything in the taxi. He toyed with the button on the cuff of his shirt and tried to neaten up his curls. We hadn't really given him enough time to be ready. Julius chattered away aimlessly about what his brothers had been up to since all six of them had landed in Paris and it was enough to keep everyone occupied in the ten-minute journey to the restaurant.

I could see, as I led the guys into the restaurant, our families were already taking up half the space of this small, French bistro. Straight away I spotted his mother and sisters, they all shared the same nose. Plus, I recognized them from the photo on his dresser. Tom and Lucas were still talking animatedly behind me about the episode of *Brooklyn Nine-Nine* which Tom had watched last night, but I turned around just in time to catch the moment Lucas realized his family were at the table too.

His eyes glassed over in shock and before he could even let the first tear slide, three high pitched screams rang out through the restaurant. Chairs scraped across the floor behind me and I quickly moved out of the way before the three dived on to him, pulling him into a hug.

Julius and Tom quickly stepped around them to go greet their own families, but for a second I lingered back to take the four of them in. These three were pretty much Lucas's whole life, and watching them wrapped up in each other, all of them crying, I could see exactly why. The huddle radiated nothing but love. It was strange for me to watch. I adored my grandparents, but this kind of familial love was obscure to me, having grown up without my parents.

I let them have their moment and moved towards my grandparents, who were waiting for me at the end of the table. Gran looked up at me with the biggest of smiles, like I'd just made her the proudest woman alive. She'd always looked at me like I was her world and it never got old; it always filled me with a burning warmth.

"Little man," she cried as she stood from the table and pulled me into her arms. At almost a foot taller than she I towered over her, but she had the might of the strongest woman alive and with all her strength, she held me against her.

I hadn't cried in years, maybe not even since the funeral, but seeing her and Granddad right now, even though it'd only been a couple of weeks, had me completely choked. It could have been the weight of the qualifiers being just around the corner or maybe it was all the emotion of the last week or so with Lucas weighing on my shoulders, but I felt like I just needed to stay close to her for a second longer to soak up some of her strength.

"Hey Granddad," I said over her shoulder, and he raised his bottle of beer at me with a smile. He was everything I aspired to be: happily married for fifty years, still enjoying a beer as he watched his only grandchild grow up.

I pulled away from Gran as Lucas tapped on my shoulder. His eyes were swollen and bloodshot, but his cheeks were stretched so much from smiling to the point it looked like it hurt. "Sorry to pull him away from you both, I just wanted to introduce him to my family." It all sounded very formal, but I was excited to meet the girls who made Lucas who he was today.

"Oliver, this is my mom, Debbie, my twin, Lucy, and my little sister, Lauren." Debbie was a stunning dark-haired woman. She looked incredibly young to have two almost twenty-four-year-olds, but there were crow's feet around her green eyes which told me she'd had a ton of life experience in a short amount of time.

"Oliver," she said softly, opening her arms to pull me into a hug. "Thank you so much for doing this." Her voice was about to break again and if she cried, I'd have probably cried too. Emotions were running crazy high. "I can't believe we are here. You'll never know how much this means to be here for Lucas."

I think, in some weird way, I maybe got it a little. I had so much of his time now. I was sharing in his experience of the Olympics and it was amazing.

"You're welcome, I'm glad you're here. He talks about all of you literally all the time." I pulled away from the hug only to be eyed warily by his sisters. They both knew. There was no doubt about it, even if Lucas hadn't told them, they knew. I could see it in the way they were looking me up and down to make sure I was good enough for their brother.

I must have been pretty okay, because very quickly Lauren's face cracked and she started to smile as she stuck her hand out for me to shake. It seemed a little obscure, but then I remembered what Lucas had said about her struggling to settle in at school. I quickly shook it which only made her smile harder.

That just left Lucy. Her white, blonde hair was half up in this ponytail and the other half was curled and down her back. She was stunning, which wasn't difficult when she and Lucas had almost identical faces with their grass-green eyes, sharp noses, and soft jawline. She wasn't about to crack, not yet anyway.

"Hey, Lucy, it's nice to finally meet you. I feel like it's a long time coming," I said quickly to break the stony silence.

"Uh huh, you too," she said wearily. I knew she was grateful to be here, but whatever she knew/thought was making her hold back. Which was fair enough, she and her twin were crazy close—she probably still harbored the hatred he used to hold towards me.

Before I could say anything else, I was swept off to Julius's side of the table. Julius's brothers all greeted me with brotherly hugs and when we finally all got seated the sheer amount of us looked crazy. The nineteen of us around one table looked like a huge, dysfunctional family. It was wild. The pure energy of it was amazing, especially as we got settled around appetizers and everyone started to catch up and get to know Lucas's family.

Dinner flashed by in a blur of food, drink, and wonderful conversation, to the point I wasn't sure I wanted it to end.

"Nice guy," my grandma said as we lingered outside of the restaurant after, waiting for her and Granddad's taxi. "Thought you hated him?" The way she looked at me from where she was leaning against the lamppost told me she clearly knew that was no longer the case at all.

"Turns out he isn't as bad as we thought he was." We both shared a coy smile that said my words were a complete and utter understatement.

"I like him. From the way you always used to talk about him I thought he was some quiet weirdo. He wasn't weird at all tonight; I'm impressed. I hope we get to see more of him."

I pressed a kiss to her cheek as her cab arrived. Some stupid part of me hoped we got to see more of him too.

"Look after him," my granddad said as he clapped me on the shoulder and climbed into the seat next to her. Had I been obvious all night? Yes, Lucas and I had been playing footsie under the table and yes, maybe at one point we'd both been missing from the table, but I thought with so many people around nobody would notice.

"Love you both." I quickly shut the door behind them both and tapped the back of the cab for it to drive off before either of them could make any more comments on Lucas and me.

"I'm going to hang out with Jules and his brothers," Tom said as they all stumbled out onto the path, some of them looking worse than others after the several beers they'd consumed at lunch. "You coming?"

I shook my head. I knew Lucas still wanted to get in some time with Alicia and his mum and I needed a jog to burn off all the bread and pasta I'd just consumed. "Nah, Lucas needs to get back and I'm gonna work out. We'll all hang out after the games, right?" Julius's brothers nodded behind him as Lucas flagged down a taxi to take us home.

"I can't believe you did this," he said as we climbed into bed together later that night. "My mum told me about the call and all the lengths you went to make sure they got here. I can't believe they are going to get to see the qualifiers now. Like I know we probably are going to qualify for the all-around team finals and I have a good shot at floor finals, but—"

"A good shot? You're currently ranked number two in the world on floor, I think you can afford to be modest. I didn't do this because I was concerned they wouldn't see you perform, but because you only get one first family day at the Olympics and there was no way you were spending this one alone."

"Where's Oliver Ramsey and what did you do with the guy who once drew dicks all over my Fitbit commercial pictures?" He grinned at me like an absolute idiot, strawberry blonde curls falling over his eyes as he snuggled into the pillow.

I quickly pushed the curls out of the way and pulled the duvet over the pair of us. "He's still here. I stand by doing that and I can't wait to do it to all the press pics which get taken of you when you win gold."

"That's probably the nicest thing you've ever said to me." It probably should have been the moment to make my move, to pull him on top of me and kiss him until neither of us could keep our hands off each other. It was all part of this arrangement we had going and whilst it would have been nice to touch him, have him naked on top of me, he looked exhausted. So, instead, I pressed a soft kiss to his temple and wrapped my arms around his waist to pull him closer to me.

We fell asleep perfectly slotted together, my arm wrapped around his frame, holding him against my chest. Part of me never wanted to let go, and the other part was scared to death about what that might mean.

On the mat the next morning we were still Lucas and Oliver, coach still drilled us about being ready and not getting distracted the week before the competition started, and nothing felt different except a knot in my stomach I couldn't undo.

Chapter Fifteen

Lucas

"So, I got us passes for the diving finals today," I said as I presented him the passes I'd frantically texted Coach Jacub for yesterday evening after the family dinner. I wanted to do something, both to say thank you for the fact he'd helped me integrate into the team over the last week or so, and for dinner last night. But also, so we could just get out of our room, just the two of us, and do something together other than have sex. I wasn't about to suggest it be a date, but I couldn't deny my mind hadn't wandered there a couple of times.

"Who are you and what have you done with Lucas Evans?" Oliver grinned in reply and snatched one of the passes from my hand. "Are you suggesting we...skip practice to go and have fun, has someone brainwashed you?"

"Yeah, you." I pinched his forearm, before swiping back the pass from him. "I mean, I can ask Tom or Julius if you aren't interested..."

"No, I'm good. Let's go watch some guys in tight trunks flipping off boards. I'm sure this was a completely selfless act on your behalf and you just wanted to take our minds off of the games, not so you can ogle men in speedos."

I pinched him again and he yelped, but I couldn't

help but laugh. The men in tiny swim trunks were a complete bonus to going on a maybe date with Oliver. What I'd give for it to be Oliver in those speedos though. I bet he'd look so damn good.

"So, I might have also been in your wardrobe this morning and stole a hoodie of yours so you can wear it to the event and then we can sit in the stands instead of the VIP section with the other athletes. Is that okay?" I just wanted for us to be normal for a little while, see what it'd be like to be just the two of us outside of our own bubble.

"Am I going to have to get a lock for it? What do you plan to steal next, my underwear?"

"Why would I need to go in your wardrobe for those when they live all over our bathroom floor?" Now that we were having sex, I found them everywhere: on the floor, under our bed, under my pillow—which was probably the strangest place so far. When Oliver whipped them off, the destination they ended up was always unknown. It was one of the only things which really irritated me about sharing a room with him now. Besides his annoying personality of course. Even though we were having sex he was still annoying. Oh, and his tendency to hog our makeshift covers.

"Haha," he mocked. "When did you become such a funny guy?" His actions completely undermined his words as he wrapped his arms around my neck and pushed me into the locker room wall. "You have such a smart mouth." He pressed his lips to mine and no matter how much I wanted to indulge in this feeling, we were in public.

"Hey, Oliver," I mumbled against his lips. "Don't forget Julius, Tom, and all of our coaches are just in the other room."

He groaned and untangled his fingers from my curls, which I swear was now his favorite place to put them, making no further attempt to kiss me. "So, when do these finals start?"

I glanced up at the clock before I started to unpack the bag of supplies I'd brought with me for this mission. I'd packed like we were about to become undercover agents. "In literally fifteen minutes so you should put these on." I chucked the hoodie and my spare pair of shades at him.

"These aren't mine," he pointed out like I didn't already know. Was it weird that I'd become so comfortable sharing his shit? I'd even borrowed his towel this morning because he'd used my last remaining clean one to mop up our cum.

"Nope, they're mine, just like this hoodie isn't mine either, it's yours because I seem to only have hoodies which have some kind of Olympic or gymnastics branding on them. No time to discuss though, we need to go otherwise we're going to miss all the men in tight speedos."

He slipped the hoodie over his head and I followed suit before we donned the sunglasses and slipped out of the training room in the direction of the aquatics center. As we walked, I had this strange desire to reach out and take his hand, maybe if I'd been just a little braver I would have, but if I fucked this up now, I had no clue what I'd do. The desire lingered as we climbed the steps of the spectator stands to a less crowded area and sat down just in time for the first diver.

"So, outside of gymnastics, this is my favorite sport to watch and sometimes even participate in. I say that lightly, because I've only jumped off the middle tier and it was only because I was scared Tom Daley was going to push me off the board if I didn't," I whispered to him as the competition kicked off and the first set of pairs dove.

"Hang on, you've dived with Tom Daley? How did I not know this?" he said, way too loudly, almost drawing the attention of the couple sitting three rows in front of us.

"It was for his YouTube channel. Management asked me to do it so I did. If it hadn't been him asking, I doubt I would have done it, but I have a lot of respect for him after he paved the way for other athletes to come out." My manager practically hated me, I hardly ever said yes to anything unless she forced me to do it or said it would harm my career if I didn't.

A few summers ago, I'd seen Oliver, Julius, and Tom all over every social media app posting about various engagements and press events. Then Julius's YouTube channel took off so I'd seen them all over that too.

At one point I was convinced they all just lived on social media. Tom's page was filled with step-by-step guides to different sections of various routines he could perform and Oliver's stories were always shirtless pics, workouts, and them hanging out as a team before we were even put together as the Olympic team.

At the time I'd hated seeing it because I couldn't understand why they couldn't just focus on training and being a gymnast, but now I knew I'd probably been a little bit jealous. It was like even after the virus lockdown of 2020 had been lifted, I'd still stayed indoors, my habits unchanged.

However, when Tom Daley started a series engaging with Olympic hopefuls to fill the void of the 2020 Olympics being canceled, I'd bitten his hand off. My manager had been overjoyed. Tom had even kept in touch over the years, offering up all his support for a fellow gay athlete.

"Okay, well, now I'm offended he never asked me. What do you have that I don't?" Oliver asked as he stuck out his bottom lip like a child about to have a strop.

"Clearly he only films with the best of the best." I stuck my tongue out in reply, but when he jutted his lip out further I didn't want to tease anymore, I wanted to kiss him. But, even with the noise of the crowd and our disguises, that would not be a good idea.

"If you say so." He rolled his eyes playfully, and I had to draw my attention away from his lips before I did something I'd really regret. "I wouldn't tell Julius about this though, he's already plotting ways to get you involved with the vlogs and he has all these crazy challenge ideas. If you ask me, some of them are way too dangerous for any of us to be engaging in just days before the qualifiers, but you know he's persistent."

"You can say that again. After the games though, when we have some downtime before the closing ceremony, I'd be down."

"Tell him that after we've won gold okay? He wants to move the mirror challenge that he did on floor with you to a huge trampoline and he's not at all graceful like you. He'd probably injure you and ruin your Olympic chances."

"You think I'm graceful?"

For a second Oliver looked flustered, a tinge of red to his cheeks as his eyes struggled to meet mine. It wasn't something I'd ever seen from him before. He was a leader and his confidence never wavered when we were in the gym; he always seemed so sure of himself and everything he did. Seeing a tiny bit of his vulnerability only made him that little bit more attractive to me.

In the midst of our discussion, I'd almost completely forgotten about the diving going on, but I looked up just in time for the British pair to be announced.

Oliver and I both cheered with everything we had as they prepared to dive. And dive they did. As gymnasts we had to have a ton of rhythm and be in control of every movement. Yet the pairs dive was a hundred times harder than what we did. Not only did they have to be flawless in their own dive, but they had to be completely in sync with each other as well. It would be like me doing that mirror challenge on floor that Julius keeps bugging me about, almost impossible. Our guys smashed it and as we waited for their scores to be announced I couldn't help but relax into my seat. Today had been great. Yes, it was a bit out of my comfort zone and a small part of me ached with guilt because we'd missed quite a bit of training, but it was amazing to support Team GB and to spend some time alone with Oliver.

That rush of endorphins was enough to push me to finally be brave. As we sat there patiently looking up at the screen for the results, I slipped my hand into Oliver's and squeezed in appreciation.

For a second he froze, his fingers tense beneath mine and I started to convince myself that I'd made a mistake in doing so. Then I felt him loosen up and when he squeezed back, I let out a sigh of relief.

We sat there, hand in hand for a further hour, enjoying the atmosphere of the diving wrapping up and then the medal ceremony. Watching Team GB win silver had my heart lurching in my chest with pride towards our fellow athletes. It was a potential glimpse into how we might be feeling towards ourselves in less than a week's time. I'd dreamed night and day since I was just a tumbling teen about what it would be like to stand on that podium, the heavy weight of the medal draped around my neck as I waved out to the crowd. It was completely overwhelming, like performing on a stage, but I craved it, I craved standing there like nothing else but that moment mattered in the world. That everything I'd worked for over the last decade had been worth it, that the exhaustion and crazy schedules had resulted in something amazing. If that happened next week everything would slot into place and I'd feel complete.

Something about that had shifted though. When I'd dreamed about it the night before it wasn't just me on that podium anymore, it was the whole team.

"Hey," I said as we walked across the gravel towards the training center, hoping that the fact that we disappeared by ourselves for over two hours had gone unnoticed by Julius and Tom. "I just wanna say thank you."

"For coming with you to the diving?" He stopped for a second, pausing in his stride to take a measured look at my face to grasp what I was thanking him for. "You're welcome, I had a great time. It was nice to have a break from everything for a little while." His smile told me that he was just as grateful as I was to spend time together, just the two of us, today. But that hadn't been what I meant when I'd said thank you.

"No." I shook my head. "For everything right now. I don't do this, you know, skip training. But you calling me out on not being a team player and forcing me to try harder even though I really didn't want to, well it kind of triggered something inside of me. The guys are great, even if Julius's life is just a constant innuendo, but I'm glad I gave them a chance and that was because of you." I wanted to thank him for everything else, but it felt beyond weird to both be thanking him for having sex with me, and saying it whilst we were out in public where anyone could hear. So, instead, I settled for squeezing his arm. His eyes danced as he looked down at where my fingers had just been, a genuine grin spreading across his face as we made our way back to the training center.

No one batted an eyelid as we walked back into the hall. Julius was clearly making the most of me being away from the mat as he tumbled across it straight into a double twist front rollover; Tom not far from him chatting to Coach Jacub. I did a double take as no one moved to find out where we'd been. Instead, we had to approach them as Julius finished his routine and ran across the mat to get feedback from Coach.

"Are we in the upside down?" Oliver whispered to me as we crossed the floor, as still nobody even blinked an eye that we'd returned.

"Oh, hey," Julius finally said as we came to a stop next to the three of them, interrupting whatever Jacub had been saying about his routine. "How was the interview?"

I side glanced towards Oliver to check that he looked just as confused as I felt and as he cocked his head at the pair, I knew he was.

Thankfully, we were saved by Jacub and his mind working in the most mysterious of ways. "Yeah, I told them you two had been asked to do a last-minute interview with a local sports magazine and hadn't had time to let anyone know where you were going."

I could have hugged him. Whilst he clearly knew that there was now something going on between Oliver and me, Coach Jacub obviously had our backs and was going to great lengths to cover for us. I was almost sure after how he pulled us into his office the other day that he disapproved, but this gave me some hope.

"All good, we got a bit waylaid as their interview with some Spanish cyclists ran over. Did we miss anything?" Oliver replied confidently, as I stood in awe of what had just happened, unable to form a reply.

"I've now nailed my floor routine. It's no Lucas Evan's but it's as good as it's ever going to be for my standards."

"Your double twist rollover looked great. I wouldn't be worried at all with that move under your belt." It was looking very strong right now. If I was anything of a coach, I'd be pushing him to do the triple twist we'd practiced, but it definitely wasn't my place to interfere.

"Thanks man." Julius shot me a grateful smile, no mockery, nothing, just bright, pearly white teeth that almost pushed me to become emotional as I finally started to slot into my place on the team.

"You guys can get out of here for the day. Please eat a good dinner and get a good night's sleep. Not you pair though." Coach Jacub directed his words towards Oliver and me. I almost wanted to shrink into the ground at the thought that he could say something embarrassing about what might be keeping us up at night, but instead he just said, "You have missed training hours to make up for."

Oliver sighed heavily, but I just smiled and nodded. I'd train till midnight if it meant I could have more days like this.

Chapter Sixteen

Oliver

"Hey, are you asleep?" I whispered into the half-lit room. We'd sort of fallen into bed after a late dinner and several rounds of sex, with neither of us bothering to get up and draw the curtains properly. It was only just after nine, so the setting sun seeped orange into the room, highlighting the auburn undertone of Lucas's strawberry blonde hair. His curls were nestled into my neck, tickling the underside of my jaw, but I was starting to wonder how I slept before they were there.

"What's up?" he asked as he rolled over to look at me, his green eyes bright in the darkening room. Our heads were so close they shared a pillow, so close I could lean in and kiss him right now if I wanted to, but I was way too tired to go at it again.

"Can you get up and draw the curtains please?" My playful grin was short-lived as he reached over and pinched the side of my naked stomach.

"I was just about to fall asleep and that's all you fucking wanted, are you kidding me?" He tried to sound angry, but his curls flopped over his eyes and he struggled to hold back a laugh.

"How were you falling asleep when it's literally still so bright in this room right now?" I asked. But, if I was honest with myself, I could sleep in pretty much any environment if he was curled up next to me. It was a bizarre feeling that I quickly pushed down. I couldn't believe it was Lucas Evans who helped me relax. That my stomach slotting into the dip of his toned back and my arms wrapped around his abs was what cured my insomnia. There was something about the coarseness of his snail trail beneath my hands as I tried to sleep that soothed my nerves and pushed every thought that tried to intrude my mind right back out.

"I'm absolutely knackered, that's why, how are you not? We've literally not stopped all day. I could probably sleep for a year right now." His eyes were completely hooded as he lifted his head up a couple of inches so I could wrap an arm around his shoulders to help him get comfortable again.

"Talk to me about anything, my brain is still wide-awake right now. Tell me something I don't know about you."

"Then can I sleep?" He asked.

I nodded and he snuggled into the crease of my elbow. "So, in December I've been asked to go be part of the celebrity version of The Great British Bake Off and I've said yes. It's the stand up to cancer special and well, I love that show. It's like a serious guilty pleasure for me."

"Well damn, I genuinely thought you were incapable of watching anything other than *Brooklyn Nine-Nine* to be honest." I chuckled and he licked the back of my hand. "But that's actually really cool. My gran loves that show, now I can tell her I've shagged someone who's been in the tent."

"You would not dare say that to your grandma." He all but gasped as he looked up from where he was practically in the fetal position against me. He looked so fucking cute.

"No, I definitely would not, but at least when we sit and watch your episode together I can know, in my head, that I've seen exactly what your hands can do."

He shook his head at me in disbelief, but I just pulled him closer until I could feel him completely up against me.

"Sleep now," he whispered, before dropping a kiss to the arm I had wrapped around him as he closed his eyes once more.

Only for us to be disturbed moments later, as we started to fall asleep, by a knock at our door.

"Fuck sake," Lucas grumbled, as I started to pull away from him to get rid of whoever had decided to disturb what was about to be the perfect night sleep.

"Do not move. I'll be right back." I slipped carefully out of bed and started the search for wherever I'd discarded my boxers. Whoever it was, there was no way I could open the door to them with my dick still hanging out. "One second," I called out as I tried to put my inside out boxers on.

They either didn't hear me or chose to ignore me, because instead of waiting they started to turn the doorknob and I couldn't for the life of me think if we'd locked the door behind us earlier that evening.

Before I could find a shirt, Tom had already stepped into our room letting all the light in from the corridor, illuminating my half naked body.

"Oh shit, sorry man. I didn't realize you were already trying to sleep. I was going to see if you wanted to get in a late-night workout or something. Jules is on FaceTime with Estelle and I felt so weird just sitting there whilst they talked."

He leant up against the wall and whilst I felt for him, I had no desire to leave this room before sunrise and it wasn't like I could invite him into hangout with Lucas and me. Then it hit me. Lucas. Fuck. Tom was looking directly into the space where our beds were pushed together. There was no way he wouldn't see the situation I had going on. I grabbed a shirt, that I wasn't even sure was mine, from the ground and in a rush of panic slipped it over my head before silently herding Tom out of our room.

"Sorry," I started as he stared at me, his eyebrows raised and eyes widened like he was trying to figure out what the fuck he'd seen. "Lucas is literally just about to fall asleep and I really don't want to wake him right now. He's exhausted."

"Ollie, I, well, I'm guessing you're probably too tired for another workout this evening?" He shot me a knowing smile and I wanted to be sick. I really didn't want the guys to find out about me and Lucas, period. That would not be good for the team dynamic at all, but then in strode Tom, uninvited, letting himself in, literally, on the secret. "I'm gonna leave you two to it. Do you wanna go for a run in the morning?"

"Definitely man, I'll see you then." I nodded and watched him walk away, past his own room and into the lift. He waved to me, a coy smile spread across his face as the doors closed in front of him.

"Did he see us?" Lucas asked as I re-entered the room, his body now wrapped up in our crumpled sheets, his bedside lamp switched on as I closed the door behind myself.

"Yeah, I think so," I replied as I drew the curtains to

shut out the night sky. "He won't say anything though, trust me."

He peered up at me from where the duvet cover was practically up to his chin now. I smiled, reassuringly, down at him as I pulled off the shirt and slid back under the sheets next to him.

"Are you sure? I really don't think people knowing about this would be a good idea right now. Jeez if the press caught wind of this there would be an absolute shit storm." He nuzzled back into my side, his whole body warm against mine, hands tracing lazily over my thighs.

In that moment it felt like the right time to tell him about Tom's previous experience with keeping a relationship of mine a secret. "When I was fifteen, almost sixteen, I started a new school in London. The first secondary school hadn't worked out for me and I needed a fresh start. On the very first day I met this girl, Amber. I fell in love with her so quickly that I couldn't even cope. You've heard about Julius's girlfriend, well Estelle is Amber's older sister and that's how me and Julius first started to get close." Lucas nodded along, like things were slowly starting to make sense to him.

I wished I didn't have to see his reaction to this story or that it wouldn't be awkward if I reached over him and turned off the lamp so we could talk in the darkness. "Julius and Estelle had already been together for like a year or so when me and Amber got together. He was already a rising star in the gymnastics world and was destined for the 2020 Olympics. I basically wanted to be him. I'd already had some luck at big national competitions and I definitely had Team GB scouts after me. So I joined the gym that Julius trained at, signed with the same agency, and we became inseparable. Things had been going really well with me and Amber for around a year when I was selected to go to my first Worlds at almost eighteen and that's when we met Tom. I medaled during that competition and the press on me took off. I loved Amber, but I didn't want her in the press, so the three of us hid her, shielding her from the spotlight. It was hard work, but we did it because I needed one thing in my life to be private and mine."

I knew Lucas understood, he hated being in the limelight and he hardly ever used any kind of social media. I was sure that if he could get out of any of the interviews and photoshoots we were required to do, he probably would. I stroked my hand softly up his cheekbone and into the back of his curls, as if I could hold onto him forever. It would have made this story a whole lot easier to tell.

"It was so fucking hard, but it was worth it to be able to live in our own little bubble without any intrusions. We finished Sixth Form. Amber got into UCL to do an economics degree and we started to rent a one bed in Kings Cross. I had to sign for it myself, all her post still had to go to her home address and all the utilities were in my name so we could exist outside of the spotlight. First year of Uni was fine; she was smashing her degree and I was building up my reputation as a strong rings man plus I was unbeatable on high bar. Remember we went to that London and Essex club meet in 2019? That's when you and I first met. Julius already knew who you were though, he really liked to keep tabs on the competition especially when the Olympic team qualifiers were right around the corner. He pointed you out and told me how you were some super smart gymnast at Uni whilst competing. I couldn't stop looking at you.

Like I really looked because you weren't like any other gymnast I'd seen before. You don't meet many getting a politics degree."

He grinned at me stupidly, like it was the most ridiculous thing. Which it was because seeing him at that competition was nowhere near relevant to this story, but the image of him on that day had popped into my head randomly.

"You remember we invited you to that after party because we'd all medaled that day? You walked away before even giving us an answer. That's part of the reason Julius wasn't your biggest fan. Anyway, yeah, Amber was there that day. Even though we were in hiding as a couple she found a way to make it to every meet and competition. She said you were interesting. I remember her words, she was obsessed with your hair." I couldn't help how wistful I sounded, they were all such good memories.

"Anyway, skip forward like eight months and it was the night before the 2020 qualifiers. I'd been at Amber and Estelle's folks house with Julius having our weekly dinner and I was so exhausted we decided to crash in Amber's old room. Amber, being a complete star, drove back to our place in Kings to grab my uniform and paperwork for the next day and, and…" I choked over the lump in my throat as tears bristled against the back of my eyes. I had never told this story to anyone. Hadn't had to, as Julius had told Tom and Estelle had told my grandparents. That was as far as the circle of truth extended. "Well, she didn't get a next day. A bus pulled out on her at an intersection and she was gone before the emergency services even arrived at the scene."

Lucas slid his hand into mine and gripped it hard,

squeezing like his life depended on it and it was the only thing in that moment that truly stopped me from breaking down. "Gorgeous, I'm so sorry," he said in his smallest voice as I rested my free hand in the dip of his back. "You didn't have to tell me any of that, but I'm glad you did. Is this why you've been so tense recently?"

I should have said no, I should have told him about the other anxiety and fear that sat heavier on my shoulders, literally. Sometimes, more so than Amber dying four years ago did. But I didn't.

Instead, I told him the other thing I'd never told anyone before. "We were both just twenty years old when she died, but a few weeks before she'd sat me down and I swear I thought she was going to tell me it was over. Instead, she told me that she was three months pregnant." Lucas audibly gasped and I had to remind myself, as he breathed out sharply, to breathe as well. "I thought that was it: I was about to make the Olympic team, I had the perfect girlfriend, and I was about to be a father."

"Fuck, Oliver, I'm so sorry. You'd have been the best kind of father. I see it in you with the guys and how you lead the team as captain. How you know how to handle Julius when he gets a little weird and how you put up with all my shit even when I didn't want you to." Lucas placed the sweetest and softest of kisses to my temple as I reached out to push the curls from his face. In that moment I knew I'd made the right choice to open up to him.

He turned out of my grip to reach over and pull the cord on the lamp, the room finally descending into darkness as he settled back into my arms.

"Since her death I haven't properly been with

anyone else. I don't want to get heavy with you, but I've literally avoided women like the plague since she passed because I didn't want to replace her. I felt like I wasn't allowed. So, when I kissed you it shocked the both of us. I'm glad we've been doing this though. I feel like I can finally speak about her without losing it. She's been gone for four years and, except to the guys, I haven't said her name out loud. When I attended the funeral, they printed in the papers that I was there to support Julius and his girlfriend."

"That must have been so hard. I get it though, you don't want your whole life in the headlines - good or bad."

"Us fighting hasn't really helped with that has it? I'm sorry. I've been angry for a really long time, not at you, but at the world and I took that out on you because you were an easy target."

"We don't need to rehash any of that now, what's done is done. We've made it since then. Look at where we are." In the dark I could still see Lucas gesturing down to the ridiculous blue and pink Olympic sheets. That even though they were part of the memorabilia of our time here at the Olympics, it still kind of made us feel like we were sleeping in a child's bed.

"I know, I know, but I'm still so—"

Lucas never let me finish. Instead he pressed his lips against mine and kissed me until I could hardly even remember my own name. Kissed me until the conversation we'd just had was a distant memory. Kissed me to the point we were both so exhausted we fell asleep clinging to each other.

Chapter Seventeen

Lucas

"Time to get up," Oliver sing-songed like it wasn't only a few hours after we'd fallen asleep.

I rolled over to check my phone and groaned when it was only a little after seven. Today was our only full day off, except for family day, whilst we were here and I'd planned to spend that day training anyway as my family couldn't make it.

I groaned into his pillow as I pulled it over my face to block out the early morning sunlight he was letting stream into the room. "I set my alarm for ten so I could work on my dissertation, not seven so you could wake me up by blinding me."

"Okay, well, the dissertation might have to wait because we need to be out of here in the next half an hour. I've already been next door and woke the guys."

"They must have loved you for that." I couldn't imagine a world in which Julius was a morning person. He groaned about ten AM workouts.

"I mean, they complained a lot more than you've done so far, but they are both up and getting dressed. I said we'd meet them outside in the hallway in the next half an hour so you need to move your ass."

I was still curled up with the duvet wrapped around me like a burrito and if it had been anyone other than

Oliver asking, I'd have just rolled over and gone back to sleep.

"Okay, okay," I replied as I shuffled out of my cozy zone and planted my feet on the floor. I stretched out my body and grabbed my towel on the way to the en-suite.

"Hey," I said as I hovered in the bathroom doorway, towel slung over my shoulder. "Do you mind if I invite Alicia? The guys would be cool with that right? I feel like I haven't spent a ton of time with her since we've been here and I'm sure she'd love to get out of the dorms too."

"Yeah of course, the more the merrier. I'll drop her a text and let her know to wear trainers as it'll be a lot of walking. Oh and to bring a jacket, it's going to be nippier later."

"You've got all this planned out, haven't you? How long have you been awake?" He'd already showered, dressed, and woke up the guys next door so it had to be over an hour.

"I dunno, since like five. I know we only fell asleep at like one, but I felt wired when I woke up so I just rolled with it. Then I started scrolling through walking tours of Paris and now I have one mapped out with breakfast and lunch stops." Oliver was practically bouncing on his heels as he waited for me to go in the shower. It was almost as if he'd consumed several coffees already. "Come on, we need to go."

I hadn't seen Oliver this excited before, maybe because we'd never really hung out outside of practice, but it was truly a sight to behold. I slipped into the bathroom, showered quickly, and ran my fingers through my curls to try and give them some kind of life. I knew I didn't have enough time to do a full hair wash.

When I emerged from the bathroom in just my towel, Oliver was already lacing up his trainers to get out and about. I grabbed some comfy clothes and threw them on before he could hurry me again.

"I hope breakfast is on the agenda first," I said as I shoved my wallet and phone in my jeans pocket.

"I've found a great café." He threw a hoodie at me and I wrapped it around my waist. "It's supposed to rain between one and three so you'll need this." It wasn't one of mine, but I wasn't about to comment on that at all.

He really had found a great place. We'd rounded up the other three and set off to a tiny Parisian breakfast place where Oliver had booked us the balcony table so we could look out over the cobbled streets as they became alive for the day.

The first rays of warmth shone down on us as we got comfy at the table, all of us struggling to translate the menu.

"Okay, this one's called 'sexy benny egg'. I have a feeling that from the title it might be eggs Benedict and as that is what I'd go for at home, it's what I'm going for here," Tom said, sharing his menu with Alicia so she could take a peak too.

"I think I'll go for the same," Alicia agreed, trading a sneaky glance at Tom. I shook my head. *That* could not happen. Had we not intermingled this team enough?

"Well 'avocat' is one hundred percent avocado and I'm fairly sure I remember from GCSE French that *pain au levain* is toast, so I think I'll get the avocado toast," I said passing, or well trying to pass, the menu to Oliver; who looked completely disengaged from the conversation as he tapped away at his phone, a wicked grin tugging at his lips. Instead I passed it to Julius, as my phone vibrated in my pocket.

Oliver:—*How much more French do you know?*—

He was such a glutton for punishment. We couldn't do this here. Not whilst we were sat around the table with our friends.

Lucas:—*You should order too*—

Oliver:—*Kill joy*—

He slipped his phone back into his jacket pocket and stole the menu from Julius. "I'll have the pancakes," they both said in sync. "Bacon and banana." They exchanged a devilish grin with each other and I couldn't help but smile. They had the same kind of best friendship as me and Alicia.

She pushed back her chair and headed downstairs to place our order at the till whilst Julius whipped out his vlogging camera. "So, it's the crack of dawn and Ollie's dragged us all out of bed into central Paris to eat breakfast."

"Okay, first of all," Oliver interrupted. Julius panned his camera straight on to him. "It's after eight and I didn't drag you, I asked you if you wanted to come, you big old liar."

"Like I said." Julius smirked straight into the eye of the camera. "Dragged, like physically manhandled out of my bed to walk miles to this place. But, apparently the lad has our day all mapped out and I haven't explored any of Paris so far, as we've been slammed in the training center getting ready for the qualifiers in two days' time." He stood up from the table to lean across the balcony to get a good view of the lane of small shops and little bistros. "Ollie did good though, this place is beautiful and it sells pancakes so we're winning already. I'll make sure to get some shots of the food, don't worry."

He clicked the camera off and sat back down as Alicia re-joined us with a tray of multi-colored smoothies. "I have no clue what is in any of them, but the reddy-purple one is definitely berry something." Oliver snatched that one straight up. "There's that team captain spirit," she commented, and Oliver swirled his tongue around the glass in reply. Oh the things that tongue could do.

Breakfast was only the start. After we'd demolished the food we set off on a planned walking tour to see The Louvre, Arc De Triumph, The Orsay, and the Cathedral of Notre Dame. Afterwards we stopped off at a local bakery and deli to pick up fresh baguettes, meats, and cheeses to make incredible sandwiches which we ate in the gardens of Jardins du Palais Royal. Everything was beyond beautiful and Julius had been making sure to catch it all on his vlog. He'd been ranting and raving all day about how this was going to be the best vlog ever.

Tom had fallen asleep for a solid forty minutes of the ninety-minute Seine River cruise that Oliver had booked tickets for; but it had only made the cruise more hilarious as we all snapped photos of Tom asleep in front of all the landmarks the cruise highlighted. Oliver had already put a picture of Tom asleep in front of the Pont Neuf bridge up on Instagram and got over twenty thousand likes within minutes. The official Team GB Instagram had shared it on their story and we'd all had texts from our PR team to say we were doing a great job. That was a first from them.

Our last stop of the day was the most famous landmark in Paris. The sky was a dark shade of purple, a slither of orange peeking through the sunset as I looked up at the Eiffel Tower. I could see exactly why Oliver had saved it for after dark. The other three had hung back, finding a free spot on the grass to get comfy for the light show. Oliver and me, however, had ventured right up close to get a better look and some pictures.

"I thought you'd love this," he said as we stood underneath the tower, close enough to be touching but still not quite there. "Me and the other pair did a summer vacation to the south of France last year and then instead of flying home with them I road tripped up here on my own. It was Amber's third year death anniversary and we'd always said we'd go to Paris."

The thought of Oliver completely heartbroken made my gut wrench. He was always so strong and loud, but his voice cracked when he spoke about her. It was one of the saddest things I'd ever heard.

"She'd have loved it here, I'm sure. Paris, huh, City of Love."

"Yeah, it really is," he muttered to himself but I heard every word.

Standing under the flickering lights of the Eiffel Tower it was almost too easy to do something stupid, like fall in love with Oliver Ramsey.

"You wanna get a picture?" He pulled out his phone and lifted up an arm for me to slide in next to him. This was the closest we'd ever been out in public. With his arm wrapped around my shoulder, our cheeks pressed up together, it felt good. If I could have quickly put four walls up around us I would have kissed him.

He snapped a couple of selfies and just when I thought he was done he caught me off guard, planting a kiss on my cheek whilst catching it all on camera. I'm sure one day we'd look back at that photo and realize how ridiculous this whole fling had been, but for now I'd savor it.

We made our way back over to the other three. Julius trained his vlogging camera on us as we approached them. "Thought we were going to have to come shower you with rose petals," Julius joked. Tom and Alicia laughed behind him, but I knew they were cracking up because they were in the know, not because of Julius's hilarity.

He turned the camera off as we sat down next to them all.

"I'm glad you dragged us all out here, Ollie," Tom said, drawing all the attention away from what Julius had implied. "It's been a great day."

"It really has," I murmured in reply.

"How much are you all going to object if I ask to go to the Sephora on the shopping street?" Alicia asked. "They only really have the store in America so I've never been inside and they do so many amazing make up brands." She hadn't asked to do anything all day, letting the guys lead the way as we ventured across Paris. They'd spent the day getting to know her more, seeing her for the amazing person she was. Full of wit and banter. I didn't think they'd say no.

"Sure, why not, I never say no to a chance to try on a couple of lippies," Tom replied as he jumped up from the floor, offering his hand to Alicia. Julius rolled his eyes, but happily complied with the majority.

"It's Estelle's birthday in a couple of weeks, maybe you can suggest some stuff that I can pick up for her?" He asked as we walked away from the tower towards the famous shopping street in Paris.

"Oh man, stick with me and we'll get that girl some treats. She probs needs them to put up with you." Alicia took off down the street, Julius chasing after her, both of them howling with laughter.

It was delicious, like a complete endorphin rush. Something I usually got when I finished a flawless floor routine.

I snuck a peak at Oliver and unsurprisingly he was watching me for my reaction. I shook my head at him as his lips curled upwards. "I'm not going to let you say I told you so, so you best stop looking at me like that."

"You two are so obvious," Tom commented before taking off down the dimly lit street after the other pair, leaving me and Oliver staring at each other like Tom had confirmed our suspicions that he knew. I'd had too much of a great day to care, I knew he'd keep our secret.

We left Sephora with several bags of products, everyone looking knackered, which was absolutely ridiculous for a group of five athletes. I could feel the energy of the group dropping, but for some strange reason I wasn't ready to head back to the dorms yet. I'd actually had a really good day with everybody. Was this what I'd been missing out on for the last few years?

As we slugged down the Champs-Élysées, all the shops around us starting to close, I realized there was only one way I'd be able to keep these guys out for longer. And it wasn't something I'd ever thought I'd hear myself suggest.

"Anyone wanna go get a drink or something?" The words were so foreign to me. I didn't do this, yet here I was prepared to sacrifice my sleep and usual reluctance to hang out with everybody for a little bit longer.

"An alcoholic drink?" Julius asked, raising his brow at me in complete suspicion. Oliver stood next to him in a similar state of shock.

Had I really been that much of a kill joy that they couldn't even imagine I was serious? Okay, maybe I had. Oliver had been right when he said they'd invited me to several things over the years and I'd always said no. But I was here now, and I was really trying.

"I mean not for me, but yeah, why not. I'm sure there must be a decent pub or something around here."

"I'm in," Alicia said quickly as her and Tom caught up to where we'd come to a stop. They'd been whispering about something or other, looking completely inconspicuous, but it had been such a good day that I didn't even have the energy to reprimand Tom for flirting with my best friend.

"Lead the way," Oliver said and, with a quick Google maps search on my phone, I did.

Chapter Eighteen

Oliver

"You know his mum runs a pub right?" Alicia said around a gob full of crisps as we settled into a booth in the pub, each of us with an alcoholic drink except Lucas. He was drinking Pepsi.

Julius was bugging everybody to play darts and suspiciously Lucas had straight up volunteered to go first, completely unlike him. Now I was realizing why.

"Your point?" Julius challenged back.

"In between collecting glasses, your boy here would play darts with the regulars. He's practically a pro," Alicia answered.

"You're about to get your ass whooped." Tom added as he leant back in his chair so he could take it all in and I couldn't help but laugh. This was going to be priceless to watch.

"We'll see," Julius replied as he grabbed the darts from the board, handing a set to Lucas. "Three hundred and one?"

Lucas nodded and Julius took his first shot.

For the first couple of rounds Julius was fluking decent scores, but I could see Lucas actually understood the game and when he said he was aiming for double seventeen that was what happened. He wasn't aimlessly throwing at the board and hoping for the best. Five rounds in and Lucas was below a hundred and Julius was struggling to hit the board. He was seconds away from having a strop. A twenty-six-year-old grown man having a strop.

"You take over. He's kicked my ass enough today." Julius groaned, palming the darts off on me. I'd never say no to a bit of competition with Lucas, that was one of the best ways to get him all riled up.

The first dart had been absolutely fine, I'd smashed a double twenty and had Lucas grumbling like an idiot as he realized that I was a better player than Julius. The second dart, well, my shoulder felt like someone had tried to tug it out of its socket in one swift movement. The dart hit the outside of the board and everybody cheered. The final dart felt impossible. Something exploded within my shoulder to the point the pain made me feel lightheaded and almost like I was going to be sick. I bit the inside of my cheek to the point I could taste the metallic liquid on my tongue over the beers I'd consumed.

I'd throw this last dart and I'd escape. Make my excuses so I could breathe through the pain on my own. I wouldn't let this stupid shoulder ruin my night, or anything else again.

Lucas eyed me carefully. I wasn't sure if he could tell something was wrong or not, so I quickly flashed him my teeth in the briefest of smiles and threw the dart. It hit the wall and bounced to the floor.

Lucas and Julius high-tenned like they'd just won the lottery which gave me the chance to get out of there.

"I need to piss, here." I passed the darts to Tom and slowly walked to the bathroom. Once inside a stall, I locked the door behind me and leant against the wall.

This wasn't a twinge like I'd felt before. Yeah, I'd forgotten to put deep heat on it this morning, but I'd consumed enough alcohol to numb the pain of a tiny twitch. My whole shoulder throbbed to the point I was unable to raise my arm above my head without wanting to scream.

Nothing felt right. Air was lacking in my lungs as I tried to take a deep, calming breath. My busted up shoulder wasn't what today was supposed to be about. Today was about bonding as a team and enjoying a beautiful city with friends.

I just had to push through this. I'd wake up tomorrow after a good night's sleep feeling fine. *Deep breaths.* I slammed my fist against the cubicle wall, breathing wouldn't fix this. I had to walk out there and get through the rest of the evening, then I could take some painkillers and pass out for the night. I could do this.

"You okay?" Lucas asked as I returned to the booth, the darts clearly long over as everyone, except Tom and Julius, sat comfortably at the table.

"Yeah, I think I had a little too much to drink. My bladder and liver are confused. I'm sure two weeks ago me and the guys made a pact to consume no alcohol for the time we were here." I squished back into the booth next to Lucas and I quickly caught on to how Alicia eyed us and then grinned at her best friend. I wasn't surprised that she knew, not at all. Maybe I should have properly told Julius and Tom too.

"Hey," Alicia said, leaning over the booth to talk to Lucas beside me. "I'm going to head back. We have an early practice in the morning and I don't wanna wake Izzy coming in late."

I waited for Lucas to grab his hoodie, and to ask me to slide out so he could get by to leave with her. Except he didn't. The only move he made was to lean over the table and place a kiss to Alicia's cheek as she pulled on her jumper.

"You ordered a cab?" He asked.

She nodded as she slipped out from her side of the booth, grabbing her jacket along the way.

"Leaving so soon, Miss Jones?" Tom asked as returned from the bathroom. "The night's still young."

"For you, maybe, but not for someone who has a six a.m. practice."

Tom could hardly take his eyes off of her. At some point during the evening she'd shed her jacket, leaving her in only a sports vest. His eyes had flickered over her like he was seeing her for the first time. Alicia was gorgeous and she had the most beautiful, toned body plus she could keep up with the banter of every guy around this table. Lucas was going to be so pissed if Tom tried to hook up with her.

"See you guys later," she said, blowing a kiss across the table to Lucas before disappearing out into the Parisian streets.

Julius reappeared with a pitcher sized jug of beer and five glasses. "Where'd she go?" He asked as he set them all down on the table, even putting a glass in front of Lucas who hadn't drank at all tonight.

"Home. Early practice." Lucas stared at the glass like it was about to jump up and kill him. "So you didn't grab me a Pepsi then?"

"They are all out and the bartender told me to tell you to stop being so boring and have a drink with us. One won't hurt." Julius winked at him like an idiot.

"You say that now, but this guy doesn't drink. We don't want him drunk after one beer," I said quickly, but Lucas pushed his glass forwards so Julius could pour him a pint.

"I guess one won't hurt. I did go to Uni, so I've been on a few drunk nights out. I don't think one beer will obliterate me." He sounded unsure, but Julius still filled the glass right up to the rim.

"What were nights out like in Essex?" Julius asked as he topped up everybody else's glasses and shuffled back into the booth. "Did you used to pull on nights out?"

Great, we were back on Lucas's least favorite topic. He wasn't shy in bed, maybe a little inexperienced, but once he'd gotten comfortable in what we were doing he started to let go. I grabbed my pint and went to take a sip in expectation of Lucas either erupting or getting completely embarrassed.

"They weren't awful. There's a few clubs in Colchester that are decent. In terms of pulling, there were a couple of guys after nights out," he replied.

I almost choked on my beer. I definitely didn't want this conversation to continue. "Sorry, sorry," I coughed out as I spluttered beer across the table. "Can you pass me a napkin from behind you, man," I said to Tom, and luckily as he reached around to get one he spotted that we were the only group left in the establishment.

"Fuck, it's almost midnight," Tom commented as he checked his smart watch. "We should probably get out of here." He stopped to chug down his pint, as did Julius whilst Lucas pushed his away from him. I knew there was a reason I liked him; he wasn't a dumb ass like the other pair.

The walk back to the dorms had been going so well

until a neon light flickering in the front window of a store caught our eye. And by our, I mean everyone's except Lucas's who was intent on herding us home without permanently marking our bodies. If I hadn't consumed several beers that evening, it wouldn't have been so appealing, but it had completely drawn me in. The guys all came to a halt with me and as they looked up at what was so mesmerizing, a wicked grin spread across Julius's face.

"I'm down," he said quickly as he walked close enough to peer through the window to get a better look at the designs that littered the walls of the store.

"No way," Lucas protested, not at all to my surprise. "You're all pretty drunk and this is like some back alley place."

"I'm in too. Fuck it, we're only going to be here once so we need to get something to remember it by," Tom chipped in.

"Yeah and we'll get that in a few days' time. You know, in the form of medals."

"Well you two can argue about it out here, but we're going to go look at the designs and see if this guy is any good." Tom herded Julius into the store leaving me with a very unsure looking Lucas outside.

I slipped my hand into his and pulled him into the alley next to the store. "Come on," I whispered against his lips, "it doesn't have to be anything big or anything crazy. We'll get them in concealed places if that's a big thing for you. Take a walk on the wild side with us."

Even in the dimly lit alley I could see it was still a solid no from him by the way he glared at me.

"Okay, what about a weeks' worth of massages and I'll let you watch the proposal episode of Brooklyn Nine-

Nine on repeat whilst I do it."

His narrowed eyes started to widen like my bribe was doing its job, but we weren't quite there yet.

"And I'll make sure to give you some quiet time so you can work on your dissertation. Just you and your notes."

His resolve started to break down as he leant his forehead against mine, his green eyes scanning mine as if to check I was being completely serious. "Something small and something small only," he muttered back to me and, without even thinking, I closed the gap between us and kissed him.

The evening air was warm and muggy around us and the bar had made me kind of sweaty, so I wasn't surprised to find the curls at the back of Lucas's neck sticky as I nestled my fingers into them to dominate the kiss.

He tilted his head a little so I could get better access and he walked us backwards until he had me pinned to the tattoo shop wall. "Do you not feel how hot it is?" I muttered as I played with the hem of my hoodie that he had on.

"I haven't consumed half the amount of beer you have. It isn't actually that warm right now out here." He quickly reattached his lips to mine and as they moved softly I wasn't about to stop him.

Even in my tipsy state I should have been scanning for cameras or press or something else completely ridiculous. But, as I peeled myself off of Lucas there were no signs of any of that, thankfully.

"Come on then, let's go get inked."

Lucas rolled his eyes at me, but it was playful and not full of signs that told me he was going to probably regret this in the morning.

"We're getting Olympic rings," Tom announced as the pair of us stepped into the store. The late-night artist behind the counter nodded along with him before holding up a design he must have quickly sketched whilst Lucas had been stalling outside.

"You aren't the first athletes to come in here this week and I doubt you'll be the last," the guy said with a knowing smirk. He clearly knew who we were, but he made no further comments as he beckoned us all to follow him to the back of his store to where the magic happened. "So, where do you want them on your body?"

"I'm saying like stomach or chest or something," I said, because I'd promised Lucas it would be easy to conceal and Julius seemed intent on us all getting it in the same place.

Julius whipped out his vlogging camera and whilst it wasn't the best thing to capture, us all a little bit tipsy being irresponsible, it would be hilarious to watch back later. "So, me and the guys are about to get a permanent marking of our time at the Olympics. If any of us wake up in the morning full of regret, I'm letting you know now this wasn't my idea."

"Yes it was." Tom jumped into the shot of the camera, wrapping his arm around Julius's shoulders before pulling him into a headlock.

"Who's first?" The tattoo artist said as he finished setting up his station.

He'd hardly finished asking when Julius passed Tom his vlogging camera and stripped off his shirt hopping on to the laid-back chair. "Are we thinking like lower stomach? I'm saving my chest tattoos for my kids."

Me and Tom nodded in agreement, but Lucas was still eying the now prepped needle cautiously.

"I feel like my mum might actually kill me for this, but okay, sure, I'm in too." I did not want to be there with Lucas when he showed his mum.

"Fantastic. This is the stencil I used on the last lot of athletes that came through here. Is this okay? I'll do the simple Olympic colors on the ring."

"Looks fine to me," Julius agreed and the tattooist got to work on the art. "Maybe me and Estelle will come back after the games if she agrees to marry me. I could get like her initials or the date or something somewhere."

"One tattoo at a time man. She might not even say yes." Tom warned. If Julius hadn't been pinned to the table at needle point he'd probably have smacked Tom. I couldn't imagine a world where Estelle didn't say yes.

"Are you asking her to marry you in Paris?" Lucas asked. I'd forgotten he hadn't been privy to that conversation. We hadn't even kissed at that point.

"Yeah, after the closing ceremony. You'll have to meet her soon. She wasn't here in time for family day but she's staying at the hotel with her family and mine."

"All done, let me wipe it down and wrap it and you'll be finished." Julius squirmed as the guy rubbed on the cold gel, before covering it in cling film. Then he jumped up from the chair.

Tom's tattoo was done within a blink of an eye and before I knew it, it was my turn. With the pain in my shoulder running through my whole body, I hardly felt the needle as it pressed ink into my skin. It was a pin prick in comparison. The guys watched on until it was clear I was going to have no reaction and Julius got distracted by some other tattoos on the wall. If we didn't get him out of here soon, he'd probably have a whole sleeve. It'd be like when he got his ear pierced, and then did his eyebrow and nose just days later. Except Julius got bored of those after a year or so and took them out. You couldn't really do that with a sleeve.

Lucas was last to climb up into the chair, his knee jigging like there was no tomorrow. If we'd have been alone, I would have reached out and taken his hand to help him calm down, but that would look so weird in front of the guys.

"You need your hand holding?" Julius asked as he continued to parade around the store shirtless.

"Not helping," I replied through gritted teeth. "Would it help though?" I asked and Lucas's eyes boggled like I was speaking a foreign language.

"Just let him hold your hand. We don't need you flinching all over the place and you ending up with wonky rings," Tom said, but I'm sure he had an ulterior motive. He probably wanted to watch us squirm.

Regardless, I held out my hand for Lucas and he death gripped it to the point my knuckles turned white. "You actually need to remember to breathe," I said as the needle touched his skin for the first time. "Think about something else, tell me about one of your happiest memories with Alicia."

"We were fifteen and the girls at the gym were having a parents evening show thing." Lucas closed his eyes, face softening as he relaxed into the story. "I'd decided that even though I clearly wasn't a girl I wanted to participate, because me and Alicia and Lucy had been practicing this ridiculously artistic floor routine. It was a lot more dance than it was tumbles. So I wore a girls leotard to take part and Lucy put me in a wig and did my make-up. The whole evening was so much fun." He was no longer gritting his teeth, which was a relief, but my knuckles were still white.

"I'm texting Alicia for those photos." And now it seemed that Tom had her number, which was interesting. At least Lucas was too busy focusing on being stabbed with ink than Tom's words.

"And that's all four of you finished," the tattoo guy interrupted before anything could get out of hand in his store. He peeled off his plastic gloves and led us back to the front of the store. "How would you like to pay, card or cash?"

"I'll get these lads," Julius said, whipping out his debit card.

None of us protested. It was way after one in the morning and I, for one, was desperate to get some ibuprofen gel on my shoulder.

"I've also ordered us an Uber. I'm too tired to walk the half an hour to the dorms." Julius was my savior.

We were all so tired that Julius and Tom hardly even grumbled out a good night as we got to the floor of our dorms. We left them to it and made our way into our own room.

I slipped into the bathroom, coated myself in the gel, pissed, and brushed my teeth, only to come out of the bathroom to find Lucas already fast asleep. He looked absolutely exhausted. He'd been an absolute trooper today and in the strangest way I was proud of him. He'd thrown himself into the group while being out and about today. I knew that didn't come easily to him, but he'd done it.

I brushed some curls from his face and placed a soft kiss to his forehead, before climbing into bed as the pain medication and gel kicked in. The burn from the gel soothed my shoulder and I melded my body against Lucas's, holding him close as I fell into a deep sleep. It was easily one of the best night's sleep I'd had in forever.

Only to wake up the next morning to hundreds of notifications, several missed calls from my agent, and a screen shot from Julius from The Sun newspaper picturing me caught on camera kissing some guy in an alleyway.

Chapter Nineteen

Lucas

Something wasn't right the next day in training. I'd just finished an almost perfect run through of my floor routine when Oliver hopped down from the parallel bars and followed his agent into Carson and Jacub's office. Something really wasn't right.

I was about to chalk up and put in some work on the high bar, but I couldn't focus on anything other than what was potentially being said inside those four walls. Oliver hadn't mentioned anything about a meeting this morning—which set my nerves on edge, because it must have been something bad for his agent to call an emergency meeting. But the Olympics were just days away now, so I ignored it. Until several hours passed and Oliver hadn't left the meeting room. The blinds remained drawn and at some point one of the teams PR guys had rocked up to join them.

"Do you know what's happening?" I asked as I moved closer to where the other pair were standing on the brink of the training mat trying to get a sneak peek inside the office.

They shared a look that told me they one hundred percent did, but weren't sure if they should tell me or not.

"I'm serious, whatever you guys know isn't it important that, as the fourth member of this team, I know too?"

"Do you not check social media at all?" Julius asked. Whilst I'd tried to upload more at the request of the Team GB social media guy, I hadn't checked anything yet today. My phone was still in the dorm room.

I shook my head. "I haven't looked today. I got up late after some, uh, early morning studying for my master's and literally showered and showed up." A smirk spread across both of their faces and if I wasn't already nervous after Oliver's agent showing up, I definitely was now.

"Studying, huh? What's your degree again, biology?"

Oh fuck, they knew. How the heck did they know? Oliver had made it clear he wasn't going to tell anyone.

I looked to Tom and he shook his head. "You might want to see this," he said, grabbing his phone from his team jacket pocket.

I peered over his shoulder as he clicked into the group chat of him, Julius, and Oliver before he loaded up a print screen of a photo taken from The Sun's website. *Oh no.* It was a blurry set of Snapchat pictures, but there was no mistaking that they showed Oliver being kissed up against an alley wall by another man.

Luckily, I had my back to the camera and my hood up. Thank god for the chilly summer air. It didn't change the fact that in the final photo you can clearly see me rearranging myself in my jeans and that Oliver was making out with a guy.

"That is you, isn't it?" Julius asked. "Ollie didn't pick up some random guy in the five minutes we were inside the tattoo shop talking to the artist, right?" I zoomed into the photo and was incredibly grateful that you couldn't see my face.

Julius had seen me that night in Oliver's hoodie, so even if I wanted to deny it there was no way it would fly with him. "Yeah, it's me."

"I fucking knew it," Tom said in the kind of tone that usually required a fist pump straight after it. "I saw you that night. You two, with your beds all pushed together and looking all cuddly." Clearly there were no secrets between any of us anymore.

"I'm sorry what? I feel like I've missed something here. Is this more than the kiss in the picture?" Julius asked, and something seeped into my veins.

It was something like how I'd felt when I'd told Lauren at age four she couldn't have a princess costume like her friends. I couldn't understand for the life of me why I'd felt guilty about not telling Julius, but it probably had something to do with us becoming friends.

"They've been fucking," Tom said and I shook my head, "you haven't been fucking?" Tom asked in reply, eyes narrowed in confusion.

"Yeah, we've been sleeping together, but there's no need to be so crass about it."

Tom rolled his eyes. I'd clearly forgotten who I was talking to here. I should have been more surprised that they weren't already asking about the ins and outs of our sex lives.

"So you two are what, together? I know we've all been hanging out and you're like one of our friends now, but is it more with Ollie?"

"Well he hasn't been sucking your dick, has he Jules?" I elbowed Tom in the stomach for that one.

I didn't think this was Julius trying to be a twat about this. I could see he was genuinely a bit shocked about finding out his best friend of almost a decade had been with a guy. Especially as Oliver had made it clear he wasn't out to them.

"Does it really matter at this point? Rather than discussing mine and Oliver's sex life, I think we should be worried about what's going on in there. How much shit do you think his agent is giving him right now?" I didn't know his agent very well, but she'd been in the sporting world for the last decade, which I thought was amazing for somebody who was only in their early thirties.

"All of you," Coach Carson called from his office door, "in here now, please."

I guessed we were about to find out how shit this situation actually was. As the three of us stepped into the way too small office for seven people, I realized exactly how much shit we were in. Oliver's hair was pushed in every single direction, almost like how it looked after sex. This was probably from him running his hands through it because he was stressed out.

"You know us," Jacub started. "You know we don't care what you get up to in your personal lives and we will support you regardless of who you're sleeping with, because neither of us are homophobic nor actually care about who you put your dick in. But, when it blows up like this, we have to have a contingency plan."

"Me and my team have been playing damage control all morning, but there's no denying it's Oliver and the press are going crazy trying to figure out who the guy is," Oliver's agent, Helena, said.

"So what do you want him to do?" I asked, because I wasn't quite sure if they'd figured out if I was involved or if Oliver had told them anything.

169

"That's up to you two, I guess," Helena answered, "and how you want the story to run. We can get the teams PR people to start feeding the press lines about you two being in a happy committed relationship or we can run it on the basis that Oliver is choosing to focus on the Olympics right now and when the games are over he might comment further on his personal life."

Oliver turned in his chair to look at where I stood behind him, I looked down at him and it was almost as if we could read each other's minds. "I don't think we should lie to the press," he said at the same time I said, "we can't tell the press something that isn't true."

"We aren't in a relationship," Oliver cleared up quickly, and only for the briefest of seconds did I feel the slightest bit upset about that. Okay, maybe it was longer than a second. And maybe the words hurt my heart, like a lot. I couldn't tell him that though.

"Well it would be a whole lot easier if you were. Gay, straight, bi, whatever, it would look better if you were kissing someone you were in a committed relationship with." Helena groaned, but neither me or Oliver budged. "Okay, well then, for now we'll put out a statement saying Oliver is focusing on training and will be making no further comment about it."

Oliver didn't look a hundred percent pleased about that, but I knew it was the complete and utter wrong time for him to be saying anything else that would only distract from his gymnastics.

His agent talked through what would be written as the four of us hung around awkwardly half listening, when Brayden knocked the door. "Sorry I'm late, coach." *Late?* We'd all been here for six hours already. Oliver audibly groaned. "Oh hey, Ollie, I just saw the picture all over Twitter. The rough life of being a famous athlete, huh?"

I literally wanted to tell him to shut up. Could he not read a room? I bit my tongue instead.

Oliver did not. "Oh yeah, I love being a famous athlete and having my relationships splashed on magazine covers. Such a great perk."

"I didn't mean it like that, I meant—"

Oliver swiftly cut him off. "If we're done with this meeting can we leave?" He was already standing up, so I wasn't sure his agent or our coaches were going to have a say in it.

Coach Carson nodded at Oliver and gestured towards the door. "Yeah, we'll email you over a copy of the press release. Let's call it a day in the gym, except you, Brayden, we still need to work on your vault still."

Oliver had already left the room. The rest of us followed him in a train-like fashion. We grabbed our gym bags and struggled to keep up with him as he stormed back to our room.

"Are you really not together?" Tom asked as we arrived back in mine and Oliver's dorm. The pair of them seeing our beds pushed together for the first time in the daylight.

"This is weird as fuck. We sleep on the other side of that wall and you guys have been banging on this bed. How have we not heard you?" Julius was eying our rumpled sheets, which felt all kinds of gross considering what we'd done in them that morning.

Not only was I completely drained from a tough training session, but from the stress that the circle of people who knew about me and Oliver had now expanded. Oh, and the press had basically outed Oliver, which had my blood boiling. That was nobody's right, it was *his* story and *his* choice to come out and they'd taken that from him.

"Why are you both in here?" Oliver asked as he ducked into the bathroom to piss, the door still wide open. I'd busied myself by remaking the bed that we'd left thrown all over the place. If I stopped for too long, I was probably going to scream.

"Because we're your best friends and we want to check that you're okay after everything that went down today. I don't understand why you didn't tell us, like we both give zero fucks about who you bone," Julius said and whilst it was crude, I was glad that Oliver had both of them and neither seemed to care too much that he was bisexual.

They made themselves comfy on the end of our bed and it felt a little weird for them to be sitting on it. This was where Oliver and I slept and had sex.

"I knew you two wouldn't have a problem, but it felt unimportant to mention when I've never been with a guy in a serious way before. Plus you two would make a big deal of it exactly like you're doing right now by being in here coddling me. What's done is done, the story is out there now," Oliver said as he washed his hands and emerged from the bathroom sans his shirt, which he lobbed towards his laundry basket, only missing slightly. I'd let that slide today.

"Hey," I said as I fluffed up our pillows. "It's all good, we don't have to talk about it." Oliver's mouth slipped into a smile.

Julius cooed. "I literally don't know how we missed this when you two talk like that."

I rolled my eyes at Julius, part of me could see why

Oliver didn't want him knowing, he was going to be even more insufferable asking us every detail about our relationship and sex life.

"Oh yeah, we are so romantic. I often whip out the rose petals and a romantic playlist whilst we make love on the very spot you're sitting on," Oliver replied, and Julius's mouth dropped slightly, clearly a little unsure if Oliver was being serious or not.

"Your face man," Oliver laughed. "We normally fuck with Brooklyn Nine-Nine on max volume so you don't hear anything and think it's actually just Lucas working and being inconsiderate."

"Hey," I said again, my tone harsher than it had been before.

"I don't care what either of you say," Tom added. "Smells like more than just sex in here, whether you wanna admit it or not your friends, at the very minimum."

"No-one said anything about us not being friends, Thomas," Oliver replied, his back to us as he rooted through my drawers for some sweat shorts.

"You need to do some washing. You can't keep stealing my shit." I turned on the TV, because if the pair were sticking around, we could probably watch a film and unwind a bit before dinner.

"More than sex," Tom coughed, before Oliver threw the dirty sweatpants he'd just taken off at him.

"You two gotta stop. I already clean this floor daily because Oliver treats it like a floor-drobe. Are you two staying? Do you wanna watch a film or something?"

"Nah, I'm gonna go get dinner and call Estelle before crashing for the evening," Julius replied.

"And I'm going to go for a run. We'll leave you two

love birds to it."

They both quickly leapt up off the bed before Oliver could throw another article of clothing at either of them, and left without a second glance.

Oliver breathed out deeply as he pulled on the sweat shorts and climbed into bed. I quickly followed suit, stripping down till I was in only my boxers and climbed in next to him, wrapping an arm around him and pulling him close.

"You okay?" I asked.

"I have no clue. I haven't even looked at anything being said online yet, so I have no idea what the reaction is. I didn't think it would happen like this. Like, I was thinking the other night about coming out to Jules and Tom after Abbie came out. Didn't think I wouldn't have a say in the matter."

I wanted to wrap Oliver up and protect him from the world and that wasn't normally how I felt towards anyone other than my best friend and my family. Yet Oliver had wormed his way into a place quite close to my heart and even if I didn't want to admit it right now, this was way more than sex for me.

"It shouldn't have to be like this at all. I swear I'm so angry that they've printed this and outed you, Oliver. Like fuck." He draped his legs across mine as we got comfortable under the duvet, him being more of the little spoon for once. "I'm so angry, but I think you've got a good agent behind you if she's willing to print a statement about you being focused on the Olympics and whatever. We'll just have to be more careful, save any kissing for inside the bedroom from now on."

"You wanna know what I was worried about?" He asked, leaning up on his elbows so he could look up at me. I nodded my head. "Whether you'd still want to do this. I saw the picture when I woke up this morning and all I could think was 'fuck, Lucas hates being in the press, he isn't gonna wanna do this now the paps are on my back'."

"You're an idiot, that should not have been priority number one." I laughed, but my whole body filled with warmth. He'd found himself at the center of a scandal this morning and he'd been worried about losing *me*. My mind was in overdrive; what did this mean? Why was he worried about losing me? Was it the sex or was it more? I'd stupidly started to hope for the latter.

"How many blow jobs would I have to give you for you to go grab dinner and bring it back here. I'm not trying to hide, but like I'd rather eat in bed with you and then fall asleep."

"None," I said, pressing a kiss to his head before sliding out of bed, leaving him tucked up peacefully. "But if you're offering, maybe after we've eaten?"

"Mmmm, you're too good to me," he replied sleepily, his eyes half lidded as he watched me leave the room.

I returned with two take out containers of some kind of pasta dish, but he was already fast asleep—star fishing across the bed like he owned the damn thing.

I decided to leave him sleeping, grabbing my phone from the bedside drawer before climbing up onto the dresser to sit cross legged and eat. I hadn't touched my phone all day, so when I unlocked the screen I found over a hundred notifications across all my social media apps.

The only one I was interested in opening was WhatsApp to check in with the family. However, when I clicked on to the app I found seventeen new messages from my twin all ranging in different levels of excitement. I'd never seen so many full cap messages and exclamation marks in my life.

They ranged from a casual 'good morning' to her teasing that 'Alicia had sent me pictures from last night' of me and the guys, to her screaming about 'Oliver kissing a guy' to the last message that simply said 'call me', but in all capital letters.

I glanced over at Oliver to check that he was still sound asleep and then clicked call on Lucy's name. "Hey, Luce," I whispered, "is everything okay?"

"Is everything okay?" She screamed into my ear to the point that I had to pull my phone away.

I gave her a second to calm down and when I returned it to my ear all I could hear was her ranting. "I can't believe you didn't tell me that there was something going on between you and Oliver Ramsey. We sat next to him at dinner and you didn't think to mention it? Who else knows, huh? Alicia? I'm gonna kill her. Do your teammates know? I hate all of you."

"Are you finished?" I replied in a hushed tone.

"Why are you whispering?" She paused for a second before lightning struck. "Are you with him right now? Is he there, asleep?"

"You know we're roommates, right?" I rolled my eyes as I shoveled a fork full of pasta into my mouth.

"It's about the only thing I knew, apparently. I can't believe you, I've *always* told you everything about the guy I'm dating. How long have you been keeping this a secret?"

Too long was the only acceptable answer when it came to my twin. I usually told her everything straight away.

"Can you chill, we weren't planning on telling anybody at all. I only told Alicia because I was freaking out after the first time I slept with him."

"Okay so you're screwing around, good to know. Do you like him? Is it something more?"

Yes was the easy, but stupidly hard answer. I liked him, I really liked him. My heart was crashing headfirst into something more and I couldn't stop it. I wasn't sure if I even wanted to.

"Yes, I like him. Is it something more? Who knows. I'm not sure anymore. We live in this easy-going bubble right now where we can be glued to each other without anybody questioning it because we're teammates. And now that he's been outed, we've been told not to be seen out alone, and I don't know Luce. He's, he's…" How did you describe the guy you were falling for? How did you summarize someone like Oliver Ramsey, someone I'd thought I'd despised for so long, only for him to turn out to be the most incredible guy. "He's wonderful."

"Well, I'd be happy to be a third wheel if you guys want to get out and about. We still have a week in Paris so you might as well make the most of it. "

"I might take you up on that. Anyway, I just wanted to let you know I'm alive and well, but I have practice in the morning and need to sleep. Message you tomorrow."

"Love you, Luca. Sleep well. I mean, I'm sure you will with that hunk next to you."

I rolled my eyes. She wasn't wrong though. "Love you too, Luce." I cut the call, shoveled another couple of mouthfuls of pasta down before tossing the rest, and slid back into my spot next to Oliver.

Chapter Twenty

Oliver

I yawned as I stretched in front of the pommel horse. I wanted nothing more than to lie down on the mat next to it and have a nap. Luckily, with the events of yesterday, I'd been allowed pretty much a whole day off of training. It probably wasn't the best thing to do two days before qualifiers, but it gave my shoulder a break. I could only hope that a day's rest would be enough.

"Late night?" Julius wiggled his eyebrows at me. Any other day I'd have probably been amused, but my exhaustion sliced through his humor and it fell flat against me.

So I said nothing, instead opting to chalk up my hands in silence as he watched me curiously, not used to silence between the pair of us.

"What's going on?" He asked, sneaking a peak at where Tom and Lucas hovered by the parallel bars on the other side of the gym, chatting aimlessly before Tom hopped up on to the bars to demonstrate something for Lucas.

"Nothing, I'm tired. Lucas hogged the covers last night and he was restless from about one in the morning." It was an outright lie. I'd not been able to get comfortable in any position despite the four painkillers I'd taken before bed.

"I still can't believe we're having a conversation about you and Lucas sharing a bed. Do you snuggle? Is that like a thing for you guys?"

I didn't want to be short with him, but I really just wanted to get to work to see how my shoulder was feeling. "I dunno, I think we do what normal people do in bed together. Sometimes we cuddle, sometimes we don't. Sorry, I'm stressed about this routine as I don't seem to be nailing that dismount, which ain't great a couple days before qualifiers."

"Nah, I get it man. I'm going to go bother Lucas because he said he'd watch my floor routine with the triple rollover added."

He clapped a hand on my shoulder and I had to bite my tongue to stop myself from wincing. I nodded at him and, like an excited child, Julius sprinted off across the mat towards Lucas, tugging on his arm until he agreed to go to the floor with him. He really was something else.

My eyes burned hell fires into the pommel horse as I stared at it rather than climbing straight on. One of the big parts of gymnastics, that not a lot of people seemed to talk about, was the mental game. I'd struggled with it for a while after I'd fallen on the vault during the 2020 qualifiers and destroyed my shoulder the first time. I'd have panic attacks when I'd go to do run ups and I'd often skid to a halt before I even got all the way up to the vault. We put a lot of trust in our bodies and the apparatus and sometimes they betrayed us. Having fear about it only made the mental game worse.

This time, I wasn't scared of the apparatus, I was scared of how my body would react to it. Whether I was strong enough to get on it and do a whole routine. If I didn't climb back on the horse, quite literally, I'd end up being scared forever and that was no way to live. So I pushed through the fear, gripping the two handle bars to ease into my first position. So far so good.

One practice run through on the pommel horse and everything was feeling strong, my shoulder hadn't even twinged. Which felt amazing after the whole darts fiasco. Yet the second I pulled myself up on the high bar, everything started to strain like a mother fucker. I'd hung in the air for a solid minute trying to figure out what was the best thing to do. I could have pushed through and tried to get a swinging motion, but the tugging feeling I was experiencing in my shoulder socket was so intense I didn't even dare try.

So, instead, I discreetly scanned the room to see what everyone else was doing. When I noticed they were all caught up in their own shit, I dropped from the bar, grabbed my gym bag, and disappeared into the bathroom.

Everything felt shaky. My whole body was alive with vibrations as pain shot through every nerve. I found myself leaning up against the wall to keep myself upright as my head started to spin and light-headedness took over. I had to breathe, breathing through the pain would help. So I moved myself to the mirror above the sink and watched as the glass fogged up with every long exhale until the pain dulled and my shoulder went numb.

I shouldn't have relished that numbness, it was one hundred percent a sign that something was wrong, but it was nice to not feel like the pain was going to push me to be sick. The second I could move, I scooped up my gym bag, rested it in the sink then rummaged around for the tube of pain relief gel I kept in there.

Peeling off my vest quickly, I dropped it into the top

of my bag. I poured out a steep amount of the gel onto my hand, wincing as it came into contact with my shoulder, reigniting the pain all over again. I'd just started to rub it in when the door behind me, that I'd clearly forgotten to lock in my pain filled haze, creaked open. Julius caught me red handed.

"What are you doing?" He asked as I pulled my hand away from the jagged scar across my shoulder. "What's going on?" He asked again, this time louder.

There was no getting out of this. "Putting some gel on, is that okay?"

"On your bad shoulder?" He quickly stepped forwards to get a look at the shiny spot over my scarred shoulder.

"If you need to piss, can you give me a moment to put my shirt back on and get out of here?"

"Are you having issues with it?" I had no clue why I'd expected Julius to leave it, but it had been worth a try. He snatched the tube that I was trying to smuggle back into my bag. "This is the strong stuff. How bad is your shoulder?"

"It's fine."

"Clearly not. When did it start hurting again?"

"Leave it, Jules," I said, reaching for my shirt so I wasn't standing completely exposed to his criticism.

"If it's bad, you need to see a doctor. You can't compete if you're injured," he said it like I didn't already know that. I wasn't injured though, not to the point he was probably imagining. "There's no shame in admitting that you're hurt, man. Why are you being so stubborn about this?"

"Because I don't want to be a retired, injured athlete at twenty-four." I wanted to cry and scream at Julius because he didn't seem to be getting it. Maybe it was because he'd already done one Olympic circuit so this one was just a bonus, but that wasn't how it was for me. If I didn't compete this time around I wouldn't get another shot. This injury was only getting worse, and I knew that in four years' time I'd be screwed.

"What about if you make it worse or, I don't know, fall from the bar and break your back because you're too injured to be in control of your movement?" Julius practically screamed back at me.

It wasn't that the thought hadn't crossed my mind, but if I had really thought I was putting myself in serious danger, I'd stand down. "With the pain relief my shoulder is fine. It's been a little bit twingy and sore after a days' practice, but it isn't to the point where I feel like I can't compete. This is the process of being an athlete, right? Like when you wrap your wrists, Jules."

"I wrap my wrists because I'm practically ancient in this sport and my main apparatus has always been pommel. It's precautionary, not because I'm in pain."

"I'm not in pain," I wanted to scream it in his face, anything to get him to back off.

"Then why does your shoulder currently smell like a deep heat factory?" I didn't have an argument for that. I'd gotten through almost a whole tube since being here. That should have told me something, but I had believed that I was managing the pain like a normal athlete. It wasn't unbearable by any means, so it wasn't a cause for concern.

"Can we just drop this, please? I don't know what you expect me to do with literally twenty-four hours till the qualifiers?"

As I said that, Lucas and Tom must have caught

wind of the commotion and decided to join us in the bathroom.

"Do you have nothing to add? Do you really want to let your boyfriend compete with a fucked up shoulder?" The way Julius directed the question at Lucas made me feel sick. Not even because he'd used the word boyfriend, but because I didn't want to hear what Lucas had to say. I also knew how hard this would be for me if I was in his shoes. If he was injured and still wanted to compete, I'd probably be saying the same thing, but I also knew I wouldn't stand in his way. I couldn't, not when I knew how much competing meant to him.

"We're not boyfriends," we both said practically in sync. I looked over at him and whilst he had the most serious look on his face in regards to the conversation, he still offered me the smallest smile.

From the outside, we probably did seem like boyfriends. Sometimes, well maybe even most of the time, it felt like we were boyfriends, but that was not a label I could see either of us agreeing to any time soon. And in a little over a week our Olympic bubble would burst, and we'd go back to our own lives.

"It's Oliver's choice. I have my opinions on it, but we are all adults here and if he had any real concerns I'm sure he'd have them checked out," Lucas said.

Bile churned in my stomach. Maybe I should be doing that, but if I was able to manage it myself then I didn't see the point in concerning the coaches. We'd all had physio check-ups since we'd been here and I'd passed mine with flying colors.

"You've been together two minutes so I'm sure it doesn't matter much to you anyway." Julius always took it too far, there was no reason for him to bring Lucas into this.

"I literally can't do anything right with you, can I?" Lucas's face flustered as he pushed past all of us to the tap to try and splash water on it to cool down. "I don't try with any of you, I get shit. I try and I still get shit. Oliver isn't my partner, he's made that clear, but he knows that if I'd seen him in a lot of pain, I'd have called him out for it."

Clearly I'd hidden the pain from the other night really well, and that didn't help the sickly feeling that shot up my esophagus. It was the 'he's made that clear' part that resonated with me. Had I? We'd never even discussed anything more than sex. Had I been that out of practice in a relationship that I hadn't realized he'd wanted more? I hadn't even thought about that myself. Well except in my dreams or when I couldn't sleep at night and I'd play with his curls to help me relax.

"Let's not fight, Lucas is right, Jules. He sees me every minute of the day pretty much. We sleep in the same bed, if there was a really dramatic problem he'd know. Can we chill the fuck out?" I wanted nothing more than this conversation to be over before Brayden caught on to the argument or, even worse, the coaches.

"You see that scar on your shoulder?" Julius gestured to where I'd had surgery before.

"Not really, it's on my back," I said, trying to lighten the mood but absolutely failing, as I watched Julius grind his teeth like he was trying to bite back his anger.

"Not the fucking point man, it's there because you've already suffered one tear and had to have surgery on it. Wasn't that traumatic enough? Because I remember it like it was yesterday. You were in a dark place and you were drinking a lot and you'd just lost

Amber." The room went pin drop silent with the mention of her name, almost as though everybody was holding their breath.

"Don't bring her into this," I spat back. Everything inside of me burned at the fact Julius thought now was the right time to say her name, after all these years of it hardly being muttered. "This isn't like that. I was depressed and in a completely different head space. I can't believe you!"

"What's all the shouting about?" Coach Carson asked from where he was now standing in the doorway with one of the assistant coaches at his side. Brayden was lingering behind them, no doubt trying to get a look in at my place on the team.

"Ollie's hurt his shoulder, the one he's already had an operation on, and he's trying to tell us it's nothing when we caught him putting pain relief on it," Julius tattle tailed like a child on the playground. Except this wasn't a kids game of tag on the line, it was my career.

"Is that true?" Carson asked.

I nodded a little. "Small twinge, that's it. Went a little too hard on the high bar, but it's fine. I just wanted to put a bit of gel on so I could finish up my routine on the bar."

Coach Carson wasn't having any of it though. "Step out so we can have a look please." The four of us emerged from the bathroom and into the gym. "Raise both arms above your head," Carson commanded.

I bit the inside of my cheek to keep me from wincing and followed his instructions. As I stretched both arms to full extension I desperately tried to keep control of my shaky breaths, in the hopes that I looked steady and in control of my movements.

He placed a soft hand on my bad shoulder and worked my arm back and forth, every movement feeling like he was trying to remove my arm from its socket. I didn't whimper or cry out like I wanted though, I kept my face as neutral as possible, lips pursed as I waited for this nightmare to be over.

"See, all good," I said, not only to Carson but to my other four teammates who watched on almost as if they were waiting for me to fail. "Can we get back to practice?"

"He does have a full range of movements, even with a layer of ibuprofen gel on. If there was a real problem he'd be crying in pain," Carson commented, and I shot Julius a narrowed eyed look that said, '*I told you so.*'

Without another word Julius stomped off, Tom following behind him to make sure he was okay. Carson dragged Lucas and Brayden off to the floor to run through their routines, which left me standing by my angry self to stew with my thoughts.

In some ways Julius had been right. If something went wrong whilst I was twenty feet off the floor or swinging between two metal bars, I could end up killing myself. Yet on the other side of things, everything could be absolutely fine if I laid up on my shoulder until qualifiers. I needed to try if I wanted to have any kind of shot at a gold medal. Every other scenario that passed through my mind contradicted the one before, but the only situation I could even imagine involved me competing. So compete I would do.

Chapter Twenty-One

Lucas

Oliver was beyond tense as we got back to the room. In the five years I'd known both Oliver and Julius, I'd never seen them come to blows like that. I imagined it would feel like if me and Alicia had a huge argument the night before the biggest day of our lives. If that was me, I'd be crushed. I'd probably want to curl up in bed with Brooklyn Nine-Nine and try not to cry myself to sleep.

That wasn't Oliver's style though. Knowing him he probably wanted to be out and about right now and I had this strange desire to make that happen for him. We'd promised the coaches yesterday that we wouldn't be seen out just the two of us, in case the press put two and two together and figured out I was the mystery guy in the hoodie, but I had a way around that.

"You okay?" I asked as he peeled off his team jacket, discarding it on the end of our bed.

"I swear if I have to hear that again today, I'm going to absolutely lose it. I'm fine. Was my shoulder a little sore? Yes. Did I put some pain cream on it? Yep. Why is this such a big deal? I've been practicing my rings a lot as it's the apparatus I'm most likely to medal on and I overworked it a little. I've rested it, I've used the massager on it, and the coaches don't seem to think there's a problem. Can we move on?"

Part of me understood. I spent so much time crashing onto the floor that sometimes my back killed me, but it wasn't from a previous injury like Oliver's. But I had to trust the experts and they'd signed off on Oliver being okay to compete so who was I to say otherwise? "Yeah, we can move on."

He flopped down on to the bed, kicking off his shoes and sending them flying up against the radiator on the far side of the room. Bucking up his hips he peeled off his sweatpants and gym shorts in one swift motion leaving him in a vest and his boxers.

It would be so easy right now to climb into bed and bang out the anger that was currently bubbling up inside of him, but I had a better idea; one that would get us out of the room for a little while.

"How about we get out of here for a little bit?"

"We aren't allowed to be seen out there together on our own in case the gay relationship press spots us and figures out it was you I was kissing in that alleyway."

Tonight was not the night to revisit that mess. For a couple of hours we needed to get out of the village and out of our own heads.

"Well, what if it wasn't just the two of us?"

"I swear if you say Julius and Tom right now, I'm going to go share with Brayden and I'd actually rather break all of my limbs than do that."

Poor Brayden not only had he been forced on to another floor because this one was full, but he was sharing with some guy he'd never met before. He didn't seem to mind though, we'd spotted him at breakfast the other morning with a whole crew of friends.

"Well, before you get completely dramatic, I was actually going to suggest my sister and best friend. If that's okay with you?" I'd already texted both of them on the way back from training after he'd left scorched earth in his tracks as he burnt his way across the village. They were both in to go to this arcade and bar thing that my mum and Lucy had visited a couple of nights ago.

"You serious?"

I nodded.

"What do you have in mind?" He asked sitting up on the bed, parting his legs so I could slide in between them.

He took my hands in his and brought them to his mouth pressing soft kisses to each knuckle. I wasn't up to date on the rules of being friends with benefits, but I'm pretty sure they didn't look like this. No wonder the lines had become so blurred in my mind. "You'll see. Do you want to shower?"

"Only if you're coming with me." Who was I to say no? With his hands linked through mine I pulled him up from the bed, grabbing two fresh towels before pulling him into the small space they called a bathroom.

We lost almost half an hour in the shower to messy hand jobs and an impromptu massage from Oliver that I didn't even realize I needed. Which left us rocking up many minutes late to the arcade style bar where we were meeting the girls. As I assumed, they'd already seated themselves in a booth and were watching us intently as we arrived at the table.

"Struggle to find the exact Google map pin I sent you?" Lucy asked as Oliver and I slid into the opposite side of the booth to the pair. We probably should have taken separate sides in case anybody was watching, but I really wanted Oliver to breathe tonight and enjoy himself. That wouldn't happen if he was stressed about the press.

Oliver laughed as he realized we'd been caught. "So you're the funny Evans, good to know." He winked at me and I pinched his arm.

"You're such an asshole," I replied, but I couldn't help but lean into the side of him nudging him playfully. Everything tingled. My whole body was completely fuzzy. I wasn't sure how a normal person felt when they were out with a guy they liked, but I was guessing it was something like this.

Both of the girls exchanged a look that I hated to recognize, it was how they looked at each other when I did something that bewildered them—like when I'd moved out of the house to go to university after they'd expected me to stay at home to study. I shook my head and mouthed, *stop it,* across the table at them, but it only caused them to giggle more.

"I feel like I'm missing something here, like some sibling/best friend communication shit," Oliver commented, his eyes flicking between the three of us.

"Well, you know, Lucas has never had a boyfriend before," Lucy started.

"He's not my—" Oliver laid a hand down on my thigh to stop my protests and I quickly came to a halt. Don't get me wrong, I knew he wasn't saying we were boyfriends, but his actions still flooded my heart with his unrelenting warmth.

"What I was trying to say," Lucy continued, "is that because he's never had one before, we've never seen him like this with another guy. All blushing and content looking. As his sister it makes me feel stupid happy because he deserves a good guy."

"And what, that's me? The great guy? I remember

you chewing me up and spitting me out when I first contacted you about flying out here."

"Opinions can change, can't they?" My sister, the wittier and quicker twin, shot back. She could match Oliver, and probably even Julius, pace for pace.

"Touché, touché," Oliver replied as he finally peeled his hand away from my thigh, the loss of contact from him immediately noticeable for me.

A waitress headed towards us with two extra-large oval plates, placing them down between the four of us.

"We've ordered food," Lucy said, like that wasn't clear to us.

The plates of food were completely beige, delicious looking, but probably not what we should have been consuming so close to the games.

"How is the littlest Evans enjoying Paris?" Oliver asked, snapping up an onion ring in the blink of an eye.

Alicia raised an eyebrow at me across the table, clearly as confused as I was at Oliver taking an interest in my family. I appreciated it though.

"She's absolutely loving it. The night before we flew out we watched that show, Emily in Paris, that came out a few years ago and now she's running around taking pictures like she's going to become Insta famous," Lucy replied, dunking a mozzarella stick in the ketchup.

"She already has like ten thousand followers on TikTok, so I wouldn't be surprised if that happened."

"How do you know that?" I asked him, as even I hadn't seen that yet.

"She followed me, so I followed her back. She's got a killer voice for such a young girl. I was impressed. I think she's hoping I'll share her videos with my five million followers," he chuckled, which had us all chuckling. If Oliver shared anything of hers she'd die.

The conversation flowed like four old friends catching up, until the platters were completely empty and we were all stuffed to within an inch of our shirts busting open.

"I need a drink," Lucy said, gesturing towards the bar, "you coming?" She looked at me and I nodded, waiting for Oliver to shift out of my way so I could get past.

"You wanna try some of the machines?" He asked Alicia and she jumped straight up from the table to lead the way to an air hockey machine.

Whilst Alicia and Oliver battled it out at the air hockey table, me and Lucy stood at the bar waiting for her complex cocktail to be made.

"You really like him, huh?" She said, elbows resting on the bar as she twiddled a cocktail stick, that once held olives, between her fingers. I went to say anything other than yes, but she held her hand up to stop me. "That wasn't a question, more a mere observation. You've been mooning over him all night. Plus, I saw you two sneak off to the bathroom at family lunch. You can't hide anything from me."

"Okay, fine, I like him, but like I don't know—he's Oliver. What am I supposed to do? We both thought this was going to be just sex, but now it isn't and I don't know what I'm meant to do about that." It was probably the stupidest thing I could ever do, falling for Oliver Ramsey. We hated each other, except now we kind of didn't. Now we woke up in each other's arms, took showers together like it wasn't uncomfortable for us to cram into the tiny cubicle in our en-suite, and shared moments that I imagined felt like falling in love.

"He's good for you. I'm not sure if you see it, but look where you are." She gestured around to the arcade style pub. It felt very homely, almost like the one mum ran at home, with its vintage jukebox, dart board, and air hockey table. Big booths littered the pub and I'd always choose a booth over a table any day of the week, they were so much more intimate.

I wasn't quite sure what she meant though. "We're in a pub?" I replied with a raised eyebrow.

"Yeah, but you don't have to be here. You aren't at work, and this wasn't a compulsory outing. You wanted to be here, you wanted to get out with Oliver when you could be fitting in an extra work out or working on your dissertation. I like that he's pulling you out of your comfort zone a little."

She wasn't wrong, I just wasn't sure if I wanted to give Oliver that much credit and power. Once I did that, how did we go back? This wasn't going to be life forever, in like ten days we'd both be back in the UK living our own lives and not waking up to each other. It wasn't possible to make this work when we got back home. He was out now too, and he'd have his pick of the guys or girls when he got home. This was a relationship of convenience.

"I can see your cogs turning, trying to figure out how he fits into your five year plan and your life back in Essex. Stop it, enjoy the now with him and then see what happens. I know that isn't your style, but you can't plan for love." That made me want to gag. I didn't love Oliver.

"Don't say love," I replied as the bartender handed her the overelaborate cocktail she'd had him make. As she paid, I headed back to our booth. I needed a second to breathe without her making me talk about my feelings. Did I now care about Oliver? Yes, a lot. That didn't make me in love with him. Although, as I'd never been in love before, I wasn't even sure what it would actually feel like.

"Still sticking to the water though," she commented as she slid into the booth opposite me.

"We do still have the qualifiers tomorrow afternoon, you know. We should probably head back to the Village after this last drink." I took a sip of my water and tried not to overthink. It wouldn't pay to deep dive into mine and Oliver's relationship less than eighteen hours before the biggest event of my life.

"I'm really proud of you, Luca," she said as she stirred her drink with the straw, "and I'm so glad to be here. I can't believe Oliver did this. Like I know you don't want to talk about him anymore and after this I promise I'll stop, but you must see that he really cares about you. He got us here, paid so I could take time off and then flew us all first class. That's an act of love if I've ever seen one."

I'd already over thought his actions a million times. He'd gone out of his way for me, but I could imagine he'd do the same for Julius and Tom and all they were to him was friends and teammates. I'd started replaying things he said in passing or little things he'd do when we were alone, like let me rewatch the same episode of Brooklyn Nine-Nine over and over again if I was writing my dissertation or before we slept.

"I'm a mess," I groaned.

"Wow, Lucas Evans admitting that things aren't perfect. I'm definitely proud of you now, bro." She smirked at me as she took a sip of her bright pink cocktail before continuing. "Seriously though, he seems great. I think we misjudged him and if he's making you happy, then I think you should roll with whatever the pair of you have going on."

"I thought we were going to stop talking about him?" I was almost at the point of wanting to rest my head on the table and call it a day. We should have stayed at home. Although, when I looked over at Oliver doubled over, laughing to the point of tears as Alicia smashed yet another puck off the table, it was all so worth it. Mum had always said give and take was the key to a perfect relationship. Was that what this was? I was in over my head here.

"Okay, okay no more for the rest of the evening." Thankfully, she stuck to her word and we made our way over to the other two and convinced them to play a two against two game of table football. The Evans siblings versus the losers. Which is exactly how it went down. We'd been raised on pub games whilst mum worked behind the bar, our areas of expertise being table football and the bingo games machine that we knew how to play without paying.

It was a surreal night, being surrounded by my sister, best friend, and Oliver. Seeing how they all got on like a house on fire. It flipped a switch in me as Oliver told a story about something that had happened in training. I'd tuned out halfway through, completely distracted by how attentively the girls were listening and howling with laughter. I'd never thought about the criteria for the perfect guy for me, but being adored by my sister and best friend had to be top of that list. Oliver had that all sewed up already.

I was screwed.

Chapter Twenty-Two

Oliver

Nothing felt the same as we stood in the wing of the arena waiting to be called into the hall to start the day. Every other team waiting around us was talking animatedly about the day ahead, stretching together and motivating each other. Team GB were all stood at least six feet apart. Lucas with his wireless earphones in like he always did before every other competition, but normally the other three of us would be huddled together getting fired up.

We were about to compete as an Olympic team for the first time together, yet the atmosphere felt more like a funeral. It was bullshit. Yet I didn't know how to break the frosty atmosphere between me and my best friends, and I couldn't disturb Lucas—he had to be in the zone, as he wasn't used to the distractions before a competition.

I went to go and say something, anything to the other pair, but it was too late. Coach Carson and Jacub were already calling us over to go through final logistics and before we knew it we were walking out into the jam packed Olympic arena for the first time. It took everyone's mind off the atmosphere between us all. No matter what, we were all able to keep our eyes on the prize.

We were in subdivision three with Canada, Ukraine, and Japan, as well as a mixed group of individuals from countries like Spain, Poland, and the Netherlands, who's teams hadn't managed to qualify as a whole. Canada were called into the arena first and as I heard their individual names being called, I felt like I was on tenterhooks, in seconds that would be us.

"From the United Kingdom, Team Great Britain. Julius Reed, Lucas Evans, Oliver Ramsey, and Thomas Hines," the announcer called over the microphone to the audience. We all walked into the arena and stepped forwards individually and waved to the crowd in a manner we definitely hadn't practiced enough in comparison to how in sync the rest of the teams looked. It was messy, but over in a blink of an eye so nobody caught on.

We got into formation and neatly marched around the area to our first apparatus, high bar. After that everything blurred into one huge day of anticipation and nerves. Nothing felt right, and I struggled to enjoy it without my best friends embracing every moment with me. Plus, Lucas had kept his distance all day to focus on his routines. The tension between all of us didn't stop everybody killing it. Julius knocked every athlete except his Chinese competitor out of the park on both pommel horse and high bar, and of course Tom had killed it on parallel bars.

I stepped up first for Team GB on the vault, my run up smooth as I ventured towards the vault, but the second my palms hit the vault a bone shattering pain splintered through my right arm. My muscle memory kicked in and I still nailed the Yurchenko, but the second my feet were on the floor again, I knew I was in trouble.

Julius was watching my every move, so I plastered a smile across my face, gritted my teeth, and made my way back over to the group.

"Still the best vaulter in the team," Tom commented, which was nice, considering I'd probably just wrecked my body to land one of the hardest moves.

Words formed in my head to reply to him, but my whole body was in shock and yet it knew I hadn't finished with it today. There were still two more apparatus to go and I had to perform well to keep us in fourth place to qualify for the all-around team finals. Plus rings were my last shot at qualifying for any apparatus individually.

Everything sucked. My routines were good enough, but not great and so far I'd been finishing in like tenth or below on every apparatus. It was a mess. I was supposed to be a shoe in for vault this year, as I went into the event with one of the highest difficulties. Yet even landing a Yurchenko wasn't enough. It felt like this huge let down—this was my first time competing in the Olympics, it was supposed to be special.

I thought it was going to feel like the best day of my life, but as we waited for the fifth round of apparatus, floor, nothing felt special. By the time I stepped onto the floor I hardly cared how the routine went. I wasn't going to qualify for the individual event on floor. I wasn't artistic, my tumbles were messy on a good day and none of my lower ground work looked great. The score was okay, a 14.3, but it wasn't qualifying material. Julius and Tom both scored higher 14.8 and 14.9, but neither of them qualified individually either. We were all waiting for Lucas to step out on the floor, despite everything going on between all of us, Lucas never failed to wow us. There was something about his floor routine that could unite anyone, it could probably solve world problems if he let it.

Except for the first time ever, it wasn't the stunning piece of art that it normally was. His handstand was loose and he rolled out of it half a second too early. Then on his final tumble, the Arabian double front he'd worked so hard to master, his foot landed out of bounds. He smiled and waved to the crowd as he finished, but the second he was off the mat and back with us on the side his face crumbled, his eyes watered and he looked distraught.

He chucked his hood up over his head as he sat on the side and waited for his score, the hood crumpled around his face so no-one could see the tears as they fell hard. When he looked up to his score of 15.566, his eyes were red and puffy and I thought he was going to end up crying some more. Instead I watched him take a deep breath and collect himself, smiling hard as the cameras found him to celebrate his score.

My whole body felt exhausted at this point. I'd slipped two painkillers between round four and five, but there was still an oceans worth of pain resting on my shoulder. As we walked around to the final rotation of rings, nothing in me felt right.

"You ready?" Jeremiah asked as I clapped chalk on to my hands and checked that the straps on my wrist were tight enough.

I wasn't sure I could even open my mouth to reply to him, as doing anything right now was exhausting. Pain had chipped away at my body all day to the point that I felt like I'd ran a marathon non-stop, and without water.

I nodded towards him, but my vision fogged and I

had to stop and close my eyes for a second to be able to see properly. The announcer had already called my name, but if I started now I'd probably pass out before I could even do my first move. "Can I have a second?" I asked, as I grabbed my water bottle from beside the mat and chugged half of it down in the hopes that I'd feel somewhat refreshed by the icy water. It didn't squash the drowsiness though—I still felt as rough as I did when I woke up at four a.m. this morning and couldn't get back to sleep.

The two assistants said nothing as I wiped the chalk off my hands with a rag and rubbed my eyes, clearing the fog so I could focus enough to push through my rings routine. I chalked back up and gave them the signal that I was ready to go. The announcer called my name again and the crowd roared back to life as I was hoisted up on to the rings.

My muscles constricted beneath me as I pulled up into an Iron Cross, but everything felt too tense for me to hold it for any period of time. So I pulled back into a stronghold on the rings to save me from straining anything. Falling out of my iron cross so early was going to cost me points, but if I could get a rhythm going I could fit the move back in at the end of the routine. For a moment I just hung there, my upper body strength feeling weaker than it ever had as a familiar pain tugged at my shoulder.

None of my movements felt controlled, my swallow hold must have looked a complete and utter mess as I struggled to complete a full extension of all my limbs. My transitions were messy instead of smooth like they had been in every practice before-hand.

Even if I stuck the dismount right now I'd still be

looking at a poor execution score. I allowed myself to drop out of the swallow hold and attempted to transition back into the iron cross I'd missed the first time around. Everything around me sounded fuzzy as I tried to remember the best way to move from a swallow hold into an iron cross. I ran through the routine in my head and I could see it; a single flip, release, grab, swallow hold, but what used to come next? How could I not remember when I'd been practicing this routine for months and months and months.

Oh shit. It was my dismount that came next. I was running out of time. I had to try and fit in an iron cross before the dismount if I was going to get any kind of good score. So I went for it, the move that would cause my shoulder all kinds of stupid pain. An absolutely fantastic move to try and put my body through when it already felt stressed and strained.

Despite the pain, I pushed my hands flat into the rings and hoisted myself up into the Iron Cross position. I took several deep breaths and stretched my arms out completely into the correct position. From the ground it probably looked great. I tilted my chin up and attempted to count the beats, but every time I got past two all I could feel was the tug in my right shoulder. A tug which hurt so much I couldn't even focus on whether my toes were pointed down or arms extended perfectly.

I was so in my own head that I didn't realize I was slipping until my hands were already uncurled from the rings and gravity had hurled me into the mat, landing in unbearable pain on my shoulder.

I heard him scream, over the thousands of people in the crowd *his* voice was crystal clear. Lucas must have been watching me, must have seen my grip break from the rings and how I'd dropped through the air with brutal force. Everything was hazy around me as I laid there, eyes half lidded trying to focus on anything other than my shoulder. But the pain was sucking all the life out of me and I knew any minute I'd pass out so my body could deal with the pain. I was right. Seconds later everything went black.

Through the crippling darkness I heard the murmurs of concern, felt hands on my lifeless body, and then cold metal beneath my back. The next thing I knew I was waking up in a foreign hospital, a nurse hovering above me, my whole body completely numb as they wheeled me down the corridor.

Chapter Twenty-Three

Lucas

Everything stilled around us as Oliver was carted out of the arena on a stretcher. I'd held my breath as they walked past me, watching intently to make sure he was still breathing. His chest rose and fell and I heaved out a breath. That fall could have been deadly.

Some part of me was thankful that this was the final round of apparatus and we'd gone into this round in fourth place for the team all-around finals, so we'd still qualify.

Seeing him in so much pain, how he'd screamed as he crashed to the mat. It had shaken me to the core. I had no idea how Tom had performed on rings moments after, without even being able to make sure his best friend was okay.

"Coach Carson went with Ollie and the ambulance," Julius said as I grabbed my team jacket and sweats, pulling them on over my shorts and leotard.

"We need to get out of here. Oliver's going to be freaking out. We need to be with him." At this point, I couldn't have cared less about what they chose to do next as I was already dashing down the tunnel that would hopefully lead me out of the arena.

"Wait up," Julius called from behind me. "I've booked us an Uber, it's going to be at the north exit so head there." We all sprinted around the back end of the arena until we spotted an emergency exit and burst through it.

Following the map on Julius's Uber app, we made it to the taxi, all three of us hopping into the back; Tom telling the driver to put his foot down as we had a medical emergency.

We were banished to the waiting room for several hours when we arrived at the hospital, waiting for Oliver to return from tests and scans. None of us were family and despite us all being in the team clothing he'd been brought in with, the doctors still wouldn't let us wait in his private room. However, the second they wheeled him back into that room the three of us raced past the doctors, regardless of their protests.

"It's fine, they are my teammates, they can stay," Oliver said groggily, struggling to keep his eyes open as the fluorescent light from the overhead lamp blinded him.

Julius drew the blind across the single window in the room. The second that it was closed I was reaching for Oliver's hand threading my fingers through it before pressing a kiss to his forehead.

"I don't think I've ever been so scared in my whole life," I muttered as I moved my lips to his and covered them quickly with a swift kiss.

"I'm okay, I'm okay." He squeezed my hand, and maybe he was. His right arm wasn't in plaster, there was no sling on or anything.

"What happened up there?" Tom asked from where he was leaning against the end of the bed.

Oliver glanced over at where Julius was leaning against the wall next to me. "I was in pain." Julius sighed and both me and Tom glared at him. Now was not the time or the place for 'I told you so's'. "I know, I know, I was a fucking idiot. My shoulder is probably completely fucked now and that's my own fault, but I was managing the pain. That vault completely knocked the wind out of me and by the time I got up on the rings I could hardly see, I was in such blistering pain."

"I swear, if you weren't in a hospital bed right now, I'd punch you," Julius said, "nothing is more important than your life and by trying to perform whilst in major pain you risked your life and I'm so fucking angry at you right now. We've lost enough in this lifetime." He was on the verge of tears. I could see it in the way his hands trembled at his sides and how he bit his lip to keep them from spilling over.

"You don't have to tell me—I'm paying the price. They've done some scans to see how bad things are, but they've said the Team GB doctors want to have a look at them with the coaches, so I have no clue what's going on."

"I also can't believe you two just kissed in front of us. I think it's one thing knowing you two are shagging, but another thing seeing it. You're pretty cute together," Julius commented, settling the atmosphere, even though if I knew Julius how I thought I did, his blood was still boiling over from Oliver acting so idiotically. I'd forgotten that they'd both lost Amber and it must have felt like that could have happened again just now for Julius.

"Shut up," Oliver said with a roll of his eyes before groaning. "Oh fuck, that was a mistake, I passed out in the ambulance and my head is banging."

All I wanted to do right now was pack him up in my

suitcase and take him home with me so I could look after him. I'd never wanted to take a guy home with me before, never mind taking care of one. Oliver was already one step ahead as well considering he'd met my family. My mind was spiraling and I needed to get a grip. Oliver was still in a hospital bed.

"You two look good together, is what Julius was trying to say after he weirdly watched you two kiss," Tom added, "I'm glad Jules drew the blinds though, the hospital staff would be gawking like crazy right now otherwise."

The wall behind us started to vibrate like crazy, distracting away from the topic of me and Oliver. "Sorry, sorry, I've cut whoever it was off. It's probably my mum or Estelle trying to check in. I'll call them back afterwards." Oliver nodded at Julius and brought my hand up to his lips, pressing them to my knuckles.

"I'm so glad you're here, but what happened? Where did we rank?" he asked.

"Fourth, behind the Chinese, US, and Japan." We were lucky Oliver's fall didn't completely tank our score and move us down the rankings, but luckily we'd killed it in the rounds before."

"That's good, I'm glad I didn't fuck it up for everyone. Probably only myself," Oliver replied sleepily, his eyes half lidded as he leant his head against the side of his pillow. This could so easily turn into a pity party if we let him and I wasn't about to let that happen. Or well, Julius's phone wasn't as it started to vibrate like crazy again.

"Who the heck is messaging you?" I asked as Julius's phone vibrated in his pocket for what felt like the hundredth time since we'd arrived at the hospital.

Oliver was on the verge of falling asleep, the pain relief finally beginning to knock him out. I could feel it as the death grip he'd had on my hand started to release. I really didn't want Julius's fans keeping Oliver awake.

Julius pulled out his phone, as Tom's started to ring. Whoever it was, I was glad that I'd turned mine off the second I got to the hospital so I could avoid anything that was being said about Oliver's fall. I'd lived through it. I didn't need to read about it or have to keep explaining it to people asking.

Tom answered the call, but halted in the doorway as he went to step into the hallway. "Apparently we all need to hear this, it's the team's PR. Yeah, Dan I'm putting you on loudspeaker now."

"Julius, you fucking idiot, why aren't you checking your phone?" Were the first words that bellowed from the loudspeaker and straight away Oliver jolted awake. Julius immediately pulled out his phone and started to scroll through the messages and missed calls.

"Oh fuck," he groaned.

"Yeah, oh fuck indeed. We had a plan guys. We were going to keep this under wraps not to distract from the games and you guys as a team, but you had to push it and now it's out there." Dan sounded furious, a grit to his voice that I'd never heard from the PR guy.

"I'm sorry, but what have I missed here?" I asked. It sounded exactly like my biggest worry but, right now, with Oliver laid up in bed unsure of his future, I wasn't sure what my biggest concern was anymore.

"Everybody now knows that it was you Oliver was kissing in that alleyway," Dan said, confirming that my greatest fear had happened. We'd been exposed and my name was a headline.

I looked straight to Julius wondering what he had to do with this.

"I'm such a twat, I forgot I'd already edited the video of us getting our tattoos and I scheduled it to go live after the qualifiers because I thought the fans would be buzzed to watch more of us after our win today. It's not hard to put two and two together from this video as you can see the hoodie you have on is the same as the hoodie in the picture."

Oh fuck. I snatched the phone from Julius and pulled up the first article about the two of us. It was scathing. It talked not only about the kiss, but how it could be related to Oliver's fall. How it could have been a distraction to him. I opened up a second and it was more of the same, except now they'd somehow gotten photos of us walking around the Olympic Village together. The third was the worst though, as it contained comments from a waiter at the restaurant we'd gone to for family day and how he'd seen us go to the bathroom together for a solid fifteen minutes.

I couldn't move. I couldn't even breathe and at that point I'd missed everything Dan had said. Phrases like 'distracted by Lucas', 'charmed into bed', and 'the gayest Olympics yet' echoed around in my mind and I wanted to run. This shouldn't have happened. If I'd have stuck to my guns and trained and written my dissertation this wouldn't have happened.

"Lucas?" Oliver whispered, breaking me from my thoughts to realize I'd let go of his hand and practically backed myself into the corner of the room.

"Is he still there?" I heard Dan ask through the phone, and as I stared at the final article once more I really wished I wasn't. I should be back in my room by now, TV on playing Brooklyn Nine-Nine, and my laptop open as I typed away about political systems and how they could be tailored better to be more democratic.

"This shouldn't have happened. Fuck, this is literally everything I was worried about when I climbed into bed with you. I didn't want this. I wanted to come here and train hard and win gold, that's it. It was supposed to be that simple, yet I stupidly let myself think that I could have it all. And I can't." I couldn't stop the way my hands balled tightly, nails imprinting the palms of my hands.

"Lucas, come on—"

"No, Oliver," I interrupted, "can't you see this was exactly what I didn't want? Like, for fucks sake! I don't want my name in the papers. I don't want journalists speculating if we were hooking up in a bathroom or not." I felt disgusted that those words had even been printed in an article, never mind read by what would probably be hundreds of thousands of people by the end of the day. It was a scandal. *I* was caught up in a scandal.

"How are you the one screaming at me right now, when I'm the guy laid up in bed," he screamed at me the best he could through the pain. "You get to walk out of here, and yes, there's some nasty stuff about you on the internet right now, but I'm stuck in the hospital with what could be a career ending injury."

I thought it'd shut him up, but I'd forgotten what we were like in a fight, and I bit straight back. "Look, I'm sorry that you decided to compete whilst you were clearly hurting. I wish you'd talked to me about it like I'd talked to you about my whole damn life, but I'm the one who has to go out there and face the world. Face my mum and my sisters. Now they know we were being fucking idiots in a bathroom and an alleyway. I have to go and have cameras shoved in my face and journalists asking me invasive questions, you damn well know I didn't want this. I never should have fucking kissed you." The words toppled out of my mouth before I could even stop them. The air was sucked out of the room with my words and we all stilled.

"Lucas, come on."

"No, Tom, not come on. I hate this, you all know I hate this. I wanted to just train and compete and yet I let him suck me into this mess."

"You kissed me," Oliver rebutted.

"Yeah and I regret it."

"Lucas," Julius hissed.

"I'm fucking done. I'm done. I just want the games to be over so I can go back to my life outside of the spotlight and away from doing stupid things like thinking I can be in a relationship. It's over." I threw my final words straight in Oliver's face and stormed out of that room and hospital like the angry tornado I was.

I gave the Uber driver the address of my mum and sisters hotel, and within minutes I was knocking at their door and throwing myself into the safest of arms.

"Oh baby," my mum cooed as she scooped my body into her arms like I weighed nothing and was still her little boy. "We saw the news, I'm so sorry." I collapsed against her and for a few minutes we just stood there, her holding me more than anything else.

"Your sisters nipped out to pick up pizza for dinner. If we'd have known you were coming we'd have ordered one for you too. How's Oliver?"

Oliver. Fucking Oliver. I wanted to hate him, but I still couldn't believe we'd screamed at each other whilst he was hurting in a hospital bed. My heart squeezed. I was the worst person, but I could not stop thinking about the fact that I'd been completely exposed to the world.

"Hurt. I don't know. We had a big argument and I think we broke up. If it's even possible to break up when you aren't together." I'd been behaving like a delusional teen thinking that me and Oliver could actually get it together and make something work that wasn't the friends with benefits mess we started in. That was such a joke, now our sex lives were plastered on the front of every trashy newspaper.

"If you two think you weren't together then you're not the son I raised. You care about him more than I've ever seen you care about anyone outside of your family and Alicia."

"I don't want to talk about him anymore tonight. Can I stay here? I don't think I could bear to go back to our room tonight." Sleeping in the bed we'd shared for so many nights alone would probably kill me. I'd let myself grow accustomed to sleeping with him next to me. It was stupid and naïve when in less than a week I'd be home in my student bed alone again.

"Of course you can, you know you're always welcome here. You can sleep in Lauren's bed in Lucy's room and she can sleep on the spare in here." She kissed me on the cheek and handed me a spare robe from the door and the key card to Lucy's room next door. "Everything will be okay, Luca, it always will be."

I'd stripped down to my boxers, abandoned the robe on the chair, and passed out in the bed before the girls had even returned with pizza. All night Oliver haunted my dreams. I'd been worried I'd dream about him falling, but instead it was images of what our life could

211

have looked like together if we'd been able to make our *relationship* work.

Chapter Twenty-Four

Oliver

"We were just harassed by at least a dozen paparazzi," Gran said as she pushed open the door to the hospital.

They'd messaged about coming to visit the day before, but after everything that had kicked off yesterday, I hadn't been in the mood to see anybody. Not that I felt any better at all. An x-ray had confirmed that my shoulder was looking pretty fucked and even though one of the doctors from the Olympic Village had come in talking about getting a cortisone shot and then a full medical assessment in the UK, I still felt awful.

"I don't know how they realized that we were related to you, but they were asking us how we felt about you being gay and having sex in a bathroom." Fantastic, now they were asking my elderly grandparents about my sex life, could the press get any lower?

"I feel like we raised you better than to be having sex in a public place, Oliver," Pops added as he pulled up two chairs at the side of the bed for them to sit.

"I know, pops, I know." My favorite thing about the conversation so far was the fact that they weren't bothered that it was a guy. They'd known almost since I'd known that I was into guys, but they'd never experienced me with one, so I had no clue how they'd react. "I'm so sorry you both had to read that."

"We were all young once, little man. Me and your pops have been together for over half a century, but we remember what it was like to be young and in love and unable to keep your hands to yourself." Both her and pops grinned at me and I wished I could have turned over so I didn't have to see it.

"I don't think I want to hear about what you two got up to when you were my age."

"Why? We've had to read all about your sex life on the front page of The Sun. Apparently you two are what they call exhibitionists? We googled that on the way over here and we definitely stumbled upon some disgraceful videos. You two aren't filming it right?"

"Gran! Stop," I groaned, "of course we don't film it, we didn't even have sex in that bathroom like the papers are reporting.

"She's pulling your leg. Let them say what they want, son, we've known you for the past twenty-four years and are well aware of what a remarkable young man you are. Plus, now we've met Lucas, I don't think he's the kind of guy to ever put a foot out of line." Pops always knew exactly what to say to push me to the verge of tears. He was like a father to me. I respected every single one of his opinions, especially what he thought about me.

"So you and Lucas, huh?" Gran said, and I wanted to groan so loud. I wasn't even sure there was a me and Lucas anymore. I hadn't heard from him since he ran out of here yesterday,

"I don't think that's happening anymore. I'm not even sure if we were ever together in the first place, but if we were, we definitely aren't now."

"What happened?" Pops asked as they both shuffled their chairs closer to my bed.

"He's not a fan of the headlines. I guess he blames me for it. I don't know, I've known from day one, five years ago, that he lived his life behind closed doors and me kissing him in an alley has fucked that up for him." I didn't think it was completely my fault, but it was that move by myself that had blown the closet doors off of our relationship.

"He's a grown man, Oliver, he makes his own decisions and from the pictures I've seen it didn't look like he was forced to kiss you in that alleyway. He practically had you pinned to that wall."

"Now, now Julia. I don't think we need to rehash this."

One day, the three of us would probably laugh about this, that I'd been outed by The Sun of all papers, but right now I struggled to find the humor in it. Maybe it would be easier if me and Lucas had managed to make it out to the other side of this, but I had to be realistic; he was done.

"What I'm trying to say is that the two of you looked happy. I saw you at family dinner and straight away I could see something was going on. He looks at you like you hung the moon and stars, but that you'd been blocking them with clouds from him for a while." Gran and her awful metaphors that never made one hundred percent sense. Exactly what I needed to hear when it came to this mess.

"I don't know how to go back to that though, he's mad. Plus, how would we make this work outside of the Olympic Village? We live completely different lives."

"You two will sort it, he'll have to come for Sunday

dinner and I'll make him my famous beef roast. If that doesn't change his mind, then he's not good enough for you." Trust Gran to make me laugh even when it felt like my whole world was falling apart.

The three of us laughed together and for the first time in the last thirty-six hours things felt somewhat okay in the world.

"We have to talk seriously though," Gran started, clearing her throat to stop her from laughing anymore. "Julius called us last night to make sure we were okay, and he also sent us dinner. He's such a wonderful man. I bet he's going to make a great husband. Estelle is a very lucky woman." She'd have jabbered on forever if Pops hadn't covered her hand with his to pull her back..

"Julia," Pops said, curbing whatever story she was about to launch into about her favorite friend of mine. She'd known him so long now she practically treated him like another grandchild.

"He said you knew you were injured, but still competed. What the heck were you thinking? We've always spoken to you about pain levels and how strenuous this sport can be, even when you were a little boy doing tumbles for fun. Why did you think you were okay enough to compete?" She asked with a tone that told me she wasn't amused by my stupidity.

"Because it was the Olympics. And you know I've been dreaming about a gold medal since I was old enough to understand how to get one."

"And how did that work out for you?"

"What your Gran means is that she's just sad that you didn't follow her advice. We both are."

Disappointment was worse than anger, especially from the people who raised me. I couldn't take it and as tears bristled the back of my eyes, I let them fall for the first time since I'd dropped from the rings. "I'm so sorry," I gasped out as sobs wracked my body. "I've been so stupid. I'm supposed to be a captain, yet I haven't led by example at all. I never should have been chosen as captain."

"Hey, none of that," Gran said, gripping my hand so tight it would probably end up as bruised as the rest of my body. "You can cry over this as much as you want, but we have to look forward now. Get you all healed up and see what you can do after your body is fit and healthy again. Whatever you choose to do."

"But I have no clue what that is," I replied, taking a tissue from my Pops to furiously wipe away the tears that kept relentlessly falling, "I'm a gymnast, I've always been a gymnast. I don't know how to do anything else. I'm almost halfway to fifty and I've never had a job outside of being an athlete. I don't have a degree. I don't even have Year Ten work experience because I chose to go to a competition in Scotland that week instead of doing what the rest of class did. I dedicated my whole life to doing this, only for my body to betray me."

"Together, little man, we'll work this out together. There are options: coaching, advising, teaching little kids to tumble, literally anything you want. You're still only in your early twenties, you have forever to figure this out. The world is your oyster." In the back of my mind I knew she was right, but my whole body was in a bitter pool of pain and self-pity. I didn't want to be anything other than a gymnast.

"Sadly, visiting hours are over," the nurse said as she stuck her head around the door. "We should be able to release him tomorrow, but we want to observe him for one more night to make sure the swelling on his shoulder goes down and that he's adapting to the pain relief for the bruising on his back and side."

Gran nodded, standing up from her chair so Pops could stack it on his and put it back up against the wall where they belonged. "We'll leave you to it now, little man, but we'll check in with you when you're back in the dorms tomorrow. I'm sorry we didn't bring you a charger or anything, but the nurse we spoke to before we came in said you'd be going home tomorrow and we didn't think—"

"It's okay, Gran, at least it means I'll sleep tonight without distraction."

"Love you, little man," she whispered before pressing a kiss to my cheek.

"Love you, son."

"Love you both, get out of here. Go enjoy your last few days in Paris. Don't drink too much wine without me." Gran blew another kiss at me as she lingered in the doorway and I convinced myself that she wasn't tearing up as she left me alone in my hospital room again.

Chapter Twenty-Five

Lucas

"We're coming in whether you like it or not," Julius said through the wooden door of my room back at the Village.

I'd been ignoring the pair of them hammering against it like lunatics for the last few minutes, holding my breath so they wouldn't suspect I was in here.

True to his word, he pushed open the door. Why hadn't I locked it the night before?

"No fun sleeping alone, huh?" Julius asked, and I was so tempted to roll over and pull Oliver's pillow on top of my head to block him out. We didn't have training today, so I thought I'd have a whole day of stewing over the world knowing my personal life without any interruptions from the guy who'd leaked it all out there.

"What do you want?" I asked, pulling the duvet up over my bare chest. I'd not done any washing in a week and Oliver had been stealing my tops so I was running low.

"Alicia has her finals on floor and beam today. We thought we'd go support the girls, if you're up for joining us."

Oh fuck, I pulled my phone from under the pillow and breathed a sigh of relief when I saw I still had half an hour before I planned to meet Alicia. I had hair to braid.

"I know, I'm going to meet her beforehand to wish her luck and stuff."

"We'll join you."

I groaned so deeply it almost came out as a growl.

"Oh, he's still mad," Tom said.

"Look, I know you didn't do it intentionally and you genuinely forgot you'd got it scheduled to go live and you didn't mean for the press to figure things out, but still."

"So it isn't my fault then, is it?"

"Not purposefully, no, but it set the ball rolling and now I'm having my whole life invaded."

"He did say sorry, Lucas, you've got to give him that. Julius never apologizes." That was a complete understatement. I'd never had an apology for some of the horrible things he'd said in those texts that were released a couple of years ago.

"He's right, I don't," Julius said quickly.

The rational part of me knew I wasn't actually angry with him. It was me I was mad with, that I'd been stupid enough to start feeling things towards a teammate and act on it.

"I meant it as well. I never meant to bring this level of hurt to you or Oliver. He's practically my brother and well you've grown on me. Plus, Oliver adores you." Tom shook his head to get Julius to stop talking. He must have known that that wasn't what I wanted to hear right now.

"I still can't believe you two had sex in a bathroom," Julius continued. That was what Tom was trying to get him to shut up about.

This was what I hated. That *that* was what was going to be talked about when they thought of mine and

Oliver's relationship. *'Oh, you remember those two Olympic Gymnasts who were together?'*, *'Oh yeah, I remember, didn't they hook up in a bathroom in Paris?'* That was something I'd now be remembered for, not the medals I won or the charity work I did. The bathroom sex.

"It wasn't sex. We were making out and lost track of time." Not that that was any better. We should have kept everything locked behind closed doors or literally not at all. It pained me to think about it. I couldn't lie to myself and say that if I could I'd go back and not have kissed Oliver. Now that I've looked back at it I'm surprised it didn't happen before—a lot of tension in the earlier fights in our career made a lot of sense now.

"Basically, you can't keep your hands off of each other," Julius laughed.

"I don't think you're helping," Tom said as he perched on the end of my bed. I nodded in agreement.

"Is there still press lingering around outside the dorms? Security keeps clearing them out, but every time I look out the window they are there again. I don't know what they want me to say? It's not like I can deny it, they have photographic evidence." I couldn't deal with it all, not when I was supposed to be getting ready to go support my best friend. "Actually, don't answer that. If I know, I'm just going to curl back up and never leave this room. If you insist on coming with me, then you can hang in here whilst I get showered and dressed." Thankfully, the night before I'd already pulled out a pair of navy sweats and one of my team hoodies.

"We'll be here," Tom replied, and I disappeared into the bathroom.

They didn't leave, and after my shower we ventured

off together flashing our athlete passes at the security team so we could slip backstage to find the female gymnasts getting ready for the event.

"Hey, my love," I breathed into the top of Alicia's head as she squeezed me so hard I was worried my lungs were going to burst. I tucked her petite frame into my side and inhaled the familiar scent of the Chanel perfume she'd been wearing since she was old enough to steal a squirt from her mother's bottle. It was the comfort of home that I needed right now; with Alicia everything felt grounded.

"How are you?" she muttered into my chest. I had to bite the inside of my cheek to stop myself from breaking down. This was her moment, my disastrous shit show of a life right now wasn't going to distract from that.

"Ready to braid some hair," I said as I pulled away from her, running my fingers through her curls. "What are we thinking? Fishtail or two individual braids or do we want something cooler like braids into space buns or a single bun?" I'd been practicing on Lucy whenever I could because these braids were important. They were Olympic braids and I wanted them to be perfect.

"Girls are doing buns so I think we should do two simple plaits and then pin them into buns, that cool?" I nodded and she handed me the oil to run through her loose curls and her partition comb.

"I feel like I should finally invest in some of this oil for my own hair." I poured a pea sized amount into my hands and rubbed it between my fingers to warm it before combing it through her hair. "Remember when we used to do this with coconut oil when we were kids? It was so greasy and you used to smell like a vegan deep fat fryer for weeks after." My words came out more choked than I would have liked. I wished I could have blamed it on the childhood memories, but I was so overwhelmed by everything else.

"Lucas," she said softly, placing a hand over mine as I reached for the comb to sort out her middle parting.

"No, no it's okay. We don't have a ton of time, let me do this." I gently shook her hand off mine and got back to work. I wanted to savor this moment without Oliver ruining it.

"Is he okay?" She asked as I parted her hair down the center. Using one of her spare bobbles, I pulled the other side into a ponytail to keep it from being in the way.

"No. I don't know. We haven't spoken. It's over, it's just...whatever. He's still in the hospital. They are talking about him getting a cortisone shot and still competing and, argh. I don't want to be a part of it anymore." That's what I'd convinced myself anyway, we hadn't really agreed on anything. Not that we were really together in the first place. It was all a bit of a head fuck if I thought about it for too long.

"What do you mean it's over?"

"Me, him, whatever messed up thing that was going on between us. It's done."

"Because of the papers? You can't let that ruin it, Lucas, you can't. You're letting them win."

"I love you, Alicia, but please can we just leave it be." My voice cracked. "I'm hurting," I whispered to her and only her, making sure my tone was quiet enough for the other two not to hear.

"Do you love him?" she asked.

I nodded against her shoulder, admitting it for the first time as I finished up her hair. I wasn't quite ready to say those words aloud. "Now turn around and let me get a proper look at you. Your hairs all done." She spun around for me in her team jacket and leotard, her sweatpants hung over the chair ready to go on before she entered the arena.

"You look beautiful." I squeezed back a couple of tears as Julius and Tom approached us backstage in the arena. "These two idiots bought VIP tickets for us so we'll be watching from the stands." She launched herself at me and we hugged till both of us were on the verge of crying a river. "I'm so proud of you," I whispered and then released her. "Go kill it."

"Love you," she called over her shoulder as she followed her teammates out of the dressing room towards the main arena.

"Love you too," Tom and Julius echoed behind me with a laugh. It was actually ridiculous that in this moment I was grateful to have them around so that I wasn't alone.

"I'm going to take that girl out on a date after the Olympics," Tom said. He freaking wished. Alicia had ridiculously high standards and she knew all about Tom's long list of ladies since he'd been here.

"In your dreams, man, in your dreams." Julius clapped him on the back and led us out from backstage and into the arena to find our seats.

Alicia never failed to stun me. She was out of this world good on the beam, even as the oldest member of the female Team GB gymnastics team this year. Which was crazy considering I was the youngest of the male team. She sizzled as she did a full body roll before powering into a triple aerial walk over—the move that had seen me toppling off the beam. She shuffled on to the very edge, whole body stretched from the end of her toes to the tips of her fingers as she prepared to launch into her dismount.

I'd not seen her beam routine in a good few months, so you could have colored me every shade of surprise as she perfected a double pike back Salto with a full twist. One of the most difficult moves to perform on the beam. It was stunning. She landed with the most effortless stance, a beautiful smile gracing her face as she realized she'd smashed it.

And smashed it she did. The 0.7 difficulty boost the dismount move offered blew every other female gymnast before her out of the water and, rightly so, she took her place on the gold medal spot of the podium.

"We should have bought tissues," Julius commented as the dam broke and a couple tears dribbled down my cheek. Alicia and I had dreamt about this together for over half our lives. Watching it come true for her was probably the most overwhelming moment of my life.

"Shut up," I muttered, but Julius was relentless as he threw an arm around my shoulder. I didn't protest as he pulled me half on to his seat letting my head rest against his shoulder. Everything was fucked up right now, so I'd take a hug even if it was from Julius. Especially as the British national anthem played around us and Alicia waved her flowers around in the air like there was no tomorrow. I needed the damn hug.

Tom whipped out Julius's vlogging camera, the wretched thing and hit record. "Here we are at the women's gymnastics finals and I'm capturing a rare moment on camera. A love fest between Julius and Lucas." He flipped the thing round from his face to us and zoomed in on where Julius had his arm around me.

"All is forgiven between the pair and our boy Lucas is a little emotional watching his hot, I mean childhood best friend, kill it on the beam." Luckily, he didn't catch on camera how I flicked the back of his head. "One day someone's going to write a book about these two and how they went from hating each other to snuggling, but for now let's appreciate this bromance." Tom lingered with the camera on us for a second and then turned it off.

"Do I have to worry about you starting up a channel too?" I asked as I pulled away from Julius's embrace to reach my water bottle from the floor.

"Nah, I just couldn't resist. Plus one day you'll thank me when we are all showing our kids and what not," Julius gulped, and the way me and Tom both turned to glare at him was comical.

"Estelle is four and half months pregnant," he announced, like he'd been holding the secret in for a while. "I wanted to wait to tell all three of you together but fuck it. I'm gonna be a daddy."

I groaned at his choice of words, but excitement pulsed through me for him. That kid was going to have such a fun life. "Congrats man," I said, pulling him in for a 'bro' hug. "Do you know what you're having?"

"A little girl." Tom squealed like a little girl at Julius's announcement and I had to shush him to remind him we were actually still out in public.

"Oh my god, a little baby Juliana. She's going to be adorable."

"Sadly, Estelle has already vetoed any girl version of my name, which sucks. You guys can't tell anybody. Estelle is type A and she wants to wait to announce it publicly outside of family and friends until she's six months." Tom mocked, zipping his lips and I nodded, focusing in on the event as Alicia was about to perform on the floor.

She trampled all over my floor routine, taking one of my biggest power moves and walking straight out of it into several upbeat dance elements.

"That girl's got moves," Tom muttered to himself, which I pretended not to hear.

Her groundwork was stunning, her whole body poised as she spun into a triple turn in tuck-stand position. We needed to start training again together, I could learn a thing or two.

Her two Chinese and Japanese counterparts were, sadly, that bit better on the day and she was quickly knocked out of a medal position. Regardless, she'd walked away with a gold medal around her neck and a fourth-place result on floor. That was everything to be proud of. She'd shot me a text as the medal ceremony happened that she was going to celebrate with the girls, leaving me and the guys unsure of what to do.

"Did you see this?" Julius asked as we walked back to the dorms, passing me his phone to see yet another article about me and Oliver.

"I don't think I want to look at it," I said, trying to return his phone, but he was his always persistent self and pushed the phone back into my hands.

"Just read it."

How did we miss it? The article was titled and as I scrolled through the two-page spread, I could see exactly why Julius wanted me to read it. The very first photo was one from over five years ago at an Essex/London meet that Oliver, Julius, and I had competed in. I'd probably seen the picture before, but not like this. They'd blurred everything else around the two of us, leaving me performing on the floor and Oliver watching from the side. His eyes were glued to me as he watched with a soft smile. He stared as if he couldn't look away. Completely intrigued. The article described him as besotted. They weren't aware he was with Amber then, but the look was still there.

There were a ton of photos from events over the years that they'd analyzed and their words read like a half a decade long love story. Then I scrolled down to a video. I'd never seen this before, but it was from my *Vogue* cover shoot that Oliver had come to three months ago. The video panned from where I'd been posing in my Team GB uniform to him watching in the wings, the camera catching the exact moment he looked me up and down like I was some hot girl in a movie. They'd even done a mini interview with him for some behind the scenes stuff, but had clearly never thought to release it till now.

"He's the one to watch out for at the Olympics this summer. Of course Julius and Tom are going to kill it on every apparatus, but there's something special about Lucas Evans. He wows every single time. If you've seen his floor routine you know exactly what I mean. I'm a little in awe of him." Were his words. In awe. Something special. The softness to his tone, he wasn't talking about a great teammate, it was full of adoration. I'd have cringed seeing this from anyone else, but seeing it from Oliver only made me fall harder.

I wiped furiously at my eyes as a tear splashed onto Julius's phone screen. "Don't give up on him, Lucas. He's never given up on you." Julius said as he took the phone back from me.

It was probably one of the most meaningful things

I'd ever heard from him. The second Oliver was out of the hospital and back in the dorms, I'd try to follow Julius's words.

Chapter Twenty-Six

Oliver

Waking up for the second morning in a row in a hospital bed killed me even though I knew I'd be going home at some point that day. That didn't matter when I was already missing the individual all-around finals today. Missing my two best friends competing and potentially winning medals. The television on the wall of my room only seemed capable of showing the news. It was all in French so I didn't understand a single word, plus my phone was dead so I couldn't even distract myself with that. Which was probably a blessing as I know I would have gone back and rewatched a video of my fall a thousand times to punish myself.

Everything from the day of my fall was now a complete blur. I was truly surprised I hadn't passed out before I got into the ambulance—I'd pushed my body to its absolute limits. Every inch of me was screaming for me to stop, to sit down and breathe, but I couldn't give up. I wanted to win too badly. Now that chance was probably gone.

Maybe this was why Lucas had almost two degrees under his belt, so if he ever found himself in my position he'd still be devastated but at least know he had something else to fall back on. He'd probably be able to recover and find some amazing paid job in politics and go on to be someone who did great things in the political world. He'd help people the way he'd learnt to from his mom. What was I supposed to do if this ended my career?

In the last five years all I'd done outside of training for the Olympics was live it up with the guys, do brand deals, and go to charity events. All of those things would disappear if I had to retire at twenty-four. How was that even possible? Retired at twenty-four. I knew I wasn't going to have decades in this sport, but I thought I might have at least another Olympic run in me.

The light outside my door started to flicker, illuminating my room on and off, making my head feel like something was hammering against my brain. Everything still hurt, even though it was only a small tear to my rotator cuff, the rest of my body had taken an absolute battering from exhaustion and the fall itself. The bruises on my back alone were horrific, but my shoulder was still swollen and my sides ached like somebody had kicked me in the ribs repeatedly. Falling twenty feet would do that to a body.

What came next? That was probably a question I should be asking myself right about now. Even if I could compete tomorrow, if I was cleared by the coaches and physios and maybe even with a cortisone shot, this would probably be my last Olympics. I'd already had one load of surgery on the shoulder and now it was becoming a reoccurring injury—the kind of thing that sent athletes straight into retirement.

If I wasn't doing gymnastics what would I do? I had three sub-par A-Levels and one of them was in sport, the other two being geography and religious studies. What help would they be now? I had no work experience, I'd never had another job outside of running social media accounts for myself and working on brand deals. I didn't want to be an influencer. I wanted to do good in this world. That's what my grandparents would want for me too.

I just had no clue what that good would be.

I must have drifted off amidst all my thoughts because the next thing I knew a familiar face had poked his head around the door. "Are we okay to come in?" Coach Carson said, Jacub lingering behind him in the doorway. I nodded and they stepped into the room, shutting the door behind him. "How are you feeling?" he asked.

"Not like I've been hit by a truck anymore, but frustrated that I'm in here rather than out supporting my team. How did they get on?"

"Julius brought bronze home for us. We've got it all recorded so you can watch it when you get back to the dorm. Lucas said he'd load it up on the Roku stick." That was something at least, even if he was only doing it because the coaches had asked him to do it.

"And Tom?"

"He finished seventh, but he was still amazing. It was a tough day out there and both of their attentions were still a little frazzled. You should see the press trying to get into the village now. Some pap managed to get into the dorms and was trying to find yours and Lucas's room. Luckily security got to him before he even made it into the lift."

Lucas must have been freaking out, that wasn't a journalist writing nasty words about us, it was some crazy person trying to get into our room and invade our privacy.

"Is he okay?"

"Lucas?" Jacub asked.

I nodded in confirmation. I wasn't sure how to say his name without having some kind of breakdown in front of the coaches.

"Withdrawn. He came out to support the guys today, but he lingered in the sides on his own with his earphones in. He was training on his own in the gym with the assistant coaches when we left." That was a sad, sad image. We'd worked so hard to get him out of his shell and now me being an idiot and Julius having a YouTube channel had ruined that.

"The team put out a message about supporting all LGBTQ+ athletes and respecting their relationships. All of the British teams have now released a similar message, same with a lot of the teams from the other countries. The outpouring of support for you and Lucas has been too much for the PR team to handle. We had to mute the Loliver hash-tag."

Oh jeez, we had a ship name hashtag and we weren't even together. "I bet Lucas has deleted every single app on his phone, it's probably dead in a drawer in our room." Another reason I was grateful for my phone being dead, I hadn't succumbed to messaging him to ask if we could talk about us. He'd made it very clear that whatever we were, we were over. "I definitely wouldn't tell him about the hashtag though, he hates me right now."

"Yeah we got that vibe when we asked if he wanted to do an interview to set the record straight."

"I can't believe you thought you were going to get him to an interview right now. Good try." I almost laughed, almost. This would have been amusing if I wasn't in a hospital bed. If me and Lucas could actually properly duke this out and then figure out if we were done or not. That couldn't happen right now though, we'd hurt each other enough and I wouldn't distract him when he was so close to achieving his gold medal dreams.

"We didn't try that hard, we didn't get a chance to. He shot us down before we could even tell him which magazine it was for. It was actually for Queer Sports Magazine, they'd have been good to him and let him talk properly about his sexuality and you and whatever else he wanted to," Jacub said.

"Before we try and talk you into the same interview, we need to talk about the injury. We've spoken to the team's doctor and the Team GB medical experts and as it's only a small tear and mostly bruising they would clear you to compete in the finals in two days' time. There's also an option to have a cortisone shot so if you're still in pain from your back and shoulders, that would numb it," Carson explained.

"It's your choice though, hopefully after this fall you know how much your body can handle." Jacub shook his head at me as I pushed myself up out of bed. I'd been told earlier that day that it would be these two I was leaving with.

"We're here to take you home anyway, we have the hire car parked up outside to drop you back to the dorms. If you choose to take it, your cortisone shot will be at eight a.m. tomorrow morning. So sleep on it and do whatever you feel is right, now that you've had the medical opinions. If you choose not to, Brayden will step in."

I was sure he was hoping I wouldn't compete so he

could have his first shot at a medal, even though he was young and healthy and probably had two more Olympic circuits ahead of him. It was so easy to slip into being bitter, but when I ached like fuck I wouldn't let myself go there.

"Come on, let's get you back," Jacub said, grabbing my bag from the hospital locker next to my bed before leading me out of the room.

Stepping into my dorm room, everything felt wrong. Lucas had cleared up all of my clothes and actually folded them in my suitcase like I was leaving. He'd moved all of my belongings like my phone charger and towels from where they'd mingled in the middle of the room, back to my side like it was that easy to split us apart. He'd even moved the stack of protein bars that I'd left on his dresser so we could share them, back to my own dresser. We were clearly done.

The only sign of us still being in the room was that the beds were still joined together. Even then he'd folded my duvet on to my side and was clearly only using his blanket and pillows. How were we supposed to share this bed when he clearly had deep regrets about us being together. I'd desperately tried not to think about his words from the hospital, but every time I closed my eyes they replayed on a loop in my head, making my heart hurt more than my shoulder, back, and sides combined.

So I did the only thing that I could to prevent that kind of heartache. I pushed the two beds apart, before repositioning the bedside table back in between them. It was probably the hardest decision I'd ever had to make and I knew in the coming weeks and months I'd have to make some kind of decision on my athletic career.

Chapter Twenty-Seven

Lucas

I'd expected to find him asleep, it was pretty late after all and he'd just spent two days in an uncomfortable looking hospital bed. What I didn't expect to find was him asleep in his own bed, our bed completely separated, mine now a good six feet apart from his. This was it. It was over. I'd ruined it. In the midst of being so angry at him and Julius, and becoming part of this team, and my sex life being front page news, I'd lost him.

I waited for another rush of anger towards him to wash over me for doing this and making it clear we were over, but nothing except sadness tore me apart. Something inside of me shattered and I had a feeling it might have been my heart.

Sleep didn't come easy after that. Especially when I knew that the next morning Oliver would be making the mistake of having a cortisone shot so he could compete. I didn't want to be controlling—especially as we were nothing to each other right now if the two meters between our beds said anything—but I didn't want him to have the shot.

Yeah, that would mean he couldn't compete, but it would also mean he wasn't about to do any more damage to his body.

Hence, that's why I found myself getting dressed at

eight a.m. the following morning—knowing very well Oliver's shot was at half at eight in the medical center—before sprinting across the Olympic Village to make sure I was there. Even if he went through with it, I wanted to be there. He shouldn't be on his own and I knew Julius and Tom had press to do this morning after Julius won bronze in the all-around individual finals yesterday.

"I couldn't not be here," I said as I poked my head around the door to the medical office. Julius and Tom had informed me about his shot and the time of it the night before so I could be here. When I'd started to mull it over I realized, despite everything, I really wanted to support Oliver through this. He was already laid out on the table, shirtless, ready for his shot. "I know I'm the last person you probably want to see right now, but I couldn't leave you to go through this on your own." I hovered in the doorway, his day was already going to be hard enough, I desperately didn't want to make it worse by making him uncomfortable.

"Come in." He beckoned, "I fucking hate needles so I'm kind of glad there's somebody here with me." He chewed his bottom lip between his teeth and I wanted nothing more than to reach over and take his hand, ease any of the worry I could about what was about to happen.

We sat in silence for several minutes, the ticking of the clock on the wall and the overly bright white floors enough to give me a banging headache, before he spoke again. "Even if this isn't a complete rupture, I'm probably going to need another round of surgery on my shoulder when I get home. My shoulder is now truly fucked up and this will probably be my last chance to compete at this level."

My heart shattered for him, there was only a tiny

percentage of people that could understand how much he was hurting right now. This was his whole life and it was about to be torn away from him, all he'd ever worked for gone because of a simple fall.

"Don't," he said as I looked at him, my vision blurred by the tears that threatened to fall as I thought about what he must be going through. How did you process all that on the day of the biggest competition of your life so far? "I don't need your pity, just sit with me and tell me about how you're feeling, get me out of my head before the doctor comes back and rams a ten-inch needle into my shoulder."

What could I say to that? He needed me and after everything that had happened in the last week I owed him all the words I could give him to make him feel better. "I'm landing the Arabian double layout nine times out of ten, and if I can land it tomorrow, it'll give my routine a difficulty of 7.1 on floor. I'd already be going into the finals with the highest difficulty, I just need it to be good. No, scratch that, it needs to be perfect, flawless, because there's no point having a high difficulty routine if my tumbles are loose and landings sloppy. Part of me wants to do the three and a half twist. I have it nailed, but it'd reduce my difficulty to 6.8, but if I scored a high 8 or low 9 on execution would it really matter?"

He nodded along as I word vomited everything going on in my head onto his medical bed. When all my thoughts were gone, we started to discuss the all-around team event and at some point he reached out and took my hand.

"We wouldn't have qualified without you as our team captain, you know? Part of me can't believe I was so unappreciative towards the role that you played. You whipped all of our asses into shape and the bond between us, it mattered just like you said it would. Julius has helped me upgrade my pommel horse routine a little and Tom's given me a newfound confidence on the high bar that I've never had before. He even said that when we get back to the UK, he'll show me how he perfected his gaylord."

That extracted the chuckle I wanted from him and his death grip on my hand loosened as he turned onto his left side to get a better look at me as we spoke.

"Laugh all you want when, and I mean when, we go to Worlds next year I'm going to be good enough to make it to the all-around individual finals. That's because you brought me into this team kicking and screaming. I've learnt so much, gained a couple of new friends and well, you, I hope, from all of this."

The doctor popped his head around the door interrupting anything Oliver could have replied with. "Sorry about the delay, Mr. Ramsey. The medical center is really busy today. We'll be with you in the next ten minutes."

Oliver nodded as the doctor pulled the door shut again behind us. "I was so sure lying in that hospital bed that everything was over. I started thinking about the future." An uncontrollable grin spread across my face. "Yeah, yeah you've always said it was a good way to think. But I thought gymnastics was my future, but I have to be realistic—I'm injured. This is clearly going to be a reoccurring injury and I have to think about that. I was watching a video on Nile Wilson's channel from 2021 when he retired and all the injuries he's faced and I don't want to do that, I don't want my body to be that wrecked. So I have been thinking about life after gymnastics."

"And what are you thinking about?"

"Coaching."

Of course, there was no better role for Oliver in this world. He was a leader on and off the mat, plus he understood the value of a team and young people needed some of that infused in them.

"I don't think I'll be ready to leave gymnastics maybe ever. This has been my life since I was old enough to remember and it got me through some really dark times."

I could probably cry. Was this what it felt like to be so infatuated with someone that you wanted to give them everything they wanted in the world and so much more that they truly deserved? If I could hand it all on a silver platter right now to Oliver, I would. He hadn't let a potentially career ending injury defeat him and that was exactly the kind of guy I could see myself spending my life with. I'd never imagined a guy in my future before.

"But first, I just need one more shot at the Olympics. I don't even know how I'd give that up now."

His words clawed at the back of my eyes until tears started to leak out the corners. I was so scared for him to the point his knuckles turned white at how hard I'd been squeezing his hand. I couldn't live with myself if I didn't at least say my piece on this.

"I need to tell you something."

"Lucas," he immediately interrupted, clearly sensing where I was about to go with this. That wasn't going to stop me though. He'd had his say on my life, and because of that we'd happened and I didn't regret that. I hoped I wouldn't regret this either.

"No, Oliver, you need to hear this. I don't think you should get this shot. I know it means your Olympic dream is over and I can understand that that would be crushing, it'd crush me too, you know that, but I don't think I can sit back and watch this happen. You asked me to be a part of this team, to be your friend and when you asked to kiss me you made this," I gestured between the pair of us with my free hand, "something more and I need to say this. If you go out there and you compete and because of the jab you can't feel the pain, but your shoulder fully ruptures and you fall again, it would kill me if I didn't say this. What if you fall awkwardly and break your back or your neck? I know I'm sounding like Julius right now, but I care, okay. I really care. You could die falling full speed off the high bar and that would kill me because I love you, Oliver. There. I said it, I've stupidly fallen in love with you and I know we said just sex or whatever, but it's out there now."

His hand slipped from mine as he laid there wordlessly. Absolutely fantastic, exactly the reaction a man wanted the first time he said those stupid three words. I sighed because it was probably the most ridiculous thing I could have gone and done. I'd protected myself against love and guys and all of this heartbreak for so long, only to go and fall in love with someone who'd been my rival for the majority of my career. For fucking Oliver 'Ollie' Ramsey, the guy who'd beaten me in 2020 and lost so much more than I could ever have imagined.

"Did you hear me?" He still said nothing, "I don't know what the fuck you did, but you dragged me out of my bubble of studying and training and freaking *Brooklyn Nine-Nine* and along the way I started to fall for you. I can't fucking help it and I'm not even sure I want it to stop."

I didn't want it to stop, but I did want him to say something. Literally anything in reply to my admission so I wasn't left standing there like an absolute idiot who'd fallen in unrequited love. I'd convinced myself that wasn't the case, that the last few weeks had meant something to both of us, but maybe not.

Silence engulfed us and with a clear of her throat from behind us the nurse awkwardly announced her presence in her own office. Even better, humiliated in front of someone else other than Oliver. The silence lingered even as she stepped back outside to give us a moment before she returned with the injection. My words hung between us like a bad smell. He made zero attempt to reply, he could hardly even look at me. That's when it hit me; I'd made a huge mistake. I should have just kept my mouth shut and my heart closed, saving myself from this pain.

The clock on the wall started to ping nine times and as the silence broke, so did I. The dams against my tear ducts crumbled and tears began to stream down my cheeks. There was no way I could stick around now. I pushed my chair back from the bed, the metal scraping across the floor, and fled out the door as fast as I possibly could.

Tears blurred my vision as I sprinted across the Olympic Village. I wasn't sure where I was going but my feet kept moving until I reached the training center. Of course, the ultimate distraction of getting back to training was what I needed to try and take my mind off the devastation and mess that was my life. I took a breath at the door, trying to compose myself as the wet rim of the neck of my t-shirt clung to my chest. If I went in there like this, it would raise nothing but questions, but if I didn't go in I'd probably self-combust from over-thinking Oliver's reaction. I palmed at my eyes until the tears dried, wiped my snotty nose on my already soaked shirt, and stepped into the center.

After two and a half weeks of bliss in the training room with him, I never thought I'd be glad for his lack of presence. Except there was no escaping Julius and Tom as they paraded out of the office following an interview, stripping out of their suits into the gym gear they had on below as they made their way towards me.

"You okay?" Tom asked, as there were probably still tear tracks staining my cheeks and my eyes were probably still red raw after I'd rubbed them repeatedly to stop myself crying. "Did you see, Oliver? Did he get the shot?"

I shrugged, pretty much in response to both of his questions. I wasn't sure when I'd be okay again. "I don't know. He hadn't when I left." I kind of wanted to scream at the world right now and if that wasn't possible then I needed to hit the floor and throw myself into my routine until I couldn't breathe and sweat poured out of me. That was the release I needed.

"I thought you went to support him through it?" Julius asked as he tossed his now completely crumpled shirt into his gym bag.

"I did, but we had a bit of a row, and you know what, I can't talk about this right now. My floor finals are tomorrow and I need to practice."

Julius went to open his mouth and ask something else, but Tom held his hand up and they both backed away. I'm sure, when all this was over, I'd thank Tom for that or maybe never speak to him again.

I shoved my earphones in, turned up the volume on

my workout playlist and stripped down to my vest and shorts before heading to the top corner of the mat. Hurling myself into my routine, I pummeled the floor for hours until I could no longer hear myself telling Oliver that I loved him.

Chapter Twenty-Eight

Oliver

I'd barely blinked after Lucas's admission and he was already gone, leaving me laying there, shirtless, like an absolute idiot.

He'd just bared his whole heart and soul to me, the first person outside of his childhood circle of trust, and I'd said nothing. Not a single word. I'd watched him leave and that alone had broken my heart. *Damn it.*

I laid there for a second longer, the painkillers from when I'd woken up this morning starting to wear off and leaving me with a dull throb in my shoulder. It was never going to be right again. It was stupid to think this shot would fix that.

The nurse returned and I took my moment to get the heck out of there. "I'm sorry, I can't do this. I'll talk to my coaches and let them know I'm not having the shot. It's not worth it." She didn't seem too shocked, which only confirmed my decision further.

I thanked the nurse profusely for everything she'd done to take care of me over the last few days and exited her office, only to be caught off guard by a very familiar face and long brown ringlets that sometimes haunted my dreams.

"Have a second for an old friend?" Estelle asked, her perfect smile spread across her face, arms open wide ready for me to pull her into a hug. It was almost surreal, every time she spoke to me I could still hear Amber, they sounded exactly the same with their distinct, South London accents.

She had a shirt with Julius's face and the Team GB logo on. It looked homemade, but it was perfect and I'm sure Julius would go absolutely wild for it. "Always for you, Elle," I replied, before swallowing the lump that had started to form in my throat at the sight of her. I scooped my arms around her tiny frame and squeezed hard, breathing in the scent of the perfume she always loved.

"I'm so sorry about your shoulder, Ollie," she muttered into my non-fucked up shoulder, her words making me want to squeeze her harder. I missed this, I missed her and the rest of her family. For years they'd been good to me and after Amber's death I'd hardly made any time to see them. It hurt too much to go to their house or see any of their faces, every bit of them and where they lived reminding me of what I'd lost. But, holding Estelle like this, I wished I'd made more of an effort to keep in touch after the funeral. Maybe it would have given me the closure I needed around Amber's death.

"So, I heard from Julius that you've been seeing someone," she started and my heart sank.

I'd thought about this, how she and her parents might have felt when they saw me with someone else. I never realized it was going to be such a public reveal of my relationship and that I wouldn't have had a chance to sit them down and tell them about it. Guilt encased me, this wasn't how it was supposed to be.

"Why didn't I hear this from you, huh? You know, since we lost Amber, we've always worried about how you are and we miss your dumb face in the house. All we ever wanted was for you to find love again."

"You trying to make me cry, Elle?" I said light heartedly, trying to take some of the pressure and emotion out of the conversation.

"No, I'm telling you to stop being an arse-hole and go get your man. Lucas is fucking hot and he's a sweetheart according to Julius. A sweetheart who I'd really like to meet when we are back in the UK, hopefully as your partner. Are we clear?" She may have been tiny—standing at five-foot nothing—but when she took that tone with me, it meant that if I didn't follow whatever she was saying there'd be hell to pay. I knew it well, both her and Amber had shared that quality.

"Crystal," I replied, deadly serious. Scared that if I said anything else, she'd probably punch me and even from a midget that would hurt in my condition.

"I'm happy for you, Ramsey. Amber would be too." Was what she left me with as she exited out the double doors to where I was sure Julius was waiting. What I was one hundred percent sure about now was that I needed to make things right between me and Lucas, and between me and this sport. There was no way I could leave on a note of hate from the press and a career ruining injury. I had control over at least one of those narratives. Estelle was right, Amber would be happy for me and I deserved to be happy.

I knew what I had to do to make this right not only for myself and my future, but also for me and Lucas to have any kind of a shot at a future together. So I got straight on the phone to make it happen. Luckily, my agent was happy to be finally putting my own narrative on the story they'd been running on me for the last week or so. She'd already had a LGBTQ+ friendly sports magazine reach out to her when the first image had been run, so they'd been more than happy to do an impromptu interview.

It was going to be both a written interview for their magazine, but also a video that they'd be putting on their website and social media so it would be more accessible which was exactly what I wanted. I wanted everyone to see me sit down and tell my story. Maybe I should have done this a while ago, but right now it felt right.

That's why, a couple of hours later, I found myself sitting down with the magazine to tell my side of the story.

"Today we are joined by Oliver Ramsey, captain of the Team GB Olympic gymnastics team and I have a feeling we're about to get an exclusive from the man himself. How are you, Oliver?" She smiled softly at me and there was something about her that oozed this maternal warmth. I'd got it from my Gran growing up, but I don't think I'd seen it properly in a mum until I'd met Debbie Evans. She was a super mum.

"Well, this morning I made the decision that I wouldn't be competing in the gymnastics finals over the next couple of days due to the injury in my shoulder. So everything seems a little bleak in that sense right now. But that's not what I'm here to talk about," I quickly added.

"I'm so sorry, Oliver. As an athlete who retired from women's rugby a little over a decade ago because I was injured, I can sympathize. It's the hardest decision we have to make. But I know that's not what you're here to discuss. I have a feeling it's something to do with some of the headlines we've been seeing over the last week."

She tucked a strand of mousy brown hair that had fallen out of her messy bun back behind her ear and sat forward so she could get stuck into the interview.

"Last week the papers ran with a headline about me being gay after they caught me kissing a guy, which they later revealed to be my teammate, Lucas Evans. Whilst the nuts and the bolts of the story are true, the I'm gay headline was not. They stuck that identity on me before I could even have my say, they saw two guys kissing and immediately they were both gay. They outed me regardless of the label and took away my chance to express myself for myself."

"And how did that make you feel?"

"At first, a little bit sick, but then I pushed past it and focused on the games. Then they named Lucas and I was angry. He's a private person and I was distraught that they'd leaked so many private details about him and well, then I fell twenty feet off the rings and realized that from my hospital bed I couldn't really do anything about the narrative. But now I can. And I have so much to say."

I took a deep breath. "Being an athlete at any level takes bravery. We put our bodies through a lot more than a person with an office job. In gymnastics it's the bravery of performing flips on a six-inch beam or leaping through the air to catch a bar. Just like divers who jump from twenty feet or any other athlete that pushes their body to their limits." I shuffled on the uncomfortable stool as I tried to collect myself to say what I wanted to next.

"Yet during this Olympics I've seen a whole lot more than physical bravery. I still remember every emotion that ran through me when I watched Leila Rose's coming out interview before we set off for Paris and every ounce of pride I felt as she spoke about her girlfriend at home and how they were getting ready to start a family after the games. It's all I've ever wanted too, marriage, children, a big family with somebody I loved." My heart clenched as I thought about how I'd once had that in the palm of my hands, but I pushed that feeling down. This interview wasn't about Amber or anything from the past—it was about me and Lucas and a future that I longed for.

"Then Abbie Heston came out the night before the opening ceremony. I was lying in my bed at the Olympic Village, and I was in awe of her bravery. She's a legend and an inspiration to me as someone who has three Olympics under her belt. I also felt less alone. Which was ridiculous as I was sharing a room with a gay athlete, I'd never been alone on this team.

"I've known since I was fourteen that a family could look like any combination of one or two parents of any gender. When I realized that, it allowed me to breathe a lot easier as I figured out my sexuality. I've just never really embraced it or considered my future family to be made up of two dads. I'm not sure if that was out of fear of it not being the stupid norm of society or because I didn't know how to come out as an athlete, but whatever it was I'm sad that I let it hold me back. I'm bisexual. I'm comfortable in the label and yet I've still been hiding. Not anymore. I'm injured, I have a torn rotator cuff and whilst I'm absolutely gutted that I'm not going to get to compete again this year or maybe even ever again, I still want to do some good."

"And what good is that?" The interviewer asked.

"To be brave, to lead the way for other athletes to come out and be comfortable regardless of their identity.

From other athletes so far, I've had nothing but support on social media, but some of the other media have been nothing but unkind. They've treated my relationship and identity like shit and tried to use it as an excuse for my injury when that wasn't the case at all."

"What happened up there? We've all seen it, it looked like you slipped out of a move we've seen you do a million times?" I knew there might be a chance I'd have to talk about this, but it was time to set the record straight.

"I was in pain," I revealed. "A ton of pain and I was stupid enough to think that it was a manageable pain and that I could still compete. It wasn't. The tear in my cuff meant that I wasn't strong enough to be up there and I should have known that. It wasn't right and I wished I'd been less of an idiot, because now I'm potentially out for life."

"And what about you and Lucas? Is that something you'd like to talk about more? I know there have been some awful headlines about the pair of you, but that isn't how we operate here. You saw that we released a sit-down video interview with Abbie yesterday where she spoke about her engagement to her girlfriend and her plans for retirement. We have no other motive other than to do what you want to do here and bring good to other athletes who are scared or still figuring themselves out or want to be better allies."

She was right, I'd watched that video last night on loop whilst I tried to distract myself from the pain in my shoulder and the decision I had to make about competing under the influence of a cortisone shot. I'd have been stupid to even have tried, especially with the knowledge that competing could lead to a full tear instead of a partial one. Or even worse, if while competing, it caused me to fall and break my back. Or worse, my neck.

"Whilst I can't speak for him and would never want to, I've been developing feelings for him for a long time. Yet it was only three weeks ago I decided to even acknowledge them. Not many people know Lucas, but he's not big on the world having an insight into his life. I'm sure you know that maybe more than I do."

She chuckled. "Yeah, we've been trying to get him to talk to us for years, but he always said that his coming out video said everything he wanted to say. Which is fair and we've always respected that."

"Yeah, he hates to talk. Over the last three weeks I've really gotten to know him. He's incredible, one of the strongest people I've ever met. You can see from his gymnastics alone that he's driven and motivated, but behind the scenes it's so much more. He's already got one degree under his belt and he's close to being done with his master's. Not only that, but he also works a job and helps look after his little sister." I probably sounded like a gushing boyfriend, but I was past caring. "He's the best guy I've ever met and he's always been brave. He came out in the sporting world before he'd even been to his first World's competition. He makes himself, his family, and everyone who loves him proud on a daily basis and I can't wait to see him win gold."

"Sounds like love to me." She grinned at me and whilst she was clearly trying to get the big old scoop from me, those weren't words I was planning to say to her before I even had the chance to try and make things right with Lucas.

"We'll see what the future holds," I replied, "that's what I plan to do from now on, look more to the future.

I wish it hadn't taken an injury forcing me to do this, but I'm excited. There's a whole world out there and whilst I might need a little time to grieve the loss of my dream, I'm excited to see what comes next for me."

"Thank you so much for doing this, Oliver. Every day when another athlete comes out and shares their experience it helps everyone else still struggling or questioning." She stood up to turn the camera off, signaling that it was over and anything we talked about now would be off the record. "We'll get this interview typed up, use some of the pictures your agent has allowed us access to from training and the qualifiers. Then after the finals tomorrow we'll send a copy to you and your agent, and then print it if you approve. If you and that man of yours want to do a follow up after the games let me know."

"No, thank you. Honestly, the fact that you'll respect printing this till after the games is everything to me." I needed to speak to Lucas first before I agreed to do anything for the pair of us, especially when there wasn't currently an *us*. Not until I pulled my finger out of my ass and spoke to him and apologized for being an idiot.

"I hope you two figure things out. You'd be such a power couple. Good luck." I thanked her again and set up the second part of my making amends plan for the day.

Oliver:—*Dinner in twenty minutes! Meet me on the picnic benches at the back of the dorms, I'm bringing nuggets—*

I'd hit their weak spot. As I carried two boxes of twenty nuggets, a bag full of a variety of sauces, and three large diet cokes around the back of the dorms I could already see the pair of them waiting for me.

"How are you feeling?" Tom asked as I slid on to the bench opposite them, depositing the food in front of them. Julius dove in before I could even get comfy.

"My shoulder hurts like a bitch. It's so fucked up I'm scared to even have another scan on it." That would wait till we were back on UK soil. Even if I couldn't compete I still wanted to try and enjoy the remainder of time I had left in Paris with my best friends.

"So you didn't get the cortisone shot?" Julius asked around a mouthful of nuggets, sweet and sour sauce dripping down his chin.

I shook my head, his words crushing against my heart. I wasn't sure when this decision would feel like a good one. "No, I spoke to Lucas and I guess I kind of realized that the Olympics doesn't have to be it for me and with my shoulder, they probably aren't going to be."

"Fuck, I know I didn't want you to get it but I can't imagine going out there without you. I'm so sorry, Ollie. You know we'll do anything to support you." I'd never doubted that from either of them, it went both ways, but hearing Tom's word made the decision feel that little bit easier.

"Are we about to have a group hug moment?" I asked, swiping a nugget from the box that Julius was practically cradling.

"Hang on, why was your boy crying then?"

"He was crying?" *Oh fuck.* How did I come back from that? I'm glad he'd left the room, seeing him cry would have ruined me. Those grass green eyes sopping wet would have been a sight worse than the x-ray that ended my Olympic career.

"Yeah, he rocked up to practice this morning looking like he'd just cried an ocean full of tears. He was a mess. He didn't practice anything but floor for about five hours and then he left without a single word really," Julius replied.

"He told me he loved me." The words still felt foreign on my tongue. Lucas was in love with me. He loved me. I hadn't heard them from a lover in over four years and they'd silenced me. Not because I didn't feel the same, not at all, but because I'd settled for the fact that I'd never hear them again from someone who I could feel the same for.

"Damn, Lucas Evans in love. Have pigs flown today? Did I miss that?" Tom threw a nugget at him to shut him up.

"What did you say in reply?" Tom asked.

"Nothing. I'm such a fucking idiot. I think I was in shock." I still was. That didn't change the fact that I was an idiot though.

"Okay, makes sense why he was crying. You trampled on his heart. If Estelle did that to me, I don't even know what I'd do. I'd probably have to emigrate to Antarctica and freeze to death." Ever the dramatic, Julius "You gotta figure out how to win him back, man. You two are perfect for each other, even we can see that now and we didn't like him for almost five years." His words were a little off point, but the sentiment was right. I had to win him back, no matter what it took.

Chapter Twenty-Nine

Lucas

Everything was alive in the arena. The crowd roared as the days schedule was announced. Men's Floor and Uneven Bars in the morning and then some trampolining in the afternoon. With the women then competing tomorrow. I was so excited to stick around for that especially after Alicia medaled gold on beam yesterday. She never failed to impress me and I'm sure tomorrow would be no different.

As I stretched my hamstrings on the side of the mat, I felt him creep up behind me. All that muscle didn't exactly make him the quietest sneaker. "I can hear you, Oliver. What do you want?" I tried to make myself sound annoyed with him, but it came straight out as playful banter.

"No pressure, like at all, but Max Whitlock's in the crowd with Nile Wilson."

My heart sank and I rapidly scanned the crowd, like I was going to be able to pick them out from the thousands of people seated in the stands.

"Oh and don't get jealous or anything, but Max spoke to me and I'm definitely his favorite on the team." I felt my eyes widen, ridiculously, like I was some jealous teen. "Lucas, Lucas, Lucas, you're so easy to wind up. I'm kidding, literally all he said to me was that if I saw you before you hit the mat to wish you good luck."

"Fuck you, Oliver, fuck you." I grinned, as I unzipped my hoodie a little. The heat of the arena and this conversation were getting a little too much for me.

"When this is over, sure thing, you definitely need to be introduced to celebratory sex." He winked at me and I had to check no one was listening because there were cameras literally everywhere even as the athletes warmed up. "Step out with me for a second. We need to have a chat."

"Oliver." I groaned as I took a step back from him. I didn't need to be dumped all over again before the biggest routine of my life.

"Lucas, I just, I let you speak, now you need to hear me out okay?" How could I say no to that? I'd sprung my confession of love on him when he'd been lying on a medical table completely unable to escape, the least I could do was afford him a couple minutes of my time.

We slipped down the dark tunnel that led into the arena, Oliver trying every door we walked past until he found an empty, unlocked room. "Look, I should start by apologizing. I've been a dick. You've said from the very beginning that you didn't want to be in the press and it was me that pulled us into that alleyway that night. I should have been more careful. I'm sorry the papers printed all that awful stuff and I'm even more sorry that they've found stories about your family."

"This isn't just your fault—"

He quickly interrupted me, "It's not that. I knew I was injured and I shouldn't have even tried to compete, but I'm not like you. I don't have all these amazing plans for the future. I don't have something like a crazy good floor routine that I'm known for. I'm just Oliver, another Team GB athlete and now I'm an injured athlete who will probably never compete again and I felt like everything had been taken away from me. I shouldn't have taken that out on you." He took both of my hands in his and squeezed, before pulling me down to sit on the weights bench with him.

"I'm sorry, Oliver. I'm so sorry you're injured, I wish I'd maybe pushed a little harder about you not competing like Julius and Tom did, but I have a feeling you wouldn't have listened anyway." He shook his head and I laughed. "I also shouldn't have abandoned you. Yeah I was freaking out, and all of a sudden my whole life was in the public eye, but you needed me more than I needed to drown in self-pity."

"It doesn't matter now. I'm so lucky to have you and the guys. I know I've always known it, but like I don't think you realize how much you need people until everything hits the fan and you're alone."

"You're never alone, gorgeous." I pulled away from his grip to smooth a hand over his cheek. "You're kind of stuck with us. Remember, you did this all yourself by forcing me to become friends with the guys and well, because you asked me to kiss you."

He smiled softly at me and lent in to kiss my forehead, running his fingers through my curls. Damn, how I'd missed that sensation over the last few days, before he whispered. "Sweetheart, I have no regrets at all."

I could have cried. It was everything I needed to hear. That this hadn't all been a huge mistake and that maybe, just maybe, after all of this we still had a chance together. "Oliver." He pressed the pad of his finger softly

258

to my lips to stop me from saying whatever I had been about to say.

"Today's your day, tomorrow it'll be the teams, and after that it'll be ours. We'll have every single day after that to do our thing and I'm counting down the days till we can. Now I need you to go out there and kill it, there's medals to be won, baby. Good luck, even though with your floor routine you definitely don't need it." He squeezed my hand like he meant it and then kissed the corner of my lips softly.

The kiss was so featherlight that physically I hardly even felt it, but emotionally it meant everything. It told me everything I hadn't heard from him in the last couple of days. We walked back into the arena together, him to the guys and the coaches, and me to the side of the mat where I waited next in line to compete.

The camera was on me even whilst I stretched on the side of the mat as I waited for the Chinese competitor, my biggest competition on floor, to finish up his routine. I didn't look up as his score was announced, I had no desire to see what I was up against. I needed to focus. I needed to stay in the positive head space I'd been left in as Oliver had held my hand and wished me good luck.

I looked over to where him and the other guys were standing beside both coaches. Tom sent me a thumbs up and Oliver grinned at me. My nose fizzed like I could get teary at the way Oliver's cheeks continued to stretch as he looked me up and down. Damn him, it was not the time for him to be looking at me like I was his prey. Getting a boner in my leotard and shorts was not a good idea in front of a crowd of thousands.

I scanned the crowd for mum and the girls, but amongst everybody they were ridiculously hard to find.

I could, however, see hundreds of British flags and that was enough to reassure me that they were in the crowd, rooting for me, somewhere.

Going into the qualifiers I'd been shaky, my arms had quivered in the handstand and my foot had gone out of bounds after the Arabian double layout with a half twist. It was the move that brought my difficulty up, but it was also the move that had added a points deduction to my execution score. Standing in the corner of the mat I promised myself that none of that was going to happen this time round.

This was it, sixty-four seconds that could change absolutely everything.

We were starting off strong. That's what Coach Carson loved to do with a floor routine, he'd practically bullied the team GB choreographer to let me start with a power tumble. Carson always said it gripped the judges from the very beginning with a huge amount of strength, hence why I was starting with a triple twist, punch front. It had the potential to be disastrous, but I'd drilled this move so many times it now felt natural to come out of a triple twist and into a punch front. It had become a little problematic when working on any other move with a triple twist.

Landing each tumble I had to look the perfect amount of rigid and loose, a balance I definitely thought I'd mastered over the last couple of years. As I came out of the triple twist into a punch front and landed it without a single wobble, I knew I had.

I launched into a triple layout across the floor before engaging in a double flip in the tucked position, then going straight into a half twist after, my feet planting to the floor like cement. I faced outwards of the mat which was the perfect place to start as I spit fired into the next tumble.

My shoulders leant back and I swung my arms over my head to perform three back handsprings in a row. The coiled springs thudded below the mat giving my body enough power to keep the handsprings going, each thump only motivating me more and more to go for perfection. I landed the tumble around three meters from the top left corner of the mat, as planned, and got to work on a succession of leaps. Starting with a switch leap, where I pushed my legs forwards and backwards in a scissor style motion to carry me a meter and a half forward closer to the corner. Then from that into a split leap. I made sure my legs were completely straight into the split position and as I felt every limb extend in the air to the max, I knew it must have looked perfect to the judges. When it felt good, more times than not it looked good. Call it gymnasts' intuition.

My hands didn't even shake as I performed the series of air flares my routine contained. They walked in a perfect square with every step bringing either my right or left hand off the ground to work my legs under it in a circle formation. I counted the beats in my head as the circles my legs did varied in heights, until I hit six seconds and landed in the splits. I paused for a second to smile wide at the crowd and judges, for some reason they preferred me to look happy as I worked every single muscle in my body to the limit, so I always abided.

Coming out of the selection of air flares into the splits was not only a great addition to my difficulty, but also created the best starting position for my handstand. I flattened my stomach out onto the floor, shoulders wide and palms flat on the floor, shoulder width apart, and pushed up into the handstand. My legs moved like clock arms into the midday position and I kept them rim rod straight, not even teetering in the air. It felt fantastic as I held it for two seconds and then rolled out into the corner to perform a double layout into a roll over.

There was always the urge to look across at the panel of five senior judges who followed my every move in person and then again on their screens as they scored me, but I couldn't—I had to keep my focus on the corner of the mat or the handstand I was in.

I tumbled across the mat and stretched out completely as I landed, preparing myself for the final tumbling set. The big gun of the routine, the Arabian double layout. If I landed this without any slip ups or feet outside the mat it would be a solid routine. I took the deepest of breaths as I pointed the toes on my right foot at the floor, ready to take off and leapt into action. I hardly remembered what happened in between take off and my feet planting on the floor, inside the lines, without a single wobble, but I didn't care. I'd done it and that was all that mattered.

I bowed slightly, before punching the air in victory. It felt beautiful. Only slightly like a walk in the park, and as the crowd cheered around me I knew, whatever the score, I'd done my absolute best. I lapped up the applause for a couple of seconds, before I tore my eyes away from the crowd to the men that really mattered right now.

The guys and coaches all waited for me as I jogged away from the mat. I encountered Coach Carson first who slapped me on the back and then Jacub who gave me a huge smile and raised his hands for a high ten. I was beyond appreciative of them both, but I could see Oliver a meter or two behind Jacub and it was him that I wanted to celebrate with.

Brayden had other plans first though. I hadn't even seen him with the other guys, he hadn't come out for the all-around individual finals yesterday to my knowledge so I wasn't sure if he'd be here or not as he didn't have an individual event to compete in. "Oh my god, that was amazing. You killed it, you're definitely going to win gold." It wasn't that I wasn't thankful for his praise, but there was a safe pair of arms behind him that I wanted to be in.

"Thanks," I quickly replied before I tried to sidestep around the guy only for him to block my path for a second time.

"I was thinking that I might add the punch front you do in that first pass of tumbles to my routine for the competition tomorrow. I've landed it a couple of times, but I've never thought it would work well in my routine. Yet seeing you landing it, I'm sure it will."

"I'd talk to coach first. I wouldn't recommend doing it without practice or adding it this close to the competition." My foot tapped impatiently against the floor. I was ready to celebrate.

"You don't think I can land it?" I wanted to give the young lad all of my time to help him become the best he could be on floor, but not the second after I'd just competed.

"We'll talk after this event, is that cool?" He nodded and I didn't wait for him to say anything else before I sprinted towards Oliver. I practically launched myself the second I got close enough to him, arms around his neck as he pulled me closer to him.

"Damn, damn, damn," he roared into my ear as I

clung to him like there was no tomorrow. It definitely did not look like a platonic hug, but if he was comfortable doing it then so was I. "I have no other words, freaking damn," he screamed over the crowd as he pulled away from me. "That was so freaking amazing, it was flawless, perfect, perfection."

"Okay man, please stop gushing over your boyfriend, it's our turn," Julius chuckled as he and Tom tugged me into a hug.

Oliver and I definitely hadn't agreed on the boyfriend part, but having their approval meant a lot to me and probably a hell of a lot to Oliver. Plus, it wasn't a title I'd mind applying to Oliver.

We all stood together after the congratulations as we waited for the final two athletes to compete. I could hardly watch. I kept my eyes focused on the floor whilst trying not to look uninterested for the cameras as I watched my fellow athletes. Going into the final athlete's routine from China, I was still in the gold medal position with a huge score of 16.1, the Japanese gymnast behind me sat on a 15.7. Jing Han finished his routine and I clung to Oliver's arms with both hands as we waited for the score to tabulate above us. When it appeared on the screen 15.66, I was so glad to be clinging to him because I went so lightheaded I almost collapsed.

I stood on the top of the podium, which felt like the top of the world, my medal hanging from my neck, my flowers raised in my left hand above my head as I waved gratefully at the crowd. It was everything I'd ever dreamed of. Every single second of applause made each year of training and all the strained muscles and endless sleepless nights stressing about routines feel worth it.

Hugging the girls, with my gold medal round my

neck while my mum took a million photos, felt like everything had come together. I'd made it. I'd done so much of this for them, but I'd found a place, here at the Olympics with a man I loved and friends who cared about me, where I'd also done this for me. This situation couldn't get any more perfect.

Then, I spotted him out of the corner of my eye walking towards me down the tunnel from the arena where he'd probably been on the ground to talk to his old coach as well as waving to the fans in the audience. He was such a crowd pleaser. I tried to act like I hadn't noticed him as he got closer and closer, but then Lauren spotted him and all hell broke loose. She pulled hard on my arm, repeatedly, practically ripping it out of the socket, before he came to a stop in front of us.

"Whilst I'm jealous that you scored higher than me when I won gold on this apparatus, I can't deny that routine was fucking bomb." Lauren went wide eyed as Max swore and I was incredibly scared that my mum was about to reprimand a Team GB legend, but she said nothing.

"Hey Mrs. Evans, and this must be Lucy and Lauren. Your brother spoke so highly of all of you when we last worked out together, which by the way has been way too long." He jabbed at my shoulder with his fist playfully. "Us Essex boys have to stick together even if I am retired. Congrats on your medal though, man. I've got to go find Nile, but hit me up when you're back on UK soil. Enjoy the rest of your time in Paris." He aimed the last bit at my family and the way they all smiled at him, Lucy and Lauren almost drooling, made me want to cringe because that was definitely how I used to look at all my posters of him when I was a teen. Or like maybe up until a couple of weeks ago.

I waved him off as he disappeared out of the tunnel into the backstage area and I couldn't help but hurl myself again at my three girls, crushing them into the biggest hugs.

As I released them, mum looked behind me and around us and then said. "Where's Oliver? Are things okay between the two of you? I saw you guys when they announced you were the gold medalist, and even from the crowd we could all see he was smitten with you."

I could feel the heat spread across my face. I wondered if she'd spotted it, then maybe everybody else did, and should we be worried about what tomorrow's headlines were going to say? But I was too happy to care. I was an Olympic gold medalist and I'd almost gotten my man back.

"He's around, the four of us are going to go and watch the women compete this afternoon. Oliver and I have agreed that after this is all over we'll talk properly about us, but I can definitely say we are back on track."

"Talk of the devil." Lucy grinned, gesturing to Oliver five meters away from us in his matching Team GB tracksuit to the one I'd slipped on over my floor outfit. "I think he's waiting for you. Go, we'll catch you tomorrow. We are heading out for some sightseeing."

I kissed all of them on the cheek, even Lauren who protested ridiculously, not wanting to be seen being kissed by her big brother in front of Ollie, before I gave them directions to the way out and waved them off.

"They look as proud of you as I am," he said with the most beautiful smile.

I checked that the tunnel was still empty and pecked a kiss to his lips now that I was allowed to do that again.

"Time to go watch Alicia kick ass. The guys have gone in search of those big pretzel things and said they'd meet us in the stands. You ready?" He extended his hand out to mine and I happily took it. I was definitely ready. There was nothing stopping us now.

Chapter Thirty

Oliver

This was not how I imagined the day going at all. I was suited in my competition tracksuit, but I wouldn't be taking it off when we got out into the arena. I was benched, unable to compete and whilst it absolutely sucked, there was no way I was going to miss my best friends and Lucas competing in the biggest event of their lives. It was going to hurt to see Brayden compete on vault and floor today, but I'd get through it to see Julius smash out one final pommel horse routine. I had this sneaky feeling this wasn't only *my* last Olympics.

They called for Team GB to enter the arena and because we're from just across the pond I could see hundreds, nay maybe thousands, of our supporters decked out in our colors in the crowd. As our individual names were called they went absolutely crazy, the applause was addictive.

I spotted the largest British flag I'd ever seen spread out across the crowd and I squinted at the faces around it to see if my plan had worked. While Lucas had slept soundly last night I'd hatched a plan and tried to get back in touch with Lucy again. After she'd hurled abuse at me for breaking her brother's heart, she gave me a moment of time to hear me out.

I scouted the crowd relentlessly for my grandma's

graying hair and tiny frame, but it wasn't her that I spotted first. It was the bleach blonde hair and the almost identical face to Lucas's that caught me off guard. I waved up at her as I spotted the rest of her family and my grandparents sat together in the stands. Discreetly, I poked Lucas in the back from where he was walking in front of me and pointed to his sister. At first he grinned up at her as she whistled at him, but then his eyes scooted over to the older couple next to her. As he realized it was my grandparents, he turned to look at me like 'what the actual fuck'.

I shook my head because now wasn't the time to actually talk about it, the team had a competition to win.

All eight qualified teams for this event started to line up around the arena as a megaphone announced how the day would proceed to the crowd. We'd already been through all of this backstage with our coaches and the organizers of the games. As we finished fourth in the qualifiers, the team would be performing fourth on all apparatus. Standing in front of the crowd, waving to the thousands of supporters felt incredible, but knowing that in a moment this would be it for me, was putting a real dampener on the atmosphere.

Before my injury I was set to perform on three different apparatus, vault, rings, and parallel bars, but even though Brayden was taking my spot he was only performing on vault and floor which meant the other guys were having to pick up my slack. More so, Lucas was going to have to perform on parallel bars, his least favorite apparatus.

We qualified behind the USA, China, and Japan. If we, well the team, did everything they could today, we would medal. That alone was enough for me to be proud of the whole team and how everyone had come together in the last four weeks. Some of us pretty much literally. As I'd participated in the qualifiers I'd still get a medal today which probably should have made me feel great, yet it felt more like a participation medal to me. Like when you'd get a certificate at school for attendance.

There was a gleam in Lucas's eye that threatened to turn to tears as he looked over at me. I knew it was somewhat pity, but mostly I knew he and all of the rest of the guys were proud of me for making the decision not to compete. Today wasn't my day to mourn though, I was here to support and then celebrate.

The day started on vault and rings. Lucas wasn't competing in either of these events as his four events were in the second and third rotations, so we both sat to the side wordlessly watching the other guys kick off the day in the most spectacular way. Our first rotation ended, and we moved on to the next rotation, high bar and pommel horse. It was Tom and Julius's time to shine.

Tom stepped up for his high bar routine to a huge round of applause, looking as ready as ever, but the coaches looked nervous. Tom's score needed to be big as we moved into the third rotation of apparatus. Coach Carson had no need to be worried, his form was spectacular, a real confidence to every swing of his legs and how he grabbed and released the bar on every turn. A big release move bang in the middle of his routine, a tucked full twist up and over the bar, the bar dipping inward as he caught it beneath him effortlessly. He stuck the landing, a perfectly executed double twisting, double lay out and as he raised his arms and waved to the crowd I thought maybe the news article I read this morning had it right. Maybe we did have a chance at a medal today.

Tom's score read to be a 16.1, a difficulty of 7.3 and a brilliant execution score of 8.8 with no penalties at all.

The challenge for Tom, however, came from Oleg Hashniv from the Ukraine, he won gold in the individual competition for the apparatus and had been crushing Tom at Worlds for the last couple of years. But today felt like our day.

The five of us sat to the side waiting for the Ukrainian to perform. The first two routines were subpar a low 15 score and a mid-15, but Oleg was up after and he looked fired up. However, he slipped out of a single twist release and caught the bar way too early as his routine got going, that would be at least a 0.2 deduction, as he struggled to gain momentum again.

Carson and Jacub were huddled meters away from us as they did their own calculations, both of them looking quietly confident after such a high score from Tom on the high bar.

It all continued in a similar fashion, Lucas and Julius smashed their high bars and we moved on to the pommel horse, Julius's favorite piece of apparatus.

"You've got this," I shouted to him as he stood next to the horse and adjusted the red tape around his wrist. He shot me back a smile and braced his hands above the pommel, ready to go.

All six feet of him looked incredibly nimble as he weaved in and out of the handles, up and down the length of the pommel horse. His hips stayed the perfect distance above the handles before he rose into a steady handstand and swung his legs smoothly back down seconds after to circle the bars like an absolute pro. It was the dismount that cost him a higher position in the individual-all-around competition, it was all over the place as his hand slipped on the horse and he struggled to land his round off. This time however, he landed fantastically, without a single slip and his score was the highest I'd seen all day, without a single deduction to his execution score.

We were close to moving on to the final apparatus, but before we could do that Lucas had to perform on parallel bars and he was pacing like he was about to have a huge freak out.

"I wish you felt okay enough to compete on this apparatus. I'm going to suck and ruin any chance at a medal for us," he groaned as he re-taped his wrists and chalked up his hands.

If I could have shaken him I would have or maybe I'd have kissed some confidence into him, but now was not the time, so instead I replied, "You're going to smash it and do you know how I know that? Because you're Lucas Evans. You do your absolute best at everything, your job in your mom's pub, your training, university. You make me want to work harder than ever. You're the reason that I'm here even though I know I can't compete rather than sitting in our room crying myself to sleep."

It seemed to do the trick as he relaxed from being hunched over the chalk pit. "So, how did you manage to get my family to sit with yours then?" he asked with the most beautiful smile, eyes dancing mischievously across my face, like he'd known I'd played a hand in making this happen.

"A lot of groveling to your sisters, that's what. Our families are now pals, it's going to be perfect for when they are our in-laws." The look on his face was wild as I said that and his jaw dropped before he practically inhaled some of the chalk from the pit.

"You're an idiot. Hand me my phone. I'm going to

need to be in the zone for this." He'd had one earphone in for the whole conversation, the music keeping him calm and focused instead of being distracted by the roar of the crowd. I handed him his phone so he could switch up his song.

Luckily, I was saved from any kind of reply as they called him up to the bars and he had no choice but to retreat from this conversation. He, however, did not ruin any of our chances at a medal. For somebody who hated the apparatus with a passion, he scored decently and easily kept us in the running. Plus, I think he knew that when he landed the dismount, we would be off to our final apparatus and his favorite one. This was his final chance to perform his stunning floor routine this Olympic circuit.

The Chinese, however, still looked incredibly relaxed across the hall, leaning back in their chairs as they waited to go on their final apparatus, the high bar. I pushed the image of them out of my head as we followed Carson and Jacub in formation around the outside of the arena to our final apparatus of the competition floor.

Lucas was a completely different guy as he got ready to perform on the floor. I watched him stretch on the side of the mat, his lean muscles tensing and rising with every move. He kept his earphones in until the very last second, when he dumped them in the box and lobbed it towards Carson. He looked more composed in that second than he had throughout every other routine today, like nothing was about to stand in his way of nailing this routine.

It was almost like I was seeing the routine for the first time. It was so stunning that goosebumps coated my arms and the top of my thighs. He perfected it, every tumble looked effortless and beautifully artistic as he demonstrated exactly why he was not only our number one on floor, but now number one in the world.

In some way though, this was better than his individual performance. There was a real grit to it, a determination in his eyes I'd never seen before. His legs stayed practically glued together as he flipped across the floor and sizzled into his triple twist punch front.

There was no hesitation as he rose into the handstand, his body unwavering as he held the pose for a number of beats, before elegantly transitioning into a fantastic set of air flares. Nobody did the groundwork better than Lucas.

With a single cartwheel into the top left-hand corner, he stretched up straight, eyes closed as he breathed deeply for a half a second, before he leaped into his final tumble of the routine. I still remembered the first time I saw him do the Arabian double layout, my heart had stilled as he twisted in the air and even though we weren't anything back then I had this pang of worry in my chest that he was going to land badly—it was such a hard move. This time around it was complete perfection, the twist into the layout went so quickly and before I knew it his feet were planted on the floor like he was stuck in quicksand. Everyone around us erupted into applause.

Something clenched in my chest, like a mouse trap going off around my heart, as he bowed slightly to the crowd and jogged off the side of the mat. I'd been so stupid to push someone as amazing as him away. He was everything I needed in my life right now and maybe even all along. I needed his determination, his tenacity, his work ethic, his everything to make me a better person.

The seconds that followed after were excruciating as we waited for his score to be tabulated. The other seven countries were finishing up around us on the other apparatus and I knew this would be the determining score to where we ranked.

"Incredible, actually incredible," Coach Jacub said as he patted Lucas on the back. Both him and Carson still clutched at their notebooks and as they peered down at it to do the addition, something like hope and then excitement flickered across Jacub's face.

"So, I'm not saying anything, but you guys came into this final rotation in second behind China and they've just finished on the high bar with 276.4 overall. If our addition is correct from the scores we've seen—" He was interrupted by Lucas's score being announced and when I saw the number I almost crumbled to the ground.

"Is that a 16.5? Am I seeing things?" Tom said as Lucas stared up at the screen in absolute amazement. His eyes had started to gloss over with tears and I could feel mine doing the exact same.

"I think it's some kind of Olympic World record," Carson commented as we all waited for Lucas to do anything, to take his eyes off the screen. "Like, I've never seen anything maybe above a 16.2 or 16.3 in all my time as a coach."

"I can't believe it. I cannot fucking believe it. What just happened? How? What? Why?" He spiraled into a relentless amount of questions as his eyes flickered between the screen and us and the coaches. His eyes were so wide, I was pretty sure they were going to bulge out of their sockets in utter disbelief.

"Sweetheart, you did it," I cried as we all crushed

him in a huge hug. "Not only did you do it, but you potentially broke a record and scored so high I think you probably broke the judges. It was flawless, absolutely flawless."

"No-one's going to beat that," Julius added as we pulled out of the hug and waited for everyone else to finish around us so we could get our final scores.

Lucas still looked incredibly shocked as we all sat down in our allocated seats and waited for it all to happen, for the scores to tabulate and for us to find out our fates.

The last five Olympic games had been ruled by the Chinese and Japanese teams, especially in the all-around team finals and this year had been somewhat the same.

Except, this year, we'd really put up a fight and now we sat waiting to see where we'd place amongst them. It all depended on how well the other teams on the other apparatus did. The screens were blank with absolutely nothing for what felt like years. We'd came into the final apparatus in the silver medal space with enough room between us and fourth to be almost guaranteed a medal. I sat and prayed no one had done amazing on the other apparatus.

The final rankings flashed up on the screens above us and for more than a second my heart stopped and I couldn't breathe. Right at the top of the table sat Great Britain, 277.1 points overall. Gold medalists, all of us, together.

There was a bucket of tears from three out of four of us, Julius still keeping his composure, but that was to be expected. I'd only seen him cry once in our eight years of friendship and that was at the funeral. I let mine fall all over the place, even as the media gathered around us and I could see we were being filmed for every channel, all around the world, but I didn't care. We'd just made history. The first British gymnastics team to medal gold in the all-around team finals.

I flung my arms around Lucas and pulled him close as he continued to cry. Even though I knew people could see us, I pressed my cheek to his and felt the wetness of his tears and how he smiled as the cameras snapped around us. We were never going to get this moment again and I wanted to remember being with him, embracing him and feeling every ounce of his love as the crowd applauded around us.

"I can't believe it," I heard Tom scream and in the next second both him and Julius had crashed into mine and Lucas's hug. We all squeezed each other like our lives depended on it and maybe in that moment they did. We'd done this, together, against all the odds.

"We are saving you from the press right now, by the way," Julius whispered, almost creepily, into my ear, before he licked over the shell of my ear like a complete weirdo. "Didn't want the paps to catch another intimate moment of yours. You can thank us later."

Any other time I'd have told him to shut up, but as the pair crushed us harder and the four of us jumped up and down like absolute crazy idiots, I regretted absolutely nothing. When the time had been right we'd come together like this well-oiled team and absolutely smashed it. No-one in the crowd who watched the team perform today would have ever known that we'd all been a mess just a couple of days ago. I was so happy I didn't even flinch when Brayden slipped into the huddle, he'd been a part of this team too I guess—even if he had taken my place.

"I can't believe it," I all but gulped out as I soaked in everything that had just happened, how we were all still clinging to each other like our lives depended on it. In mere minutes we would be wearing gold medals. It was completely overwhelming but less so with everybody by my side.

"I'm not sure how we did this, but I'm glad we did it together," Lucas screamed into the middle of our hug and that alone pushed a few more tears to trickle down my cheeks. We'd won gold, he'd become part of the team, and I'd fallen for him. What an absolute ride the Olympics had been.

Nothing felt better in the whole wide world as I stood on the gold medal podium with the three best men in my life, my two best friends and potential boyfriend.

"God, I love you," I confessed as my hand slid into Lucas's, the other one reaching around to clutch at the side of his face and without a care in the world I crushed our lips together. Cameras flashed around us and for a second all I heard was silence, but then the crowd did us proud and erupted into applause. I pulled away from him as the British flag lowered behind us and grinned at my best friends who hooted like there was no tomorrow at the pair of us.

We were two guys who loved each other, who'd just won gold, and achieved everything they'd set out to do in Paris 2024.

I looked over at Lucas as the anthem started to play, a gold medal around his neck, a winning smile stretched across his face. And I was in love with him. Even if we'd have lost, I'd have still been in love with him.

Acknowledgements

To my mom, for always being my best friend and sitting with me on the sofa for hours watching absolute crap on the TV whilst I write. To my God mothers, who are forever showing endless amounts of belief in me. To my dad and brother, who will always at least half listen to me talking about books and writing. To my grandma, who may not be able to read this, but know would love it.

To Ella and Paige. The bestest friends I could ever hope for. For always asking 'how's the book going?' even though you aren't part of the writing world. For being excited for me every step of the way and for always supporting me in every single thing I do. Love you both, always!

To Han, Alicja, and Lou. There aren't enough words. I will never be more grateful for the fact that we were brought together in the writing community. I could not ask for better writing pals and I can't thank you enough for the support you've given me through plotting, writing, editing, revising, querying, and then signing Olympic Enemies. You've been along for the ride every single step of the way, constantly cheering me on and supporting me through every full request and rejection.

To my AMM Mentor Brooke Abrams, this book would not be what it is without you. Getting into the AMM mentorship scheme in February 2021 changed my life and working with you to improve Olympic Enemies was the highlight. You challenged me to step up all the plotlines and had my back through every revision! You never left my side through a year of querying and cheered the hardest when I got good news and lifted me up the most when I got bad. I will always be grateful that you loved Oliver and Lucas as much as I did.

Author Mentor Match (AMM) didn't just bring me a wonderful mentor, but also so many awesome writer friends. To 'The Scribblers' & all AMM Round 8 Pals thank you for always just being one message away. For reading my query and synopsis when it was a mess, always giving me great feedback and supporting me through the query trenches.

To the authors I look up to—Rachel Reid, Lauren Blakely, Eden Finley, KD Casey, Annabeth Albert, Alexis Hall, Saxon James, Casey McQuiston—who continue to pave the way for writers like me who want to write queer sports/contemporary romance books.

A word about the author...

As an author, Rebecca started her writing career in the Young Adult (YA) section. She is the author of the Contemporary YA Cherrington duology which features the two titles—Cherrington Academy and Coming Home.

Since then, she has completely stepped away from writing YA and her focus is now solely on writing Contemporary Adult Romance. She always has one too many ideas and often finds herself jotting them down in the middle of the night.

When she's not writing you'll find her either reading all the Sports/Adult Contemporary Romance or binge watching (read: constantly rewatching) her Netflix favorites such as Brooklyn 99, The Good Place, New Girl and Lucifer. Outside of this, she is a BA Politics graduate and despite her degree being over she still has a vested political interest and is always keeping up to date with current affairs.

Where to find Rebecca Caffery:
Twitter - @BeckaWrites
Instagram - @RJCafferyAuthor
Website - RebeccaJCaffery.com

CPSIA information can be obtained
at www.ICGtesting.com
Printed in the USA
BVHW091945080223
658147BV00011B/140